N

gift BMc

THREADBARE

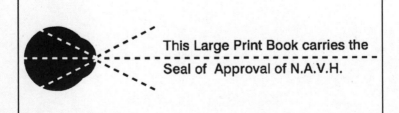

This Large Print Book carries the
Seal of Approval of N.A.V.H.

THREADBARE

MONICA FERRIS

THORNDIKE PRESS
A part of Gale, Cengage Learning

Detroit • New York • San Francisco • New Haven, Conn • Waterville, Maine • London

GALE
CENGAGE Learning·

LIBRARY OF CONGRESS CATALOGING-IN-PUBLICATION DATA

Ferris, Monica.
    Threadbare / by Monica Ferris.
        pages ; cm. — (Thorndike Press large print mystery)
    ISBN-13: 978-1-4104-4539-1 (hardcover)
    ISBN-10: 1-4104-4539-9 (hardcover)
    1. Devonshire, Betsy (Fictitious character)—Fiction. 2.
Needleworkers—Fiction. 3. Minnesota—Fiction. 4. Homeless
persons—Crimes against—Fiction. 5. Large type books. I. Title.
PS3566.U47T47 2012
813'.54—dc22   2011047437

Published in 2012 by arrangement with The Berkley Publishing Group, a member of Penguin Group (USA), Inc.

Printed in the United States of America
1 2 3 4 5 6 7 16 15 14 13 12

ACKNOWLEDGMENTS

I would like to thank Laura Melchik of the Saint Paul Area Coalition for the Homeless for her priceless aid in creating my homeless characters and describing their plight. Dr. Meg Glattly of Woodlake Veterinary Hospital gave helpful advice and information. The YWCA of Fargo was highly cooperative and informative. Roz Watnemo of Nordic Needle was and remains a valuable resource. Chris Braun and Alison Bucklin both suggested *Threadbare* as a title, for which I thank them.

ONE

Randy Untweiler, seventeen, a tall, skinny kid with dark blond hair, was the one who found her. He came out of the movie theater by the back door. He'd stayed after the last show to sweep up, and was carrying a bag of trash to be put into the huge green Dumpster near the door. He wouldn't have seen her, because it was dark and had been snowing heavily — in fact, it was still snowing. All he knew was that he tripped over something big and hard, and fell. The trash bag split open when he landed on it, and he began swearing as he picked up the candy wrappers and empty popcorn and soft drink containers by the glow of a distant streetlamp.

It occurred to him to wonder what had tripped him, and he went over to kick at the object, whatever it was. Using his cell phone to weakly light the area, he dislodged enough snow to disclose the blank cold face of an old woman with hair the same color as the snow. After an astonished few seconds, he texted his best friend, Adam, that he'd found a woman's dead body. Adam texted back, "u r joking," and Randy texted, "4 real," and Adam texted, "call 911."

But Randy decided that such things as finding dead bodies didn't happen to people like him and therefore it wasn't real after all. Maybe it was a store dummy — he pulled off a glove and touched the face and found it as hard and cold as plaster. Still, he phoned his girlfriend, Harriet, to consult with her, and while arguing with her about it, Adam arrived, still zipping up his coat. Adam, short, plump, and intelligent, looked at the body and declared in scatological and obscene terms that Randy must quit acting like a fool, hang up on Harriet, and call the police.

Which he did.

There followed a lengthy scene involving a squad car and an ambulance, made surreal by lights flashing blue, red, and orange in the blowing snow.

Though the woman was frozen stiff, the responding policeman could not declare her dead, nor could the emergency medical technicians.

Nor could the two teens leave. Everyone

had to wait for a representative from the Hennepin County Medical Examiner's Office. The man on duty lived in Maple Plain, a long way off, and he was grumpy on arrival. He prodded the dead woman's rigid face, tried and failed to lift an arm, and sighed at the obviousness of it all.

"Take her to the morgue," he said, and went back home.

Randy and Adam were dismissed with a tale they could tell for the rest of their lives — Randy would have nightmares for years about kicking an old dead woman in the head — but the story rated only two short paragraphs in the next morning's *Star Tribune.* No one knew who she was. She had no ID in a purse or pocket — no purse at all, in fact, just some old plastic shopping bags full of the detritus of her life. The sad assortment of objects — ranging from a change of underwear to a badly worn stuffed toy kitten to a half-used box of Handi Wipes — had nothing with a name on it. She didn't match the description of anyone on the missing persons list, so there was no name or age or city of residence to lead to an identification or cause a twinge of sorrow. It appeared to be one of those deaths no one likes to think about, which happen to people living on the fringes of society.

Not surprisingly, under her body there had been found an all-but-empty quart bottle of bourbon, which, in most minds, explained it all.

Because there had been a spate of killings in an inner-city neighborhood as a gang war heated up, the unknown woman's autopsy was moved down in order to discover legal medical information about the young male victims. Her body was not subjected to an autopsy for almost a week. Five days after its discovery outside the movie theater in Excelsior, a Social Security card was found in the innermost recesses of her clothing, much faded and battered. And that's when her name was revealed: Carolyn Marie Carlson.

At age fifty-three, Carolyn was known to the police as a petty thief, a public drunk, a resister of arrest, a vagrant, a disturber of the peace. She had been thrown out of a number of homeless shelters for stealing, intoxication, and fighting.

"A pity," said the medical examiner, stripping off his gloves, "that the only things we know about her are bad ones. I'm sure her mother thought she was the sweetest baby in the world."

He shut off the tape recorder he'd used during the autopsy, from which he would compile a report. The body had a number of old bruises, none of them serious enough to contribute to her death, and he'd found nothing else that could be a cause of death. Dr. Halperin suspected it was exposure, complicated by the muddled thinking years of heavy drinking can induce — he'd found all the physical damage prolonged alcoholism can cause. Still, he'd taken blood and tissue samples to be tested.

"Now at least there may be next of kin to notify," he concluded, picking up the Social Security card and rereading the name. Carolyn Carlson. Nice name. He wondered if she had been called Carol, or perhaps Lynn.

"Cousin Carrie," said Margaret Smith, "was nobody's idea of an ideal person. Our grandmother said 'she'd steal the pennies off a dead man's eyes.' "

"What would a dead man be doing with pennies on his eyes?" asked Godwin.

They were in Crewel World, Excelsior's needlework shop. The big front window faced north, and the sun had gone south. Godwin missed the morning sunlight that poured in during the summer, but not terribly; sunlight fades fabrics and paper. Artists are very fond of northern light; it's best for telling colors. And stitchers are artists in needlepoint, counted cross-stitch, knitting, and related needlework.

"I asked her that. It's from back in the days when families took care of their dead themselves, from before morticians." Margaret came to the checkout desk with a painted canvas Christmas stocking by Constance Coleman in her hand. She was a very short, trim woman with curly blond hair and big blue eyes, the sort of woman who, many years ago in high school, was the top girl when the cheerleaders formed a human pyramid. "Apparently morticians know some kind of trick to keep dead people's eyes shut, because they open on their own, and so back in the old days in England and Ireland they were weighted down with pennies, which were great big coins back then."

"Yes," nodded Godwin. "My partner, Rafael, has a coin collection, and one of them is an English penny from the reign of Queen Victoria. It's big as a silver dollar, and solid copper." He made a face. "And your cousin would steal them? Was she a really odd woman?"

"Yes, she was, but it's just an expression. People haven't taken care of their dead at home since before she was born. It's just a way of saying someone would steal anything

12

not fastened down. She didn't steal big things, just little things. She was more like a nuisance than a danger to law and order."

"Oh, I see." Godwin stored that tidbit about stealing pennies away in his memory banks — he was peculiarly fond of old-fashioned terms and expressions.

Margaret put the painted canvas on the desk and said, "Will you help me pull the yarns for this?"

"Yes, ma'm, gladly." Godwin picked up the canvas. It depicted three Scottish terriers standing with their forepaws on a windowsill to look out at a winter scene of snow and naked trees — with a reindeer just coming into view. In the foreground — in the foot of the stocking — were wrapped Christmas presents sitting on a patterned rug.

Godwin was a good-looking man a little below medium height, slender, with pale gold hair and light blue eyes. From a distance it was easy to believe he was in his early twenties, though up close the fine lines around his eyes and mouth gave away that he was closer to thirty. Once upon a time this caused him great anxiety, but now that he was in a settled relationship with Rafael (who was thirty-five), it didn't seem to matter. He was Crewel World's store manager — or as he put it, Vice President in Charge of Sales, Personnel and Displays, and Editor in Chief of *Hasta la Stitches,* the needlework shop's newsletter and web site.

He led Margaret over to the far wall, where four long rows of knobbed wooden pegs supported thin skeins of needlepoint wool yarn in colors ranging from white and palest yellow, through deepening greens, reds and purples, and ending in black. Beside it were spinner racks, with DMC Perle cotton in every color on one, and the more exotic flosses, including the hairy Wisper and furry Alpaca, on the other.

He said, "Let's start at the top. How about Crystal Rays dark blue for the sky?" He lifted a card of the shimmery ribbon from a rack. The sky on the stocking was darker at the top than the bottom, so he then reached for a lighter shade.

Margaret said, "I think I'll do the sky all one color, so not as dark or as light as the ones in your hand. You know, it was her thieving ways that killed her."

Godwin put the blues back and selected a medium blue. "Who? Oh, you mean Carrie. How did that happen?"

"Well, they found an empty quart bottle of bourbon with her body. She could never have afforded to buy a quart of that stuff, she must have stolen it. And probably from a person, not a liquor store, because she had bruises all over her, probably from someone beating her up — though it's funny he didn't get his liquor back. Maybe she gave as good as she got; she wasn't afraid to fight back. But she got so helpless drinking it, she lay down in the snow and died." Margaret was suddenly near tears, though she tried not to show it. "Such a foolish thing to do! Such a foolish, *stupid* thing to do!"

"Oh, Margaret, that's so sad! How awful for her family to learn that she died that way!" Godwin, who had a kind heart, had a brief, unsettling image of an old woman stumbling around in a snowstorm, helpless with drink, too fuddled to find her way to shelter, then falling . . . He frowned and blinked the image away.

Margaret switched from sad to angry in the taking of a breath. "It was her own fault!"

Unable to reply sympathetically to that, Godwin went back to the spinner rack and began to turn it, looking for Rainbow Gallery's Flair, a white, translucent tubular ribbon with a subtle roughness to its surface that made it glitter like snow. He pulled two cards of it. Finally he said, "How awful to have a cousin make such a mess of her life.

Were you two close?"

"No, of course not. Well, we used to be, I was the closest to her in age of all the cousins, and we played together a lot when we were children. But once we got into our teens, she started having problems, and at last she drove me away. She drove everyone away, her brothers, even her parents. It just got worse and worse. She dropped out of school, couldn't hold a job. We all tried, every one of us tried to get her to come in and get treatment, but she either flatly refused, or she'd agree and then she quarreled and fought and sneaked out of the clinic and broke all our hearts. It was finally easier to just stop trying. We did hope she'd hit bottom — that's what we were told, that she had to hit bottom before she could start back up — but we were all afraid it would come to something like this first." She sighed as if over a story gone stale with too much telling, and then shrugged. "Wisper for the dogs, right?"

"Yes, good choice. And how about this brown Alpaca for the reindeer?"

"We'll want something else for his antlers, something smooth."

They selected an off-white DMC Perle cotton floss for the antlers, and the same for the square frames of the window. They

16

chose pink, white, and maroon wool for the patterned rug, but the rest — the presents, the wooden floor, the wall — were all to be done in DMC Perle.

"What a delicious green that 699 is," said Godwin, approving her choice, "and 500, of course, for the shady side of the box."

"Yes, of course," agreed Margaret. "Poor Carrie, what a waste."

She needed a set of roll bars for the canvas — "All my others are in use," she explained, being the sort of stitcher who generally had four or five projects under way at once.

Her bill came to nearly five hundred dollars, which she put on her credit card. She thanked Godwin both for his help selecting the fibers and for listening to her distress over her cousin, and left.

Godwin described the conversation to Betsy when she came back from lunching with her accountant. "Now, I don't know a whole lot about hard liquor, but isn't it impossible for anyone to drink a whole quart of bourbon in one sitting?"

Betsy, not much of a drinker herself, replied, "I don't know. But it seems to me even an experienced alcoholic would pass out before finishing a quart of bourbon. Maybe, if she did steal it from someone, it was already half empty. Or maybe she was carrying it around, staying drunk for days on it."

"Ah. Of course," said Godwin, nodding. "That makes sense." So no mystery here; no need for Betsy to exercise her sleuthing skills over this death.

"Well, I'll be dipped," said Excelsior police investigator Sergeant Mike Malloy. "And you're sure about this?" He was scribbling notes as the medical examiner spoke. "The screening test was negative. Nothing in that bottle of bourbon that would harm a person — except for the alcohol, of course."

"We ran the standard tests on tissue and the liquor, and they all came back negative."

"Hmmmm. That's not what I was thinking at all. But thank you."

TWO

Betsy woke to the cheerful notes of J. S. Bach, played at just the right volume. The classical music station of public radio sometimes played something so raucous it yanked her awake, sometimes something so soft and gentle it didn't wake her at all. She kept her clock radio at the station nevertheless because she couldn't bear any other kind of music first thing in the early morning — at least unless NPR got all experimental, which they rarely did at this hour. "Jesu, Joy of Man's Desiring" by the Canadian Brass was just right for the god-awful hour of 5 a.m.

The mattress wobbled as her cat Sophie jumped up on it, summoned by the sound of the radio to her morning cuddle. Betsy obliged, and the big cat came under the blanket, ecstatically purring, touching Betsy's arm gently when Betsy threatened to fall back asleep.

The song ended, time to get up.

The radio started up so early because it was Wednesday, one of the three days each week that Betsy went to water aerobics. She went into the bathroom, brushed her teeth, then pulled on her old swimsuit. Over it went jeans and a sweater, then boots and a heavy coat. She picked up her zippered bag containing soap, shampoo, deodorant, and underwear, and trotted down the stairs and out the back door to the small parking lot. There were about four inches of fresh snow on the ground; her snowplow man hadn't come through yet.

She went up Highway 7 to 100 North, off it to Golden Valley Drive, and pulled into the hollow containing the Courage Center and its big pool.

The pool was Olympic size, heated to bath temperature, so the air above it was warm and very humid. Betsy could feel her winter-dry skin soaking it up as she went down the four steps into thigh-deep water. *Ahhhhhhh,* she thought, comforted. It was now six thirty in the morning, but the huge windows on the far wall showed nothing but the scattered lamps of the parking lot in the darkness.

Despite the earliness of the hour, despite the darkness out there and the heaps of snow the darkness only hid, she felt herself coming fully awake. In the pool with her were two men and seven other women, a medium-size class.

Emily was the group's newest leader. She was young, and had the slender build of an Olympic gymnast. Her button nose and merry smile combined with her build to make her look about fourteen years old.

But she knew what she was doing, and soon the group was kicking straight-legged forward, reaching for their right toes with their left hands then their left toes with their right hands.

"When you're ready," called Emily after a couple of minutes, "cross-country ski!" When she saw everyone had changed motions, she said in a satisfied voice, "There you go."

The class was an hour long. As usual, things grew less organized during the last quarter of the class, when everyone was riding on Styrofoam "noodles" at the deep end of the pool. Some relaxed and paddled aimlessly around, others gathered in twos and threes to chat. In vain, Emily called for flutter kicks or snow angel movements; half of the people either ignored her or couldn't hear her.

The music changed from beat-heavy disco

to New Age dreaminess, and Emily wanted everyone to hang their legs down and circle their feet at the ankles. Betsy, winding up a recipe exchange with Ingrid, happened to hear the call and obeyed.

"So," said Ingrid in her charming German accent, also twirling her feet, "how are things with Connor?" Ingrid was familiar with Betsy's current love interest, Connor Sullivan.

"Oh, I miss him. He and his daughter are in New York visiting her mother, Connor's ex-wife."

"That might be dangerous."

"I know. But he calls me about every other night, and so far, so good."

"I will keep my fingers crossed that it continues like that. And how are other things in Excelsior?"

"We're all right. Things are settling down after that homeless woman was found frozen to death — that kind of thing is rare in Excelsior."

"Yes, it must have been a shock to find someone like that. Do they know who she is?"

"Her name is Carolyn Carlson."

"And no one has asked you to solve the mystery of her death?" asked Ingrid lightly.

"No, thank goodness. I'm awfully busy in

the shop. Inventory is coming up so we're running a big sale."

"I'll try to get out there before your inventory — when is the deadline?"

"Saturday."

"All right, people," called Emily, "let's go back to the shallow end to stretch out."

Driving back to Excelsior on frozen roads, with snow blowing across them in sinuous curves, Betsy indulged in a daydream of retiring to warm and sunny Italy.

But once back in the cozy shop, with a repeat customer making admiring sounds at the cross-stitch patterns she was perusing, Betsy decided her occupation wasn't so bad.

Then Margaret came back in with the materials and the canvas she had bought just a few days ago. "I need to return all this," she said sadly. "I haven't touched it yet, so I can get my money back, right?"

"What, you decided you didn't like the project?" asked Betsy, surprised. Margaret had never returned so much as a skein of floss before.

"Oh, no, I love it! I was about to start on it when —" Her breath caught on a sob. "Oh, Betsy, we need to save every penny!"

Betsy asked, surprised, "Your husband's company has gone under?"

"Oh, no, not anything like that. We had to hire a lawyer. A *criminal defense* lawyer!"

"Oh," said Betsy, momentarily nonplussed. Why on earth would the Smiths need an attorney specializing in defending people accused of a crime? They were both in their late fifties and lived, so far as she knew, lives of quiet probity. Diminutive Margaret was about as friendly and harmless a creature as Betsy could imagine, and her husband, whom Betsy had met only once, had seemed every bit as much a gentleman as one might expect to find married to Margaret.

Her face must have shown her bewilderment, because Margaret said, "Oh, Betsy, we're in *such* terrible trouble!" Her big blue eyes filled with tears.

"Here, Margaret, what's the matter?"

"I'm sure Godwin told you the woman found dead last week was my cousin Carrie?"

Betsy nodded. "Yes, he did. What an awful thing to happen to someone you know, someone who's a relative."

"Well, they finally got around to doing an autopsy, and there's a detective who isn't satisfied that she froze to death but seems to think she was actually *murdered*."

"No! Oh, Margaret, that's *terrible!* Why on

earth does he think that?"

"I don't completely understand — he's not telling us much. I thought it was clear that she got drunk and passed out in the snow and froze to death. And she was a terrible drunk, an alcoholic, everyone who knew her will tell you she was. But I think he thinks someone put something in the bottle of liquor she had with her, something poisonous."

"How . . . peculiar," said Betsy.

"I'm sure it was a terrible accident, a combination of her drinking and the fact that she was out of sight behind the movie theater. What she was doing back there, I don't know, no one knows. If she hadn't been back there, someone might have seen her fall and called an ambulance. It may have been the cold that killed her, or it may have been the alcohol, but Sergeant Malloy is sure there was something in that bottle besides bourbon."

"Margaret, I'm *horrified!*" said Godwin, who had been shamelessly eavesdropping from behind a spinner rack. He came out and put an arm around her slender shoulders. "How awful and . . . *scary!*"

"But terrible as that is," Margaret continued, lifting her chin, trying to look brave, "the worse part is now he's looking for her

25

murderer — and he's looking at *me!*"

"Oh, that's ridiculous!" said Betsy. "How can they possibly think you'd kill anybody?"

"I don't know, I don't know." Margaret's voice broke over the words. She put the bag of floss and the canvas stretcher down on the desk. "It's like a nightmare, only I can't seem to wake up from it."

"There, there!" said Godwin, patting her arm. "I can't believe they're serious about suspecting you."

"But he is, he asks the most impertinent questions and looks at me as if he's going to arrest me!"

Betsy frowned at her. "But surely Mike must have said *something.*"

"But he hasn't, and it's too dreadful! He won't tell me why he's suspicious. He just says they have to consider all possibilities, and he's considering me because I'm her cousin and because I live in Excelsior and she died here and . . . and, well, I was complaining about her to some friends after church last Sunday and it turned out one of them is Mike's wife — that will teach me to *keep family matters within the family!*"

"Complaining about her?" inquired Betsy.

"Well, she came to our door to ask for the price of a bus ticket to Florida, and when I wouldn't give it to her, she kicked in a base-

26

ment window. She'd done that sort of thing before. We used to give her money when she'd come around begging, but she would never buy that ticket or the winter coat or whatever she said she needed — instead she would buy drugs or liquor. When we would offer to drive her to the bus depot or Target to buy the item direct, she'd get angry and say we didn't trust her. And of *course* we didn't trust her — she proved over and over that she was utterly untrustworthy!" Margaret sniffed. Exasperation was drying up her tears. She offered a shaky smile. "Maybe up in heaven, she is driving God and his angels crazy."

"That's the spirit!" said Godwin.

"Thank you, Godwin," said Margaret, missing the joke. "And you're right, Betsy, it's completely ridiculous, and I can't believe Sergeant Malloy is serious about his suspicions, but we've been advised to retain an attorney — and you would not believe how expensive a criminal defense attorney is! So back comes my new pet project, at least until they find out what really happened to Carrie."

Betsy looked down at the big bag of wool and floss, and at the stretcher still in its cardboard sleeve. Normally Crewel World gave only store credit for returned items.

Godwin said, "Betsy, these things are exactly as she took them from the shop. It looks as if she didn't even open the bag."

Betsy nodded. "Under the circumstances, of course I'll remove the charge from your credit card. I'm so sorry to hear about your troubles."

But Margaret wasn't finished. She raised a hand to indicate that and said, "Now that I've destroyed any measure of goodwill by returning these things, I have a favor to ask. I've heard many stories about you helping people wrongly accused of a crime. Could you possibly help us by investigating Carrie's death?"

"Why . . . I don't know." Betsy could not have said why she was surprised at the request. "We're running a special inventory-reduction sale and then the inventory itself . . ." But Margaret only looked more pleadingly at Betsy. She equivocated, "I'd have to think about it."

"Please, Betsy, we're so frightened, and we don't know what to do, who else to ask!"

"Oh, Margaret, you must know I would like to help. But these investigations of mine sometimes root out old quarrels or old secrets you might not want exposed."

This disconcerted Margaret, but not for long. She swallowed and said, "That can't matter, not now, not as much as finding out what really happened. I'll answer any questions, and I'll tell anyone you want to talk to that they must be honest with you. We have to know the truth!"

Margaret's large blue eyes were swimming with tears. She pressed her fingers against her lips to stop their trembling, then said bravely, "Somehow, we'll manage you knowing all our darkest secrets. Please, Betsy, help us. Please!"

Overwhelmed with compassion, Betsy said, "All right, I'll do what I can."

Godwin had stepped back behind Margaret to look as beseeching as she was. Now he leaped gently up and down, clapping his hands silently, smiling in pleasure.

Margaret, sensing movement, turned and caught him in the act.

"Don't mind me," he said, "I just love watching Betsy sleuth. She's very good, and I'm sure she'll get this all straightened out for you. In fact, I'm sure everything will turn out *splendidly!*"

Margaret turned back and looked at Betsy, this time with the tears loosened and streaking down her cheeks. "God bless you," she said.

THREE

The next morning dawned overcast, and by the time Betsy went down to open the shop at quarter to ten, it was snowing. Again. It had been an early winter, and although it was only January, she was already not in the least inclined to think snow romantic or even pretty.

The shop was the middle one of three in the old brick building, with apartments on the second floor. It was located in the small town of Excelsior, Minnesota, on the southwestern shore of the large and beautiful Lake Minnetonka.

For once Betsy was glad her shop was always looking toward the future season, never operating in real time. So the lights came on to shine on knitting yarns in the pale pastels of spring, painted canvases of bunnies and daffodils, counted cross-stitch patterns of blooming trees and babbling brooks and women in crinoline dresses strolling in gardens full of flowers. For just a few moments she stood basking in the scenes, ignoring the white flakes drifting down outside the big front window.

Then she started the coffee brewing, put the start-up money in the cash drawer, turned on the radio — tuned to a light jazz station — and made sure all was in readiness for any shopper who might drop in.

When they didn't come flooding in all at once, she sat down with her employee list and began making phone calls. She called current employees and past ones. She'd already talked to most of them, lining them up for inventory, now only three days off. Some had other jobs, making them hard to connect with — they didn't want a second employer to call them at their main place of work. Others were simply hard to find, perhaps because they knew it was inventory time.

Betsy didn't want just current and old employees to turn out for this tedious but necessary task; she wanted those who could come to bring a reliable relative or friend along. The more hands, the swifter the process. Betsy had allotted all day Sunday to it, and hoped it could be done in the single day of the week that the shop was closed. She would hold a pizza party to mark the completion of the inventory — no, wait, the only pizza joint in Excelsior had recently closed its doors, it would have to be a deli sandwich party. She made a note to talk to Sol's Deli next door about subs, pickles, and potato chips. And to remind herself to pick up some twelve-packs of soft drinks.

Meanwhile: "Hello, Shelly? Are you still available on Sunday to help with inventory? You are? Great! I don't suppose Harve — No, I didn't think so . . . But who? Mindy who? How do you spell that? K-O-W-A-L-S-K-I, just like it sounds. How old is she? Seventeen, you say. But a good, hard worker? Okay, I'll add her to my list. Bring her with you, why don't you? I'll pay her base wages and hope she's worth it. Eight o'clock Sunday morning, yes. Thanks, Shelly, see you and Mindy then."

A few more calls and she had an even dozen, not counting herself and Godwin. Fourteen pairs of hands, that should do very well.

No customers had come in to interrupt her phone calls, which was a disappointment.

She thought about phoning the local liquor store, Haskell's, about whether they were missing a quart bottle of bourbon. She had actually picked up the phone when she had a second thought, which changed her mind. Taking a bottle of liquor from an active alcoholic even just long enough to pour poison into it could be difficult. Easier to buy it yourself, poison it, and arrange for the drinker to get hold of it. He, or she, could have given it to Carolyn Carlson, but it would be more clever to put it out somewhere so Carrie could steal it.

Clever but cruel.

The door sounded its two notes. "Sorry I'm late." It was Godwin, arriving breathless, brushing snow off his shoulders, stamping it off his boots, shaking it off his white leather briefcase, a present from an old boyfriend. "Honestly, if it doesn't stop soon, it won't be all melted until the end of May!"

Ever since Godwin and Rafael had moved into the great gray clapboard condominium right on the lakeshore across the street, Godwin was more likely to arrive a few minutes late for work than when he had been living halfway across town.

He hurried to the back to take his coat off and get his good shoes out of the briefcase. They were old shoes, but made by Gucci and as lovingly cared for as they were long-wearing. Godwin had a keen eye and a deep appreciation of the finer things. That was one reason he liked working in a needlework shop: The surroundings pleased the eye.

Betsy watched him pause as he came out of the little back room to look around at the cross-stitch models that lined the walls in the back portion of the shop — a willowy blond in a beige sweater, a little smile on his handsome face.

But that smile faded as his gaze went forward to the front window, where snow was falling thickly. "When I think of my favorite golf course under all those drifts," he sighed, "I could just cry." Godwin was new to the game, but his enthusiasm for it seemed boundless.

The door sounded its two notes again, and this time it was a longtime customer, here for the sale. The workday had begun.

They stayed busy until about an hour after lunch, when a lull set in. Betsy took a reporter's spiral notebook out of a drawer of the desk that served as a checkout counter, chose a pen from the china mug full of them, and sat down at the library table, opening the notebook to a blank page.

She printed CAROLYN MARIE CARLSON at the top of it, then began a list of things she needed to find out. Number one, of course, was, "Did someone kill Carolyn?" She picked up the phone. No time like the present for answering that question at least.

She dialed Mike Malloy's cell number and after a couple of rings he answered, "Malloy."

"Mike, it's Betsy. Margaret Smith came to see me —"

He growled, "Let me guess why."

"You know why. She's terribly upset and frightened because you think she poisoned her cousin Carrie."

"Or maybe that husband of hers, Marty."

"Marty's too much of a gentleman to poison a female."

"Maybe you're right. Poison is traditionally a woman's weapon, isn't it?"

"I want to know what the poison was."

"That's unknown at the present time."

"Really? What did the autopsy show?"

"It didn't show anything."

"Then why —"

"Because a toxicology test doesn't show everything."

"If the test was negative, why are you so sure it *was* poison?"

"Because I know drunks. Especially longtime drunks, like Ms. Carlson — her liver announced at the autopsy that she was an advanced alcoholic. Advanced alcoholics don't pass out. They're the people you read about in the paper, arrested for drunk driving with blood alcohol three, four, even five times what legally drunk is. And yet they're alive, conscious, able to get behind the wheel, say in understandable English to the arresting officer that they are not drunk. These people can only sleep a few hours at a time because they have to drink some more, maintain that high blood-alcohol level, or they go into DTs."

Betsy said, "What are DTs anyway?"

Mike sighed but said, "Delirium tremens — alcoholics who suddenly quit drinking go into withdrawal, start seeing things, and they get the shakes. A bad case can actually kill a person. That's why they have to go to a detox center to sober up, so they can be medically supervised."

"So you don't think Carrie passed out from drinking and froze to death in the snow."

"No, I don't. She'd been in a fight days before she died, but it only bruised her a little. There was no sign she'd been stabbed or knocked in the head, so how come she laid down behind the Excelsior Dock Theater and died? Something's screwy. I want to know what it is."

After they hung up, Betsy went back to her notebook. Under her first question, she wrote, "Mike thinks so," and made a few notes about their conversation. Mike was not one to make work for himself, and he sounded very sure, so she decided not to dismiss his opinion out of hand. She was usually on the other side of Mike, trying to prove his theory wrong, but this was the first time she might have to prove there was no crime at all.

She turned to the next page in the narrow tablet, and wrote, "If Carolyn was murdered, who killed her?" She underlined the "if," then left a number of lines blank after that question, so she could list suspects and their motives. She paused for a minute, then reluctantly wrote, "Margaret or Martin Smith?"

Next was question three: "When did Carrie die?" because alibis sometimes cleared a suspect.

Number four: "Where did she die?" because perhaps she had been brought to that place behind the movie house after dying somewhere else. Which made Betsy think of number four-a: "Where was she poisoned?" because perhaps she had walked to the place where she was found.

Five: "What was the poison?" because if it was poison, then once it was identified, perhaps she could deduce who might have access to such a thing.

Godwin came by and read her list over her shoulder. "Looks as if you're making a good start," he said.

"No, it only seems that way," Betsy sighed. So many questions, and not one certain answer.

As she pulled into her driveway, Emily Hame was surprised to see a man standing on her front porch, with one of his fingers on her doorbell. Her garage door rose and she drove inside, pressing the button on the opener again to close it.

She was a young matron, not yet visibly pregnant with her third child, with long, light brown hair and intense blue eyes.

Who could the visitor be? Door-to-door salesmen were virtually nonexistent nowadays. Young Mormon proselytizers came around only in the summer. He wasn't a policeman — that was a relief; nothing awful had happened.

So who was he?

She stepped out of her car, went into the house and through it to the front door. The man was just reaching for her doorbell again. He was of medium height, hatless, with very dark brown, curly hair, a narrow, straight nose, hazel-brown eyes, and a tentative smile showing white, even teeth. He wore a navy blue topcoat open at the neck to show a suit and tie. There was snow on his shoulders.

"Yes?" she said.

"My name is Irvin Morcambe," he said, producing a business card. On it was printed, under his name, PRIVATE INQUIRIES.

"I think you must have the wrong house," said Emily.

"Are you Emily Hame?" he replied.

"Yes?"

"I'm trying to locate a Janet Turnquist. Have you seen her lately?"

"Not for months and months. What do you want with her?"

"It will take a while to explain. May I come in?"

"I don't think so. I really don't know that you are who you say you are."

He went back into his suit coat pocket and came out with a little leather folder, which he opened and showed to her. It contained a state identification card indicating he was truly a private investigator licensed in North Dakota. The photograph on it matched.

"Well . . . all right. Come this way." She led him into the living room, which was clean but cluttered with children's toys — the children were with Great-Uncle Ben and Great-Aunt Martha for the afternoon. "I hope this won't take long; I have grocery shopping to do." Emily was just coming home from a dentist appointment. She took off her coat and gloves.

"I'll try to be brief."

"Thank you. Sit down, why don't you?"

Emily moved the Raggedy Ann doll so she could sit on the big squashy recliner; Mr. Morcambe unbuttoned his coat and sat on the couch next to a floppy brown corduroy dog.

"Ms. Turnquist is your aunt, is that right?" he asked, taking a small notebook from an inside pocket.

"Yes, that's right, she's my mother's sister-in-law — she was married to my mother's brother. They were divorced five or six years ago, but I still think of her as my aunt."

Morcambe made a swift note. "You know she's homeless at the present time?"

"Yes, she's been homeless off and on for years." When Emily was a little nervous, she tended to chatter. She didn't like this trait in herself but couldn't stop it. With dismay, she heard herself explaining, "She's mentally ill but they keep turning her loose from the hospital because when they make her take her meds, she's all right. And when she's all right, they turn her loose and she stops taking her meds. Is she in trouble?"

"No, on the contrary, she has a great deal of money coming to her, and I'm trying to find her to let her know."

Emily's heart leaped with joy and excitement. "Money? From where?"

"Her uncle, Jasper Bronson, has died and left it to her."

"I've never heard of him. She never mentioned him to me."

"Janet's maiden name was Bronson, I believe?"

"Was it? I only ever knew her as Janet Turnquist. It's kind of funny to realize that once upon a time, when she was a little girl, she was Janet Bronson." Excitement made Emily even more talkative. "Of course, I was Emily Swanson until I got married, and I don't think my children know that. It's going to be less complicated nowadays, with women keeping their maiden names, isn't it? Except they get their father's last name, don't they? But that's not what we're talking about, is it? You're here to tell me about Aunt Janet inheriting money."

"No, I'm here to see if you can tell me where to get in touch with her," said Morcambe.

"Oh, that's right. Well, I can't. She's living on the street right now. She came to see me

41

in, let me think, September, yes, September. She had a bad case of bronchitis and needed medicine and bed rest and some good food. We took her in — we've done this before — and got her straightened around. But as soon as she was feeling better, she left. She wrote a very pretty note and stuck it up on our refrigerator. It rhymed — she likes to think she's a poet — and she decorated it with flowers using the children's crayons."

"Does she come to visit you on a regular basis?"

"No, only when she's ill. She hates doctors and is afraid of hospitals, but she trusts me, though she never stays here long. She thinks there are government agents after her, you see, and doesn't want to lead them to us. Kind of considerate of her, if you can look at it from her perspective. Of course, trying to stay in hiding with no money is a very hard life. She drinks but I don't think she's a real alcoholic. She says alcohol muffles the voices in her head, poor thing. I don't understand why her uncle left her money; she's not able to handle money. Or is it in one of those special accounts where it's like she gets an allowance?"

"My understanding is that it was left to her outright — but the will was made about fifteen years ago, possibly before she started having mental problems?" He looked at her inquiringly.

"Yes, she started behaving irrationally only about six years ago, though she always was kind of funny. I loved her because she'd be waiting for me outside my middle school sometimes to sneak me home with her and we'd bake hundreds of cookies or go shopping for statues of seals — she collected statues of seals, isn't that peculiar? She said seals are the ballerinas of the sea. She told me we were soul mates and we swore an oath to always take care of one another. I wonder if she and Uncle Jasper were soul mates, too. You know, it's funny he didn't change his will to put the money in trust for her after she became incompetent."

"I'm afraid her uncle contracted Alzheimer's some time between making his will and your aunt developing mental problems. Even if he was aware of her illness, he was too tangled up in his own to make a new will."

"Oh that's so sad!" said Emily. "That's just awful."

"Yes, because it appears from what you've told me that she will not be able to properly handle this money."

"How much is it?"

"I'm not sure, but I believe it's as much

as several hundred thousand dollars."

"Oh, my goodness!" Emily started to smile, she couldn't help it. Hundreds of thousands — good, good news for Aunt Janet. For a change, poor thing.

"By the way, I'm supposed to find out if she's . . . that is, is it possible she's deceased?"

"Oh, no, or I would have heard. That is, I don't think so. I keep giving her cards with our name, address, and phone number on them, so if she ends up in a hospital or jail or worse, they should get in touch with us. Though now I think about it, she pretty generally loses the cards, though not always. It's interesting how she can keep track of her knitting needles or her tapestry needles and floss, but not a three-by-five card with my name and phone number on it."

"I thought she was living on the street."

"Yes, some of the time. She goes to shelters at night, especially in the winter. Oh, you mean because she knits or does embroidery. Well, why not? You can do that in a library if you're quiet about it. It helps her pass the time."

"I see. Hmmm, maybe she thinks she's protecting you by losing the card with your contact information on it."

That gave Emily pause. "I hadn't thought

of that. I think you may be right." Emily smiled at this new evidence of Aunt Janet being sneaky-kind-clever, even if for a demented reason.

"Does she ever let you know how you can get in touch with her?"

"No, she refuses to use the telephone or a computer, she says the government listens in to all electronic communications. But you know, she's about due to get in touch with me again; she generally comes to stay for a few days in the worst of winter. We have a fireplace, and she just loves to sit and look at the flames. She gets quiet then, not so agitated. Usually it's right after Christmas, I get her a new pair of boots at the sales and some new yarn or floss. But she loses track of time and sometimes it's not until the end of January that she shows up."

"Then I'll leave my card with you, and ask you to tell her about her good fortune and that she should contact me."

Emily said, "I'll tell her, but I can't guarantee she will follow through. She may think it's some kind of trick."

"Well, then, you let me know if you see her, all right? Try to find out where she's staying, so I can track her down."

"Yes, of course."

Emily posted his card on her refrigerator

under the magnet shaped like a monarch butterfly, and went out to do her grocery shopping with a happy smile on her face. What good news this would be for Aunt Janet! Surely some kind of arrangement could be made with a bank so that the money wouldn't be lost or wasted. Maybe there would be enough to get an apartment in an assisted-living building, with the kind of supervision that would make Aunt Janet take her meds, and Emily and the children could go over and have a marathon cookie-baking session with her. What a lovely thought!

FOUR

It was a little after closing, and Betsy was tired. Her day seemed to have begun too many hours ago. The snow had just about stopped, but now it was dark out. Betsy started to put her coat on, it being her turn to shovel the front walk while Godwin finished the closing-up protocol.

The phone rang, and Godwin picked up. "Crewel World, Godwin speaking, how may I help you?" he said into the receiver. "Yes, she's here, just a minute." He held the phone out to Betsy.

"This is Betsy," she said, on taking it.

"Betsy, this is Margaret Smith. I know this is terribly short notice, but it only just occurred to me you might be interested. Carrie's funeral is this evening. It's at Huber's Funeral Home right here in Excelsior."

"What time?"

"Visitation is at six, the service at seven."

She'd already missed most of the visitation, the funeral was in twenty minutes. Too late to go? Betsy was not only tired, but hungry. On the other hand, she remembered reading that quite often the murderer would attend the funeral of his victim. The funeral home was within walking distance. Betsy wanted her supper, but this was important.

"I'll be there. Thank you for calling me, Margaret."

She shoveled the walk while Godwin concluded the closing-up routine. She made out a deposit slip for the day's income, gave it and the locked canvas bag to Godwin, and went hustling out the door — only to find that Sol's Deli had closed for the evening. No quick sandwich to eat on the way over. She was so miffed, she got in her car and drove down the block and around the corner to the funeral home.

She found the room marked with a card bearing Carrie's name. The door opened into the back of the room. It was small, but that couldn't disguise the paucity of people in attendance. A woman and three men sat in the front row, in cushioned chairs; another man sat two rows back.

The lighting was gentle on the severely plain wood coffin, with a single bouquet of mixed lilies on the closed lid. Weighty and solemn music played softly through speakers hidden in the ceiling.

Betsy took a seat at the back and waited for something to happen. After a few minutes she realized the man sitting behind the others was Sergeant Mike Malloy. She recognized Margaret's husband, Marty, but wondered who the other two men were. The woman was Margaret.

The door opened and Betsy turned to see another woman shyly enter. She could have been any age between thirty-five and sixty, with dark, curly hair and a narrow, deeply lined face. She was poorly dressed, in an autumn-weight gray coat that would have been too large had she not been wearing at least two sweaters under it. Her boots were heavy and warm-looking but shabby, and she wore a long wool pinky-maroon scarf wrapped over and around her head with just a forelock showing. She stood for a long moment right inside the door, then came to sit in the back row, four chairs away from Betsy. She pulled off a pair of badly pilled, thick black mittens, sighed as she opened and closed her fingers, sniffed once, and fell silent. After a minute, her eyes closed.

The door opened again and a slender woman in an olive green, thigh-length coat came in. In her early twenties, she wore black wool trousers and a pair of shiny black leather boots. She looked around the room, nodded at the shabby woman — whose eyes had snapped open — and unzipped her coat to reveal a black suit coat over a lavender turtleneck sweater.

She went to the front of the room, paused a few moments in front of the casket, then came to murmur to the men and woman at the front of the room, shaking their hands and touching their shoulders. She nodded at Sergeant Malloy.

She glanced up then, and caught Betsy's eye. She came to her, hand extended, to say softly, "Hello, I'm Reverend Marsha of the New Gospel Mission, and I also work at the Naomi Women's Shelter, where Carrie often stayed. I'm here to conduct the service."

"How do you do?" said Betsy. "I'm Betsy Devonshire, here at the invitation of Margaret Smith."

"Did you know Carrie?"

"No, but Margaret is a friend."

"All right. I'm pleased you are taking the time to be here." Reverend Marsha smiled and turned toward the shabby woman. "Hello, Annie," she said, moving toward her. "Sit tight, we're about to get started." She patted Annie on the shoulder as she went by.

Reverend Marsha went to the black lectern beside the casket, and somehow the music stopped. She tapped the microphone growing out of the lectern's top to assure herself it was turned on, and said, "Good evening to you all. We are here to mark the passing of a Christian soul. Carolyn Carlson spent fifty-eight years on this earth, most of it engaged in a struggle with alcohol and drugs, a struggle she ultimately lost. Let us pray."

Betsy bowed her head.

"O Lord," prayed Marsha, "we ask you to grant Your salvation to Your humble servant, Carolyn Carlson. Heal her wounds, Lord, forgive her sins, reward her undying faith in You. In Jesus' name we pray. Amen."

"Amen," said Annie loudly, over the murmured amens from everyone else.

"At this time," said Marsha, "I would like to call on the people present to talk about Carrie, perhaps to share a favorite memory of her."

There was a lengthy pause, then one of the men rose and came to the lectern. Marsha smiled up at him — he was well over six feet tall — and stepped aside.

"I'm Carrie's older brother Jack." He bowed his head for a moment, gathering his thoughts. He was a handsome man, with silver hair, bushy eyebrows, and a strong, straight nose. He wore a dark business suit with a white shirt and deep maroon tie. His head came up, and he continued, "Carrie was born in Buffalo, Minnesota, the third of three children, of whom I was the oldest. My best memory of her is as a little girl, a very pretty little girl. Her favorite color was pink, and she loved to wear this one dress covered with lots of pink ruffles. Even her socks had little ruffles on them, and Mother would tie a pink bow in her hair. She loved to be told how pretty she was, how much she looked like a little princess. Until she got into high school, she was always very careful how she dressed. And she always looked like a princess. That's how I'll remember her, as my beautiful sister, the princess."

He looked around the room with a smile and a curious air of defiance, then went back to his seat.

There was another pause, then the second man got up from the front row. He looked a lot like Jack, only not as tall. He went to the lectern. He wore a dark blue plaid sport coat, navy blue trousers, and a black necktie.

"I'm Bob, Carrie's other brother, the one in the middle. I also remember her as the little princess. I remember her sitting on the couch on Sunday mornings with her hands folded in her lap, waiting for the rest of us to finish getting ready for church, not moving so her dress wouldn't get dirty or wrinkled. I remember years later, during her six months of sobriety, when she tried to recapture some of that little princess look, took pride in her new clothes, dyed her hair and got a perm, fell in love with a good-looking man. I remember how happy she was before it all went to pieces for her again. But for those six months, she was happy, and we were happy for her. I think she was fragile but none of us knew it or knew how to keep her from breaking. We live in hope that wherever she is now, she's whole and healed."

"Amen!" cried Annie. "Hallelujah!" Then she looked embarrassed when no one echoed her sentiments.

Bob went back to his seat, and there was another pause.

Margaret stood and went to the lectern. There were dark shadows under her eyes, and her dark brown dress hung on her — she looked pounds lighter. Her voice, when she spoke, was husky. "I remember Carrie as exciting. She was the only cousin in our family close to me in age, so we played together a lot as children. She had a vivid imagination, so make-believe was great fun

— providing I let her be the princess while I was the faithful servant or the wicked witch or even, once in a while, the loyal horse. I think Bob put his finger on Carrie's problem: She was fragile in some nonapparent way, and something in her broke and could not be repaired. I think it left her angry or maybe jealous of anyone not broken. Sometimes, in these later years, when she was having a hard time of it, she would come to me for money, which I didn't always give her, because she would lie about why she wanted it. Now that she's gone, I can forgive her — and I hope she can forgive me. God bless her."

Everyone looked at the third man — Marty — but he shook his head no. Obviously he wasn't going to speak.

There was a brief pause, then Annie rose and came quickly to the lectern, unwrapping the scarf from around her head and leaving it draped around her shoulders. "Well, I liked her, she had sass!" Annie announced, gripping the lectern fiercely. "She didn't take nothin' from nobody. The way she told it, she'd been cheated left and right her whole life and so of course she was mad. Like everybody else, she had a cross to bear, and hers was like a lot of us'ns, liquor. An' don't tell nobody, but she liked some of that other stuff, too . . ." Here Annie cocked her head, winked, and sniffed sharply, as if inhaling something up her nose. "She was sad some of the time, and mad a lot of the time, but she could be sweet and she could be funny, when she wanted to be. She was a real go-getter, and while not everybody liked her, I did, so God rest her soul. That's all I got to say."

Annie returned to her seat, breathing as deeply as if she'd run a mile. She turned her head and saw Betsy staring at her, and nodded once sharply.

After another lengthy pause, Reverend Marsha returned to the lectern. "Let us pray," she said, and heads bowed.

"O Lord, we place in Your loving and forgiving hands the soul of Carrie Carlson. Bring her home to Your heavenly kingdom, Lord, and grant her the peace she sought for so long in this world. And please give peace and comfort to those here to mark her passing. In Jesus' name we pray. Amen."

A soft chorus of amens answered her prayer.

After another pause, Margaret stood and faced them, saying, "If everyone would care to come to my house, there will be coffee and cake." She gave the address.

Betsy didn't want to go, but when she

overheard Reverend Marsha saying she would drive Annie there, Betsy decided she didn't want to miss a chance to interview them about Carrie.

Glad now she'd brought her car, she went out into the cold and darkness and drove the few blocks to Margaret's home.

The house was a pale green clapboard ranch with a yellow brick front and a modest front porch. Inside, in the dining room, which was open to the living room, stood a cloth-covered table with two layer cakes, one with white icing and one with chocolate, each topped with a three-dimensional pink lily made of icing. Between the cakes was a punch bowl filled with some red liquid in which slices of oranges were floating, and near the far end of the table were two large coffeepots, one marked with a small cardboard sign labeled DECAF. A silver cream pitcher and sugar bowl were beside them.

Pretty china dessert plates and silver forks and spoons were placed on the other end of the table, with heavy cloth napkins rolled and stacked pyramid style. Evidently Margaret had hoped for a better turnout — there were easily enough plates for a dozen people.

"This looks beautiful," Betsy said to Margaret, waiting with a plate for her slice of cake.

"Thank you, Betsy, and thank you for coming. May I cut you a large slice?"

Betsy knew she should say no, but her stomach was demanding something at once, and the cake looked delicious. "Yes, please, and make mine chocolate."

Betsy took her cake and a cup of decaf coffee into the living room. It was a large room with a big purple couch, a matching love seat, a green upholstered chair, and a padded-seat armchair.

Carrie's brothers, Jack and Bob, werc seated on the couch, one of thcm cating vanilla cake, the other chocolate. Reverend Marsha was standing by the window with a cup of steaming coffee, gazing out into the night — it was still snowing, but very lightly. Margaret's husband, Marty, was standing at the table, waiting for his wife to slice him a piece of cake.

Mike Malloy, bending over Annie, who was seated in the upholstered chair, was nodding and writing something in his notebook. Annie, deeply involved in eating a large, dark slice of cake, seemed to be giving mostly short answers, and was not looking at Malloy.

Betsy went to Marsha. There was an occasional table underneath the window; Betsy put her coffee cup down on it and used her fork to separate a generous bite of cake from her slice. "Not a fan of cake?" she asked before putting the bite into her mouth.

"Oh, yes, but I had a really late lunch, so I'm not hungry. It looks delicious, though."

Betsy swallowed and said, "It is. May I ask you some questions?"

"About what?"

"Carrie Carlson."

"Why do you need to ask? Who are you?"

"My name is Betsy Devonshire, and I do private investigations. Margaret Smith has asked me to look into her cousin's death."

"I understand that man over there is a police investigator. He's asking us questions, too."

"Yes, he's Sergeant Mike Malloy. But I'm doing my own investigation. You can ask him if you like, and he'll tell you I do this, sometimes as an adjunct to his investigations."

"Is that legal?"

"Yes, ma'm."

"What could you possibly ask me that he won't?"

"I don't know — nothing probably. We just sometimes draw different conclusions."

58

Marsha fixed Betsy with a cool, blue stare, then blinked and nodded shortly. "All right, ask me some questions."

"How well did you know Carrie?"

Marsha took a drink of her coffee. "Not well. I don't think anyone in my profession knew her well. She was quite determined about that."

"You mean she didn't like members of the clergy."

"That, too. But I am also a licensed, registered counselor specializing in problems of the homeless."

"I see. She was not very cooperative, you mean."

Marsha smiled. "I mean she was obstinate, illogical, demanding, and difficult. Just like a great many other of my clients. If she had been sweet, kind, understanding, and cooperative, perhaps she could have been moved from the ranks of the homeless to renter, from jobless to fully employed. She was, under that angry veneer, intelligent and clever. But Belligerent was her name and 'None of Your Business' was her game."

"Was Carrie in need of meds?"

Marsha frowned in thought. "I think she had a personality disorder, but I'm not sure it was a kind that there's a medication for. Like Annie said at the service, she was sure that she'd been cheated her whole life of what was rightfully hers, and so was determined to have her own way as often as possible. Technically she wasn't insane, but she was a very unhappy person. She had a talent for making people around her unhappy, too."

"Do you know of anyone particularly angry with her, or who may even have hated her for any reason?"

There was a pause for thought. "No. People didn't like her, because she was quarrelsome. But what they mostly did was stay away from her, or refuse to rise to her bait. She hadn't been in a fight in a shelter in a number of weeks. Since the weather started getting bad, she'd been mostly behaving. That's proof she could control her temper, and her drinking, when the result of not controlling herself was to be thrown out into the cold."

"You wouldn't actually throw someone out into a snowstorm because they were drunk or under the influence of illegal drugs, would you?"

"There are shelters that will take people in those conditions, but they aren't nice places, and the people have to sleep on the floor. There's only so much we can do, and we have to protect the clients who aren't breaking the rules. When it wasn't awfully bad out, Carrie would resume getting drunk and picking fights. She'd happily sleep in a park or under an overpass if she thought she'd got some of her own back."

"How terribly sad. Maybe a few thousand hours in a psychiatrist's office would have helped her."

"Very possibly. Alcoholics Anonymous would have helped, too, and been a lot cheaper. But first you would have had to persuade her to go, and that simply was not possible."

"I see. Did she have any friends at all?" Betsy ate some more cake.

"She knew a lot of people, and sometimes they would form a kind of hasty, temporary friendship when one or the other had money for alcohol or drugs. I don't know why Annie decided they were friends, but Annie marches to her own drummer, too. I don't think Carrie had any friends in a way you or I would define it. She was a solitary sort of person."

"Did anyone you know of hate her?"

"No, not really. The friendships and quarrels both were . . . ephemeral."

Betsy nodded and picked up her cup of coffee. "Thank you. You've been very helpful."

She finished her coffee before going on to talk to Annie.

"May I get you another cup of coffee?" she asked, and Annie looked up at her suspiciously.

"Who're you?" she asked.

"I'm Betsy Devonshire, a friend of Margaret Smith."

"You were at the funeral."

"Yes. Would you like another cup of coffee? I'm getting one for myself."

"Sure. Milk and sugar, please. Real sugar, and lots of milk."

"More cake, too?"

"You think that would be all right?"

"I'm sure it would."

Betsy took the woman's plate and cup and went into the dining room. Almost half of the cake remained; she cut a slice for Annie, refilled and doctored her cup as requested, and after refilling her own cup — imitation sugar and just a dribble of milk — returned to the living room.

"Thank you, honey," said Annie, reaching for the plate. "Just put the coffee down right there, okay?"

Betsy put it on the saucer on the coffee table as indicated. "May I ask you some questions?"

"What about?"

"About Carrie."

"What do you want to know?"

"What was she like?"

"You don't know?"

"No, I never met her."

"Then what were you doing at the funeral?"

"Margaret Smith invited me."

Annie took a big bite of her cake. "Why don't you ask her about Carrie?"

"I will, but I want to ask you, too. You defended her very well at the funeral."

After a pause while Annie swallowed, she said, "I had a good reason to."

"What's that?"

Annie smirked and lifted the cake plate. "This. I was hoping for a whole supper, but this is pretty good. I'll have to remember to thank our hostess. Now will you kindly go away and let me eat in peace?"

"All right," said Betsy as mildly as she could. She finished her own cake, then took her coffee cup and dessert plate into the kitchen, where she found Margaret stacking a few other plates in the sink.

"May I talk with you for a minute?" asked Betsy.

"Certainly," said Margaret, wiping her hands on a dish towel draped over the handle on the oven door.

"Do you know of anyone who was particularly close to Carrie?"

"No. But I was no longer close to her myself. I was surprised at that Annie person coming to the funeral, for example. I had no idea Carrie knew her. Actually, I was surprised at Annie. I didn't think Carrie had any friends, she was a very difficult person. She'd quarrel with anyone."

"Who would know?" persisted Betsy.

"Perhaps Reverend Marsha?"

"No, I've already talked to her."

"Then I don't know, I'm sorry, but I just don't know."

"Would Marty?"

"He liked to pretend she didn't exist."

"Well, tell me about her family."

Margaret said, "We had the same grandparents, on my mother's side, Mr. and Mrs. George DuPre. They're dead, of course, and so are Carrie's parents. Carrie was the only daughter of Uncle Will — he was my mother's brother — and Aunt Marie. As you heard at the funeral, they started that little princess business, which I now think was a mistake. Carrie was very pretty, but badly spoiled. She came to think that any time she didn't get her way, it was some sort of conspiracy against her. She was bright and she could be very sweet — generally when

64

she wanted something. I liked her when we were little, even when she talked me out of my favorite doll. She was a year older than I, and my parents used to hold her up as an example to me. Nothing but A's on her report cards right up until her last year of middle school, when she discovered alcohol. She'd gotten harder and harder to get along with, being so self-centered and greedy, but in high school she became simply impossible. Her poor parents! Uncle Will and Aunt Marie spent thousands of dollars over those next few years for therapy, and then getting her out of juvenile hall, then out of jail, and then into treatment centers, paying her living expenses between times. At first they made excuses for her, then they tried Tough Love, but in the end they gave up. They refused to talk to her, to see her. They said it was self-defense. She broke their hearts and their spirits. It was so awful, just so awful."

"Did she finish high school?" asked Betsy.

"No, she dropped out after her junior year. Flat refused to go back, said all her teachers were against her and so were half the kids. Which might have been true at that point, she was always coming to school high or drunk, getting caught stealing, getting into fights with everyone . . ." Margaret

65

sighed. "I put a lot of the blame on her dreadful boyfriend, whose name was, believe it or not, Dice. A juvenile delinquent and a thoroughgoing wicked young man. I'm sure he's the one who introduced her to drugs. But she took to them very easily."

"What was Dice's last name?"

Margaret thought, then shook her head. "I'm sorry, I don't remember."

"What about her two brothers who were at the funeral? Were they her only siblings?"

"Yes. Jack's the older one, he graduated before she started getting into serious trouble, but Bob stuck up for her all his senior year, even got suspended once when he waded into a fight, trying to break it up — one she started, by the way. I had the most terrific crush on Bob for doing that."

"Do you think they'll talk with me about Carrie?"

"Yes, I'm sure they will."

Betsy halted on her way to the brothers to talk to Marty. He was a handsome man in his middle fifties, a little below average height, with very pale gray eyes. He shook his head when Betsy asked if he would talk to her about Carrie. "I don't think I ever met her," he said. "And that's probably just as well."

Carrie's brother Bob was a medium-tall

man with light brown hair sprinkled with gray and kind brown eyes. He was in his later fifties by the look of him, with broad shoulders and a trim waist, an athlete's build. His voice was surprisingly deep for a man with such a mild expression.

"I always thought it was her new boyfriend that got her all twisted around," he said. "Dice — I don't know his real first name — was a real tough guy, a greaser. Broke our mom's heart when Carrie took up with him. Looking back, I think he abused her, but the more we objected to him, the more Carrie stuck up for him, defied everyone. He's the one who encouraged her drinking and got her started on smoking dope. I wish —" For just an instant his face filled with anguish. "Ah, what's the use of wishing! It happened like it happened, nothing to do about it now. But he was the ruination of her, it was almost like that was his goal in life, to take some naïve kid and mess her up forever."

"Where's Dice now?"

"In prison, last I heard. He killed a girl."

"He *what?*"

Bob nodded. "For real. It was after he broke up with Carrie. He couldn't ruin her any more than she was, so he went after a new victim. The new one stabbed him, probably in self-defense, and he killed her. Carrie wrote to him for a while."

Betsy said, "I understand she kept going into treatment —"

"Oh, hell, yes. Over and over again. She got to where she knew the routine almost better than the doctors and nurses and therapists. But nothing took, or not for long. Whatever was wrong with her, it couldn't be fixed, not permanently. I think it was all his fault, that fellow Dice. He destroyed what goodness was left in her, and she knew it, but she blamed everyone but him."

"Did she ever marry?"

"No. She got engaged once, while she was sober; she'd been sober for almost six months. He seemed like a nice enough man, but she met him at an AA meeting. They warn you, if you're in recovery, don't date someone else in recovery. Sure enough, he fell off the wagon and got hurt bad in a car accident, driving while drunk, and she dived right back into the bottle. I don't think I ever saw her again when she was completely straight and sober." He shook his head slowly from side to side. "Hard to believe that was over twenty years ago. Not hard to believe she's dead, though. I've been expecting that for years — but not that she'd get murdered. That I still find hard to believe. I mean, she was not hurting anyone but herself, not really. Who'd want to murder a harmless old drunk?"

Carrie's other brother, Jack, declined to be interviewed as well. "She was the sweetest sister a fellow ever had, until she met Dice Paulson," he declared. "That's all I have to say."

FIVE

Betsy had virtually no experience with homeless people, so she got on the Internet later that evening to do a little research. What she discovered was disheartening.

On any given night in Minnesota, one web site declared, there are about nine thousand people without a place to sleep — although that had to be an estimate, because who could possibly know for sure? Homeless shelters can take only seven thousand, a thousand are turned away, and a thousand more don't seek shelter.

This in a Minnesota winter.

Betsy could not understand why someone would prefer trying to survive outdoors on a January night rather than go to a shelter. After all, the service was free, right?

Then she had an image from an old movie in which, in order to get a free meal, clients had to sit through a sermon. Was that what it was — they felt they were being lectured, made to feel ashamed of themselves, before they got a place to sleep?

What were the rules in these places?

But when she found a copy of the rules for clients for one local shelter, she didn't think they were particularly onerous or hard to understand. The shelter was one that accepted clients for up to forty days. No alcohol, no drugs, said the rules; no fighting, no stealing, no threats, no racial slurs. There were counselors available if a resident wanted help with a problem.

On the other hand, that shelter's aim was to turn lives around, and if a person was determined to continue drinking or taking drugs, even those basic rules for civilized behavior might be impossible to follow.

Was Carrie in that group? It seemed so.

Was Annie another? Betsy recalled her defiant attitude during the funeral and again at Margaret's house. But she hadn't smelled alcohol on her breath, and Annie seemed alert but not hyperalert, which would indicate she didn't have a drug problem. What was her story?

Betsy's impression of the majority of street beggars she encountered in downtown Minneapolis was that they were, or wanted to be, drunk. Maybe Annie wasn't a beggar.

She Googled "Homeless alcoholism" and

found a lengthy report from the National Institute on Alcohol Abuse and Alcoholism. It concluded that alcohol abuse is a significant problem among the homeless.

Well, duh, thought Betsy.

Sometimes a person becomes homeless because of a drinking problem, the report continued; sometimes a person turns to alcohol as a coping mechanism on becoming homeless; sometimes a person is mentally ill and uses alcohol as a form of self-medication.

Surprisingly, the report said that as places known as skid row were demolished, affordable housing decreased. Betsy had never thought of skid row as an example of affordable housing. But all right, maybe it was. At least it provided shelter and independence.

Alcoholism often begins in adolescence, said another article. Teens who are depressed turn to alcohol.

From Margaret and Bob's descriptions, Carrie hadn't seemed to be depressed, thought Betsy, but then she read, "Depression in teens often expresses itself in antisocial behavior — wild parties, driving while intoxicated, fighting with parents, siblings, and friends. Instead of being sad, they might become touchy, or angry. They skip school,

72

take unwise chances, and seem to hate everything."

Betsy did not think there could be a more succinct description of Carrie, both as a teen and in later life. Was hers a case of arrested development?

Interestingly, the article's author thought so. Once alcoholism sets in, he noted, the mental and emotional development of the victim stops. Problems that make a person turn to drinking are not eased by alcohol but remain and are, in fact, strengthened.

So maybe Carrie did remain a rebellious teen all her life.

How incredibly tragic.

But did knowing that move Betsy any closer to figuring out who wanted her dead? No.

She shut off her computer and went to bed.

But the next morning she woke with a glimmer of an idea. Before she went down to open the shop, she called Sergeant Mike Malloy at the police department.

"Mike, have you looked at a character named Dice Paulson? He and Carrie Carlson were very close when she was young. Several people I've talked to say theirs was a very abusive relationship. Last I heard, he was in prison for killing another woman.

But that happened a long time ago, and I'm wondering if he's been set free. And if he decided to look Carrie up. Maybe he's the person responsible for her bruises."

"Yes, that's a name I've already got. I think it's grasping at straws — after all, that *was* a very long time ago — but I'm checking it out."

"Let me know, all right?"

Later in the day, down in the shop, business still wasn't at the hoped-for level. "What do you suppose we're doing wrong?" Betsy asked Godwin.

"Nothing. Business is up, it's just not as far up as we want it to be. You know what's going on, don't you? They're waiting for the Grab-It Sale after Nashville."

Every February, The National Needlework Association held a take-away needlework market in Nashville — shop owners gathered to see the latest in needlework products, and bought them on the spot. Like some other shops, Crewel World offered a special sale after arriving back home. Betsy and Godwin priced the items they had bought but did not put them on the shelves before holding the sale the next day. Customers got to root through boxes and bags in search of that special got-to-have-it pattern or gadget or new color of floss. Betsy recalled last year, when a perfect buying frenzy happened, and a huge portion of the new products were sold. Her expression softened as she remembered the profit that wonderful day.

Comforted by the memory, Betsy returned to rearranging the painted canvases on the hinged set of canvas doors in the front section of the shop. Enough of the needlepoint paintings had been sold that there were noticeable gaps in the display. Betsy began rearranging the remaining ones so there weren't any open spaces.

Later, she was helping a customer select floss from the new Sullivan display rack when she heard another stitcher, Cathy Craig, offering advice to Godwin. "I've found that beginning your counted-thread piece with what I call the grain of the fabric helps a great deal in counting and keeping your place."

"Grain of the fabric?" queried Godwin, who was much more talented at needlepoint than at counted cross-stitch.

Betsy and her customer both paused to eavesdrop.

"Yes. By that, I mean making sure the intersection of fabric threads in the lower left-hand corner of your cross-stitch has the vertical fabric thread on top. By starting each stitch this way, you know you haven't skipped a thread, and it works as a visual aid to help you find your next stitch. The hole in the weave appears larger in these areas and your needle actually would rather go there than in the holes adjacent to it."

Betsy, whose attitude toward counted cross-stitch was that if the pointy end of the needle went through the fabric first, she was doing it right, found this amusingly picky.

She heard Godwin say, "Thanks for that great hint," which is what a good employee always says on getting advice from a customer. But Godwin went on, "I have a pattern I want to work, and if it comes out well, I want to enter it in the State Fair. I figure every advanced technique helps."

Betsy's customer murmured, "I know a needlework judge. Godwin's absolutely correct."

The piece Godwin was going to stitch was "Hoopla," a dramatic pattern adapted from the art of French illustrator Olivier Blanc. It depicted the silhouette of a slender girl stepping forward on long, long legs, her skirt flowing behind her in a dense, complex swirl of many colors.

Later, near the end of the working day, Godwin was pulling the flosses for the piece when the door sounded its two notes. An older woman with a graying forelock showing from under her green knit cap came in. She wore a heavy brown parka with the hood lying back on her shoulders, gray wool slacks, and boots that looked familiar.

"Annie?" said Betsy, surprised.

"Yeah, it's me. Can I talk to you?"

"Of course. Come in. Would you like a cup of tea? Or coffee?"

"Tea would be nice. Thank you." Annie seemed more subdued than the assertive woman of yesterday's funeral.

But perhaps that was because she was cold. Once half her tea had been drunk, she perked up again, and abruptly dropped the topic of the snowy winter they'd been having.

"You wanted me to talk to you about Carrie Carlson," she said.

"Yes, I did."

"Well, maybe I was kinda rude to you last night, and I'm sorry. Reverend Marsha said you're legit and she gave me bus fare to come out and talk to you."

"It's a very long trip from Saint Paul all the way out here."

"You bet your sweet bippy it is! So how about a refill on the tea?"

"Yes, ma'm!" said Betsy, amused. She

took the pretty porcelain cup to the back room, where a plug-in kettle lurked, and refilled it.

So long as she was back there, she made herself a cup of raspberry tea and put three shortbread cookies on each saucer before coming back.

Annie brightened up at the cookies and said, "Okay, honey, fire away."

"How long had you known Carrie?"

"Maybe four or five months? Since late summer. She knew places to hang out during the day. And most important, places to hang out between the time the skyways close and the shelter opens. That's always a hard time of day, you know, especially if it's raining. She was real good at being invisible." Annie ate one of the cookies in a single bite.

"Being invisible?"

"Uh-hmmm." She chewed and swallowed, then drank some tea, looking around at the counted cross-stitch patterns hanging on the walls, oblivious to Betsy's incomprehension.

"I don't understand," said Betsy.

"No? It's simple. You don't want anyone noticing you in particular. Regular folks don't want some smelly bum stinkin' up where they are, so the first thing is, you get

78

clean. Shelters usually have free showers, so you take advantage, and they got free clothes, so you take advantage again. Plus, you wash your face and hands every time you get the chance. And you look busy, like you're shopping or reading or checking on an important letter — the big post office in downtown Minneapolis is a good place to hang out, plus you can get General Delivery letters there — or waiting for someone to meet you — you look at your watch, or where a watch would be if you had one. You don't act up, you don't beg, and you don't catch anyone's eye. See? Invisible."

Betsy nodded. It had never occurred to her that this skill might be useful or necessary. "And Carrie taught you how to do this."

"Her and others. I've only been homeless for a year, and I was always getting hassled till I learned how to act." She held up a hand, nails forward. "See? Clean."

"What was Carrie like?"

"Oh . . ." Annie picked up another cookie and ate it thoughtfully. She sipped her tea and looked at Betsy another long moment, then said, "You want the truth?"

"Absolutely."

"She could be hard to get along with. Not eager to please, that was her. But she was a survivor, so when it suited her, she could be good to be around, even helpful. And she was funny, she could tell you jokes that'd make you laugh fit to bust. But that was usually because you had something she wanted a share of." She held up the last cookie. "Carrie'd see me with this, she'd move right in, talking trash, telling stories, and next thing I know, she's eaten it her own self."

"I guess people resented her for that."

"Oh, some, I guess. But it's a dog-eat-dog world, you know." She ate the cookie.

"Still," persisted Betsy. "I heard there were healing bruises on her body found during her autopsy. Have you got any idea who might have done that?"

"No," Annie said after some thought. "A lot of us have bruises. They don't call it the school of hard knocks for nuthin', you know."

"Could it have been because she took something? Someone said she was a thief."

"Yeah, well, she could be."

"What would she take? I mean —"

Annie looked at Betsy over the top of the steaming cup of tea. "You mean what would someone like me have worth stealing?"

"Um . . ." Betsy nodded, uncomfortable.

"A bottle of wine or maybe a little stash."

Seeing Betsy's incomprehension, she clarified, "Dope. Weed, or smack, or crack, didn't matter to her. Anything to mess with her mind. A nice-looking coat or a good pair of boots. Money — a couple dollars can make a big difference when you're trying to make it through the hungry part of the day."

"I suppose someone stealing from you can make you really angry."

"It can. But generally people get over it. We're used to bad things happening to us."

"But surely not every time. Do you know anyone who was angry with her lately? Maybe someone who hated her?"

"No." Annie read the disbelief in Betsy's eyes and said, "She'd been behaving! It's cold out there, and she needed to be a good character to stay in the shelter. Stealing can cause a fight, and fighting's not allowed. So she wasn't misbehaving like she does when the weather's nice and it's not so tough to sleep outdoors. She was still feisty, and she'd steal something she was sure she could get away with, but she wasn't starting fights or letting anyone else start one with her. She was almost easy to get along with lately."

Annie drank the last of her tea. "I better get out to the stop, there's only one bus back to town from out here. This is a nice place you got. Pretty, and peaceful. I bet you're glad to work here."

"Yes, I am." *Especially after this conversation,* Betsy thought. She wished she could offer Annie a ride, but she had a beginner's knitting class to teach in about an hour. She stood. "Thank you for coming to see me." She wished she'd put more cookies on Annie's saucer.

Annie stood. "Yeah, well, I hope I was some help to you."

"You were. Thank you."

"I hope you find out who killed her. It's good you're takin' the time to look into it. I wish I could help you someway. It ain't fair, you know, we don't bother nobody, but everybody thinks bad of us. I wish everybody who thinks we're dirt under their feet could spend a week in our shoes." She grinned, showing discolored teeth. "Serve 'em right."

Betsy was hurrying through the close-up process — she wanted to get upstairs for a quick supper before the class started — when the phone rang. Exasperated, she grabbed up the receiver.

"Crewel World, Betsy speaking, how may I help you?"

"Betsy, it's Mike Malloy."

Suddenly Betsy was not in such a hurry anymore. "Hello, Mike, what have you got to tell me?"

"Dice Paulson, Carrie's abusive boyfriend, was paroled six months ago."

"If he's on parole, you know where he is, right?"

"He never reported to his parole officer. His whereabouts are unknown."

SIX

As Betsy feared, on Sunday there were only nine people present for inventory. The calls had started coming in first thing Saturday morning. "My kid is sick," "I sprained my wrist," "A pipe broke and my basement is flooded" (that last one was probably authentic).

Crewel World was not a really big shop, not like Needlework Unlimited or Stitchville USA, so eleven workers, including herself and Godwin, were probably enough, if they got right to it.

"You don't have to count how many DMC 433s I have," Betsy explained after everyone had been served a paper cup of coffee or tea. "Just how many DMC flosses at the same price. Same with needles, not how many size thirteen, size fourteen, size sixteen, and so on, tapestry needles, just how many packets of needles at the same price." She took a sip of her tea. Everyone was looking at her very intently, even those who had done this before. It was a little scary.

"Same with the yarns," Godwin said, nodding.

"Any questions?"

Despite the intense looks, no one had any. Maybe they were just eager to get started.

"Everyone have your inventory sheet and pen?" Betsy held up hers.

In response, everyone held up theirs.

"All right. Shelly, you take the painted canvases. Goddy, you mentioned the knitting yarns, you take them. Mindy, you take the spinner racks beside the counted cross-stitch patterns." And so on until everyone had an assignment. Betsy's own assignment was "back stock," items in the back of the shop waiting for space in the retail section.

There wasn't a lot of talking after the first ten minutes, which was a good sign; everyone was bent to his or her task.

At twelve twenty, Betsy called a forty-minute halt. Betsy brought out the deli sandwiches, chips, pickles, and soft drinks. Her workers gathered around the library table or sat at the checkout desk — two sat on the floor and sneaked fragments to the cat Sophie. When Betsy noticed them, the cat quickly lay down on a potato chip and tried to look innocent. Betsy decided not to notice a scatter of crumbs down the cat's front. Sophie currently weighed twenty-one pounds, and Betsy despaired of getting her to lose any of it. How could she, with customers and employees constantly undermining her efforts?

As one o'clock approached, Betsy went through the shop, checking with each employee — everyone was back at work, another good sign — to see where she was in the counting. So far, adequate progress was being made, which was a relief. Each person had her own method; the most common was the four vertical sticks with an angled one to make units of five — though one person was counting each stroke as five, making units of twenty-five. But she was counting skeins of floss.

When Betsy came to Godwin standing among skeins of yarn, he said, "My gosh, we have a *lot* of yellow!"

"That was my error. I placed an order twice, remember?"

"Oh, that's right. We should schedule a spring sweater class. Yellow is such a cheerful spring color."

"Good idea."

Overheard on her way to the back of the shop: "I have three PHDs," which Betsy knew were not doctor of philosophy degrees, but Projects Half Done. She had a few of those herself, plus a few barely started. So many projects, so few hours in a day.

Six yards away: "Well, I hear she's sleuthing again," she heard Mindy say.

"Really? For who? The only mysterious death I've heard about lately is that homeless woman."

Betsy paused, partly hidden behind a spinner rack, to listen.

"That's who it is. Turns out that homeless woman is a cousin or aunt or something of Margaret Smith. And the police are looking very hard at Margaret over it."

"No!"

"Yes. Well, of course she couldn't be involved, not really. But there was bad blood between them, and I hear she's really scared she might be arrested."

"Poor thing!"

That "poor thing" was said in a very gratified tone, and Betsy's heart sank. Margaret was a rather proper sort of woman, and there might be people around who'd like her taken down a peg or two. If this was the sort of thing being said about Margaret, it was terribly important not only that there be found no proof whatever of her guilt, but that the real culprit, if there was one, be loudly and overwhelmingly brought to justice.

But first things first; she went back to counting her reserve stock of bamboo knitting needles.

Thanks to bar codes and computers, Betsy had records of purchases and sales for the past year to compare to the physical count of the inventory.

"One nice thing," she said to Godwin on Monday after comparing the two, "is that thefts are actually down." She knew this because the running count kept by her computerized cash register showed inventory not far above the actual count done on Sunday by her employees. Betsy attributed that to the honesty of her employees and the carefully nurtured rumor that she prosecuted shoplifters.

It was near lunchtime. Marty had called Betsy yesterday to ask for a luncheon date.

"What do you suppose he wants?" asked Godwin.

"He's probably hoping for good news about clearing his wife."

Godwin said, "Suppose you do — and it's Marty who did it?"

"Why would Marty Smith murder Carrie

Carlson? He told me he's pretty sure he never met her."

"All the more reason to suspect him. I mean, isn't it always the one you never would suspect who did it?"

Betsy smiled. "Not always."

"Well, who do you think did it?"

"I don't know yet."

"So it could be Marty."

"Sure. It also might be Margaret."

Martin Smith owned a wholesale pet food distribution company. When he started it fifteen years ago, he called it Smith and Company, and located it in a small old warehouse in the sleepy little town of Navarre, "nestled between the southwest corner of Upper Lake Minnetonka and the northeast corner of Lower Lake," according to its web site.

His wife called it, affectionately, Din-Din. Somehow that name caught on, and eventually he changed Smith and Company to Din-Din, Incorporated. As such, it was doing well. He had recently added pet medicines and supplies to his catalog, but hadn't changed the name. He was grooming his younger son to take over the company when he retired, which he had no current plans to do.

"Fran, did you make reservations for me and a guest at Biella's in Excelsior?" Martin asked his secretary.

"Yes, sir, for twelve thirty."

Biella's was a fine Italian restaurant with an excellent menu. And it was only a few blocks from Betsy Devonshire's needlework shop. He hoped to ply her with wine and good food, which would cause her to tell him what she was thinking about Carrie Carlson's death. He didn't want to call it a murder, despite Sergeant Malloy's opinion that it was. He was hoping Ms. Devonshire was not averse to finding information that would prove it a shocking accident.

They talked briefly over a shared plate of bruschetta, then Betsy had the Prince Edward Island mussels, prepared with wine, garlic, chorizo, and chimichuri. He had the caramelized sea scallops, made with shiitake mushrooms and served under a Thai coconut curry sauce. Yum!

Martin was careful to have only one glass of wine — he had two appointments with manufacturers' representatives this afternoon — and was disappointed when Betsy, despite his urging, followed suit.

He hadn't had much interest in her previously, her business being primarily of interest to his wife, of course. So now he was trying to draw her out a little. They talked business at first. She did not come to owning her own business voluntarily, he found, having inherited the shop on the death of her sister and kept it going because she had no other viable choices for income at the time. But after these few years, she knew the lingo and was comfortable in her position. She asked intelligent questions about his company and laughed at his jokes.

At last, winding down the meal with coffee, Martin said with an air of frankness, "I wanted to talk with you about your investigation. Can you share with me where you are in it?"

"I'm at kind of an impasse right now," Betsy replied after a moment for thought. "Sergeant Malloy says he has good reason to think this is a case of murder, but I'm having trouble finding anyone with a real motive for killing Carrie."

"I'm glad to hear you say that."

"Well, there is the real possibility that I'll find something in your past, or Margaret's past, that Carrie was using to blackmail you in order to get money from you."

That took his breath away. "What terrible dark secret could we possibly have?" he said after a moment.

"I don't know — and I don't think either

you or Margaret would be willing to tell me."

"But there isn't anything!" He said that too loudly, and people at other tables looked around at him. "I mean it," he said, much more softly. "There is no dark secret. How could you think something like that? What on earth makes you think there is?"

"Margaret's reaction when I warned her that my investigation might uncover things she'd rather were not brought to light."

"What did she say?" Martin asked sharply.

"Nothing. And you're not saying what it is right now, are you?"

"There isn't anything, I'm telling you! Besides, the autopsy didn't find any cause of death other than hypothermia."

"Yes, that's true."

He sat back in his chair and studied her, a handsome woman of a certain age, comfortably plump, studying him back with calm blue eyes. "What is it you're not telling me?" he asked.

"Mike said something interesting. He said the medical examiner told him there is not enough blood and tissue in the human body to test for every possible poison. So the standard test is for barbiturate and opiate drugs, the most common. In this case, the tests came up negative."

"So see? It probably wasn't poison after all."

"Or maybe it was some other kind of poison."

"Margaret doesn't know anything about exotic poisons, you know. Or common ones, for that matter."

"I know. That's one reason I don't think she's guilty of this murder."

" 'This murder'?"

"Anyone is capable of murder, under the right circumstances."

Martin felt himself growing afraid, and that made him angry. "Would that include me, do you think?"

"Certainly. Me, too."

"What do you think could move me to murder someone?"

Betsy cocked her head sideways and said consideringly, "A threat to your family. Suppose someone knew something terrible about you, or your wife, or your sons. And threatened to reveal it. You have a spotless reputation, and your wife is a model of decorum. I think both of you enjoy having people you admire think well of you. It's good for business, too. So if someone threatened to reveal that you and your wife, say, burn down houses for fun every Halloween, you might go a long way to prevent

93

that from being found out."

He started to laugh, realized it sounded phony, and shut up. "What an imagination you have!"

"Yes, I know. And it gets worse every time I investigate a crime."

Whew! Martin thought on his way back to his plant. *I wonder if she was joking, or if she seriously suspects Margaret. Or me.*

At two, the Monday Bunch meeting was called to order. The Monday Bunch was an informal club of women — and one man — stitchers, who gathered to talk and do needlework projects at Crewel World.

Bershada Reynolds, outspoken but good-natured, was working on a motto: "Sour Grapes Make Fine Whines." She wasn't sure whether she was going to hang it in her house or give it to her daughter-in-law, who, having two teens in her house, would heartily agree with the sentiment. Bershada was saying, "We have to do something about the homeless. Build more shelters, open more clinics. Get them off the streets, especially in winter."

Godwin was sitting in on the meeting today, knitting yet another in his endless series of white cotton socks. "It seems a shame that in a country as rich as ours, we have beggars on the streets." His fingers were moving swiftly through a pattern so familiar he didn't need to look.

"I say we shouldn't give anything to street beggars," said Phil Galvin provocatively, daring them to disagree. "There are plenty of programs to take care of them, and anyway, giving them money only helps them buy liquor." He was working on a small painted canvas depicting an old-fashioned steam locomotive.

Emily Hame said diffidently, "I don't know if that's true, that all they want is to buy liquor." She was working on a Kris Stott Memorial Sampler. "Some of them are mentally ill or mentally deficient."

Large and bluff Alice Skoglund gestured with a big hand holding her half-finished crocheted afghan square. "You're right, Emily. My husband, though he was a man of God, used to say that they should reopen the asylums because so many of the homeless have severe mental problems and can't manage to live in regular society no matter how many programs there are."

Phil's wife, Doris Galvin, said in her low, gentle voice, "Opening the asylums sounds like a terrible idea, perhaps, but it might be better than the life they do live, sleeping under bridges in summer and freezing to death behind movie theaters in the winter."

Lovely and reserved Patricia Fairland was working on a complex counted canvas called "Diamond Delight VI," one of a series from DebBee's Designs. Worked in a variety of threads and stitches in gold on eggshell, it was a pattern of diamonds within diamonds within diamonds, and came with a book of instructions seventy-seven pages long. It was the sort of pattern that took away the breath of anyone who knew something about needlework, but caused non-cognoscenti to nod and say, "Very pretty, but maybe a little busy."

She glanced at Doris and said, "Still, being in an asylum would be like being in prison, wouldn't it? Except there's no parole."

Since Patricia had herself served a term in the women's prison in Shakopee, her opinion carried weight.

Betsy, busy sorting a shipment of pewter charms and buttons, comparing it against the original order, said, "The problem would be separating those who have mental problems from those who are just having a run of bad luck from those who are plain alcoholics. Bureaucracies aren't always very good at making these *fine distinctions*."

Some of the women gave ladylike snorts

of agreement, and Phil said, "I understand you are looking into the Excelsior woman's death, Betsy. Why? Is it or isn't it a murder?"

"Mike Malloy says it's a suspicious death. Besides, I got a request from a family member," said Betsy.

"What family?" said Phil. "Hard to think of those people as having families."

"But they do, most of them," said Emily with unusual firmness. "It's very sad for the families when one of the members refuses their help."

"Or when you help and help and help and it doesn't do any good," said Betsy, remembering her conversation with Margaret.

"Yes, that's the hardest part of all," agreed Emily.

The door sounded its two notes, and Jill Cross Larson came in with her two children, Emma Beth and toddler Erik. "I need to talk with you privately," she said to Betsy.

"All right," said Betsy, surprised. "Come in back."

She led the way through the back half of the shop and into the little back room with its coffeemaker, tea kettle, and crowded shelves of surplus stock. "What's the matter?" she asked.

"They've found another body. She was

buried in the snow on the Fiedlers' front lawn."

"Oh, good heavens! I don't believe it! Who is she?"

"I don't know. Another homeless woman, apparently. They're still at the scene."

"This is just *terrible!* It's *frightening!*" She grabbed for Jill's hands. "What's going on in Excelsior?"

"I don't know," replied Jill. "Lars is at the scene, he called to tell me. As soon as he knows more, he'll call again."

"Please relay what he says to me, okay?"

"Yes, of course."

"Mommy, can we go now? I'm hot!" complained little Emma Beth, pulling at her mittens.

"Yes, darling, we're going right now."

"Go, go, go, go!" chanted toddler Erik, pulling at his mother's hand.

"I'll call you as soon as I hear more," said Jill, and she led the way back to the front of the shop.

"Thank you for telling me!" Betsy called after her as she and the children went out the front door.

"Well!" exclaimed Godwin in his best Jack Benny voice. "What was that all about?"

Betsy grimaced. "Another frozen dead woman. They just found her body. Lars is at the scene, at the Fiedlers' over on Fourth Street."

There were gasps around the table. Emily turned white as a sheet.

"Oh, my God!" exclaimed Godwin.

"It's a serial killer," pronounced Bershada.

"Who is she?" asked Emily in a scared voice.

"They don't know yet," said Betsy. "They just found her, they're still at the scene. It might be another homeless woman."

"How many homeless women are there in Excelsior?" asked Doris. "I didn't think we had any at all."

Indeed, Excelsior was by and large an affluent community; it only looked like an ordinary small town. Its location on the shore of a big, clean lake helped to ensure that. People seeking to relocate to its safe, pleasant, Mayberry-like environs were always dismayed at the price asked for an otherwise undistinguished house.

That two homeless women were found in town was remarkable; that both were found dead was hugely shocking.

"Betsy, you really *have* to do something about this!" said Godwin.

But what could she do? All she had was the faint lead of Dice Paulson. Could he have killed two women? Why?

"I'm doing what I can, Goddy."

"I guess I *know* that, but this is simply *dreadful!*"

Betsy sat down, but she was too distracted to continue sorting. What was going on? It couldn't be a coincidence that two women froze to death in the same small town. Mike must be right — this was murder.

Could it be that Dice Paulson was guilty after all? Maybe he wanted to divert attention from himself as a suspect by killing not only Carrie but another homeless woman. *If* he killed Carrie at all, of course; after all, she and he broke up a very long time ago. Still, it was a bad sign that he had disappeared right after being paroled from prison. She hoped Mike was able to find him quickly and that finding him would solve this mystery.

Meanwhile, this must relieve some of the pressure on Margaret. If Mike had only the thinnest reason to think she had murdered her cousin, he couldn't possibly think she had reason to murder a stranger.

Right?

SEVEN

The second body was discovered when a teenager, skylarking with a snowblower, ran it up on the lawn of his next-door neighbor and jammed the rotating blades on her boot.

There was no bottle of bourbon with this woman's body, just four bulging plastic shopping bags carrying all her worldly possessions. One was spilling its contents into the snow near the body's knees.

After the crime scene had been recorded in detail, Detective Sergeant Mike Malloy went through the bags looking for some form of identification. He was surprised to find a pair of worn wooden knitting needles and a ball of seriously crinkled yarn that looked as if it had once been a sweater or something and then unraveled. Also in one of the bags was a gray, hard-plastic case about eight inches long, with a crack in it. In it were some sewing materials: embroidery floss, needles, a pair of scissors with one point broken off, a spool of black thread, and a spool of white thread, both almost depleted. He had an uncomfortable feeling that these artifacts meant he'd really have to deal with that amateur Betsy Devonshire. She was clever enough and often provided good information — and sometimes solid conclusions — but she had no official status. He sometimes wished she'd get a private investigator's license so he could deal with her on a professional level. (Other times he wished she'd get married to that boyfriend of hers and move with him back to his home in Ireland.)

Also in one of the bags was a Social Security card that had been laminated only after it had become badly worn. It had the name JANET ROSE TURNQUIST on it.

This time there was only a delay long enough for the body to thaw before it was subjected to an autopsy. Again the toxicology screen was negative, which this time didn't surprise him. He wished they could do a wider spectrum of tests, but further testing would have to wait until Malloy could give them a clue what to look for.

One curious thing: While undressing the body, the lower portion of the back of a cotton shirt she was wearing was found to have a mildly misspelled rhyme embroidered on it.

"Last Will and Testiment" it was headed, and it read: "I leave the summer wind that blows so free, a drink or two or even three, a place thats warm in winter and dry out of the rain, a good and happy song refraine, and everything else I die posessed of I leave to my beloved niece Emily Hame." Even the signature, JANET ROSE TURNQUIST, was embroidered.

Malloy did a search for Emily Hame on his computer and was not surprised to find the name listed in the Excelsior directory. Carrie Carlson's cousin lived in Excelsior, so why shouldn't Janet Turnquist's niece? A case with one screwy element tended to have other, equally screwy elements.

Sometimes Mike Malloy wished Jill Cross Larson was still on the cops. She was good at what he considered one of the worst jobs of being a cop: bringing bad news to a citizen. But she wasn't, so he dialed Ms. Hame's phone number. To his dismay, she was an at-home mom, and was willing for him to come over right away.

When he got there, he found she was also the mom of two small children, whom she could not, of course, lock away in another room while he delivered the news that an aunt of hers had been found dead.

After the initial spate of tears, which he sat through helplessly, she gulped and said, "I wondered, you know? When I heard another homeless woman was found frozen to death right here in Excelsior." She picked up the toddler, who was weeping in sympathy with her mother, and held her on her lap. "There, there, darling, it's all right. Mommy's just sad right now. It's all right."

"Mommy, why are you sad?" asked the older child, another girl, standing with an open coloring book in one hand and a purple crayon in the other.

"Because Aunt Janet has died, and when someone you know dies, it makes you sad."

"Oh. Okay." The child, who appeared to be about four years old, lay back down on the floor and resumed coloring an elephant purple. She wielded a very messy crayon.

Ms. Hame hadn't seen Janet Turnquist for months, she said. As far as she knew, the only time Janet came to Excelsior was to see her. Janet's home was in Fargo, North Dakota. She owned a condemned house there, but she didn't live in it anymore. She traveled around the Dakotas and Minnesota quite a bit, but not predictably. Janet had been diagnosed as having schizotypal disorder — a mild form of schizophrenia — years ago. She wasn't ill enough to be locked away in a hospital. She was supposed to take risperidone for it, but she mostly didn't. She was an unhappy loner with few social skills, and sometimes she heard voices that said she was bad, all symptoms of her disease. She believed that the United States government wanted to capture her because it thought she knew something about how the moon shots were faked. She had no enemies that Ms. Hame knew of except these imaginary ones.

Ms. Hame was startled by the will, but not surprised. "That sounds just like her," she said, smiling through a refreshment of her tears. She supposed the money would come in useful.

"Money?" Mike's interest was suddenly sharpened.

"Oh, yes, there was a man who came from Fargo looking for Janet a couple of weeks ago, a Mr. Morcambe. He's a private investigator, and he was looking for Aunt Janet to tell her she had inherited a lot of money."

"How much money?"

"He didn't know, but he thought it was more than a hundred thousand dollars. Maybe several hundred."

"Did you know about the will?" he asked.

"No, of course not. And I didn't know

about the money, until Mr. Morcambe told me. Poor Aunt Janet didn't, either, I'm sure. It doesn't seem fair."

"The will may not be legal, you know."

"No?" She looked alarmed. "Why, because it's stitched?"

"No, because it's what's called a holographic will, written by the testator her own self, without the aid of an attorney. No witnesses, either. I've been told they aren't legal anymore."

"That doesn't seem right. Who will get the money, then?"

"Whoever her legal next of kin is, as determined by a court of law."

Ms. Hame considered that. "I don't know who that is," she said. "Her husband divorced her years ago, and she didn't have any children. There might be other nieces and nephews on her ex-husband's side. And I have a brother in San Francisco, what about him?"

"There are laws of inheritance, but I don't know what they are. The money may be divided among all of you. Oh, and of course, there's the house," said Malloy.

"Well, yes, the house. No one has lived in it for years. It's condemned because a Red River flood damaged it. The taxes on it are really low — we've been paying them for her, I'm not sure why, except she asked us to. She always said she'd pay us back, but of course she never did. She was living on SSI, I don't know where the checks were delivered, I don't think she had a bank account anywhere. Probably cashed them at one of those awful check-cashing places."

That was the longest uninterrupted reply she was able to make, and it was because the toddler had left her lap, climbed onto the couch, and fallen asleep on Malloy's knee.

As he went out into the bitter cold morning, Malloy thought about all that money. Ms. Hame had behaved just about right, upset over the news of the death, pleased and surprised and amused by the will. And too new to the news of it to be really upset over learning it probably wasn't a valid will.

On the other hand, a couple hundred thousand dollars was one heck of a motive.

Emily had taken Mr. Morcambe's business card off the refrigerator to give his name and phone number to Sergeant Malloy. Now she reached for the phone to call Mr. Morcambe herself. His office was in Fargo.

"Remember how you wondered if my Aunt Janet Turnquist was deceased?" she asked him. "Well, it turns out she is. She

107

was found frozen to death right here in Excelsior."

"Jesus Christ! Frozen to death? Wow, I didn't expect that. May I offer my condolences?"

Emily fought against a fresh rush of tears. "Thank you. Even though she was living the kind of life where that sort of thing can happen, it's still very sad."

"Was it some kind of an accident?"

"They don't know. A police sergeant came to tell me about it, and I think he's investigating to find out how it happened."

"This is very distressing news for you."

"Yes, it is. I really loved Aunt Janet. But there's one odd thing about this business. She wrote a kind of a will. Do you know anything about holographic wills?"

"Very little, why?"

"Because Aunt Janet wrote one on her shirt, and I was wondering if it's legal."

"I think they are, at least in some states."

"The policeman who talked to me said they weren't."

"I'm sure he's talking about Minnesota. Janet Turnquist was a legal resident of North Dakota. I don't know what the status is in our state."

Less than an hour after they hung up, Emily's phone rang. It was a woman who identified herself as Regina Kingsolver, attorney-at-law, representing the estate of Jasper Bronson. She wanted to know when Janet Turnquist had died.

"I don't know," said Emily. "I only found out about it today, but the body had been hidden in the snow long enough to get frozen. I suppose the medical examiner will have an opinion. Maybe you know Aunt Janet was a little strange?"

The attorney became circumspect. "I've heard that she had cognitive problems."

"Yes, she did. She was homeless because she wouldn't take her meds and would get all mixed up. But sometimes she'd come to us and we'd take her in and feed her, buy her things she needed, like boots or clothes. And here's the thing: She made up this kind of a will, embroidered it on her shirttail, and it was found when they did the autopsy. It rhymed, mostly — she liked to write poetry, or what she called poetry. She left everything she owned to me. The policeman who came to talk to me, to tell me about Aunt Janet being dead, called it a holographic will and he said he didn't think they were legal. Are they?"

Ms. Kingsolver became even more circumspect. "That depends on a number of things. Holographic wills are legal in North

Dakota, but Ms. Turnquist might not be said to be of sound mind when she wrote this will."

"Oh, yes, 'of sound mind and body,' I've heard that phrase."

"And there's another problem. The money was left to Ms. Turnquist on the death of Jasper Bronson. If Ms. Turnquist died first, then she can't inherit."

"When did Jasper Bronson die?"

"Eighteen days ago."

"Oh, I don't think Aunt Janet's body was under the snow *that* long!"

"I understand that another woman's frozen body was found hidden under snow in Excelsior about that long ago."

"That's true," Emily conceded. "Oh, you think the two dead women are connected somehow?"

"I have no way of knowing. Is it at all possible that Ms. Turnquist could have lain hidden in the snow for that long?"

"I don't know. Maybe." That was a very disturbing thought. "The people who own the house Aunt Janet was found in front of left for South Texas a few days after New Year's Day."

"And Ms. Turnquist was found on January fifteenth. So you see, there are a number of questions that must be answered before this matter can be resolved."

"Yes, I see."

"Could you give me the name of the police investigator?"

"Sure, he's Sergeant Mike Malloy, with the Excelsior Police Department." She looked up the number and gave it to the attorney.

"Did you know there's a private investigator looking for Aunt Janet?" Emily asked.

"Is that Mr. Morcambe?"

"Yes, that's him."

"I hired him to find Janet if he could. He's the one who called me to tell me your aunt is dead."

"Oh. I guess I should have figured that out. Can I ask you another question?"

"Certainly."

"How much money are we talking about here?"

"I believe it's on the order of six or seven hundred thousand dollars."

"Oh, my goodness! That's a *lot!* How wonderful it would have been for Aunt Janet, though I don't know if she would have been able to deal with being rich."

"Yes, that might have been a problem."

"Now suppose it turns out Aunt Janet didn't inherit the money. So then what happens to it?"

"There's a nephew on Jasper's wife's side, Alec Porter is his name. He's a veterinarian. The will stipulates that if Janet predeceased Jasper, the money is to go in equal parts to the American Cancer Society and to Dr. Porter."

"Oh. Well, thank you very much."

"You're welcome." Ms. Kingsolver said she would stay in touch as things developed, and they hung up.

Emily was shaken to find that greed had taken root in her soul. Six or seven hundred thousand dollars. And it all depended on when Aunt Janet died. Surely she hadn't lain under all that snow for more than a week! But then there was the issue of "sound mind and body." That didn't describe Aunt Janet very well. But she wasn't locked away in a padded cell raving like a real lunatic. How unsound did her mind have to be to make the will invalid?

She wondered what kind of a person Alec Porter was. Surely he would be thinking along these same lines and would be willing to fight to have the matter resolved in his favor. She'd talk to her husband; maybe they would have to hire a lawyer. Would Jim agree to do that?

Six or seven hundred thousand dollars. They could send the kids to college on that money. Pay off their mortgage. Go on a really great vacation. Hmmmm.

EIGHT

Dr. Alec Porter sat behind his modest desk in his small office, chewing on his lower lip and thinking.

Six, maybe seven, hundred thousand dollars.

He'd had no idea the estate was that large.

Of course, at the start, it had been enormously larger. But Uncle Jasper had been sick for a very long time, and doctors, hospitals, meds, and nursing homes were expensive.

Funny how long the body could linger after the mind was gone. If Uncle Jasper had been a dog, he would have been brought in to be put out of his suffering years ago.

Now there was a dangerous thought Alec had better not share with anyone.

Especially the police, whom he was pretty sure would be calling on him any day now.

This mess started when some homeless woman was found dead in Excelsior, which might have been some kind of dreadful accident. But now his cousin Janet's body had also been found, also in Excelsior, which very naturally made the police suspicious that a killer was on the loose.

The question was, who would want to murder two homeless women who apparently were not in any way related to one another?

A crazy person obviously.

But if they managed to separate the two deaths, Alec might be a suspect in the death of Janet, because with her dead, he was in line to inherit half of that six hundred thousand.

And the simple truth was, he needed an infusion of money badly. His clinic, the Small Animal Medical Center, was failing. He needed to upgrade the place, and recruit a new partner.

His attention wandered to a subject that had worn a path deep in his brain. The new veterinarian, if only he could recruit one, must have enough money to buy into a partnership. Unfortunately, with a shrinking practice and a physical plant that needed renovation, not many were interested.

The situation wasn't entirely his own fault. His previous partner had decided to go with his wife to Arizona when she got an offer of a great new job in Phoenix. So Alec had had to buy him out. Fortunately, the clinic building had been paid for, so he'd been able to mortgage it to raise the funds. Unfortunately, with the recent drop in property values, the new mortgage hadn't brought in enough to both pay off Dr. Doug *and* do some overdue renovations — a new heating/air conditioner unit, for example, a new X-ray machine, new flooring.

That wouldn't have been a problem if Alec had been able to recruit a new partner. That failure was, in part, his own fault. His manner, he'd been told, was brusque. It was possible he put off applicants. On the other hand, the prospective partners had been outstandingly unsatisfactory. Some had no funds to invest. Others were not good material — one prospect had actually come to his interview drunk.

What's more, the Veterinary Licensing Board was making his life difficult. He'd done the mandatory twenty hours of continuing education — which was damn difficult, working all the hours he did — but had mislaid the paperwork proving it. He had to find it or they'd pull his license.

He wondered if they weren't landing hard on him because he'd been a little mouthy with the woman who'd talked to him.

116

Maybe more than a little mouthy, to be honest. He wished he had the smooth and charming manners of his former partner. Then maybe his business wouldn't be dropping off like it was. For example, apart from two annual-shots visits, his only appointment today was for a routine removal of a benign growth from the skin of a pug, whose hobby, apparently, was growing them.

Every vet has his or her favorites, and Alec was no exception. For example, he liked Pugslee, and her owner, Ms. Fellows, was a nice enough woman. But he really liked Rodney, the yellow Lab whose tail never stopped wagging. Rodney's owner was a woman with almost as pleasant a personality as her dog's.

On the other hand, Alec had little patience with the sometimes casual, sometimes ignorant cruelty of several other of his human clients toward their pets — the deliberately cruel, of course, seldom brought their pets in. He had tried over and over to instill forbearance in himself. But when someone brought in a dog suffering from the final stages of a disease, a dog that might have been saved by earlier intervention, well, he could hardly refrain from pointing that out, could he? Especially when the owner's reaction to his recommendation that the animal be humanely euthanized was to ask if he knew anyone with a replacement to sell.

Dr. Doug would have known what to say to those patients. But Dr. Doug had left for Arizona. "Never liked our long, dark winters anyhow," he'd said cheerfully. And when he left, nearly a year ago now, the clinic began to wither.

Of course, Alec found these cloudy, cold, *short* winter days a huge pain, too. Going to work in the dark, going home in the dark, the high heating and lighting bills, all were an argument for uprooting himself and moving to a more forgiving climate.

But Alec was, among his other failings, a stubborn man. Someone had to stay and care for the helpless, voiceless animals who had voted (or been commandeered) to live in the too-often hapless custody of human-kind.

He was looking forward to Pugslee's arrival. He loved doing surgery and knew he was very skilled at it. It wasn't that long ago that he was up to his elbows in spays, hip dysplasia corrections, difficult births, and even, once in a while, something delicate and difficult like a mitral valve replacement. But the clients had faded away when Dr. Doug left. So, obviously, the problem was himself.

His phone rang and he picked it up to say briskly, "Small Animal Medical Center, may I help you?"

"Dr. Porter, please," said a man's voice.

"Speaking."

"I'm Sergeant Michael Malloy, a detective with the Excelsior Police Department. I need a few minutes of your time for an interview. Are you available today?"

Alec looked at the numerous blanks on his calendar but hesitated. He hadn't thought they'd get around to him so quickly.

Wait a minute, maybe this wasn't about Janet. "What's it about?" he asked.

"Have you got a cousin named Janet Turnquist?"

"Well, I had. She's deceased."

"That's correct. May I come and talk to you about her, today if possible?"

Damn. "All right, I guess so," he said. "Can you come in to the clinic around three?"

"Yes, I can. Thank you."

Alec sat still for a minute after he hung up. Thank you? *I'll be darned,* he mused, *a polite detective. Who would've thought?*

Malloy pulled into the little parking lot of the Small Animal Medical Center right at three. There were no other cars parked there. The lot was covered with snow tamped down into a slick, potholed surface; his car jounced over the ruts. The clinic was on a corner lot, a stand-alone, one-story, brick building that could have used some tuck-pointing. Its few windows were small, high up, and tinted a dark green.

He parked and climbed out, standing for a moment to take the environment in. The neighborhood was mostly residential; there was a mom-and-pop grocery store across the street, flanked by houses probably built in the early and middle of the last century, all in good repair. Up the street was a flower shop, and three blocks away he'd passed a park with a playground. A good, middle-class neighborhood, its streets lined with mature trees, its sidewalks cleared of snow. No one around, but that was to be expected during a workweek, with schools in session. Malloy went through the thick glass door into the clinic and was greeted with the heavy, sharp smell of nonhuman medicines and dry pet food — there was a shelf stacked with bags of high-end dog and cat food.

A receptionist's counter took up a third of the small room, but there was no reception-ist. Everything looked a little shopworn but very clean. One of those dome-shaped bells with a little button on top was on the counter. Malloy tapped it twice; it rang nice and loud.

Less than a minute later, a slender man in his late thirties or early forties, about five feet nine, wearing an unbuttoned white lab coat over jeans and a brown cardigan, came up the corridor that was off to the right. He had dusty brown hair cut short on the sides and a narrow, beaky nose, and his mouth stretched in a smile that did not reach his hazel-green eyes.

"Well, I believe you are Sergeant Malloy," he said.

"Yes, sir. Thank you for being willing to talk to me."

They shook hands. Porter's hand was cool and dry, but he was looking a little nervous. "No problem, except I can't tell you much about poor Janet." The smile went away. "When did it happen? I only heard about it yesterday."

"That's something we're still trying to figure out."

"You don't know how long ago she died?" He was surprised at that.

"She died outdoors during a snowstorm that covered her body. She lay there long enough for her body to freeze. Under those

121

conditions, it becomes very difficult to accurately determine a person's time of death."

"I see. That's too bad." Alec's shoulders moved in an uncomfortable shrug and he thrust his hands into the pockets of his lab coat.

"I understand you have a good reason to want to know when she died."

He froze for about three seconds, then suddenly relaxed. "I wasn't going to mention that."

"No, sir?" Malloy watched him keenly.

Porter smiled wryly. "You've heard about the will, right?"

"What do you know about it?"

Porter sighed. "If Janet died after my Uncle Jasper, the money goes to her — or now, her heirs. But if she died first, half of it comes to me."

"How did you find out about the terms of the will?" asked Malloy.

"An attorney in Fargo called me. A Ms. Kingsolver. This was after Uncle Jasper's funeral. It was a newer will than one I knew about, where he left everything to me. She asked me if I knew where Janet was living, but I didn't." He looked away, frowning. "I don't understand how her body wasn't found right away. It's not like she was in a ditch somewhere out in the country."

"That's true, but she was on the front walk of a house belonging to a couple away on vacation. We're thinking that either the killer buried her in the snow already on the ground, or it snowed the night it happened, covering the body."

"Oh. Well, that's a hell of a thing."

Malloy nodded. "Makes the case much more complicated."

"This other homeless woman that was found, was she a friend of Janet's?"

"It's possible they knew one another, moving in pretty much the same circles."

Porter nodded. "Strange that both of them died around the same time."

"Very strange."

"Could it have been natural causes, and just a coincidence that there were two of them?"

"I'm afraid you're stretching the possibility of a coincidence past the breaking point. There are other factors involved."

"Like what?"

"I don't want to go into them at present. When did you last see Janet Turnquist?"

Alec had to think about that. "A long time ago. At a funeral — yes, she and her husband came to Jasper's wife's funeral in Fargo. That would've been . . . ten or twelve years ago."

"She didn't come to Jasper's funeral?"

"No, she didn't."

"Isn't that a little strange? It was held in Fargo, after all, and that's where she's from. She must have known him well, since he made her his sole heir."

"Yes, well, that will was written back when she was just a little strange, not totally bonkers like she got later."

Mike almost smiled. Gotcha! "If you haven't seen her in ten or twelve years, how do you know she had gone, as you say, 'totally bonkers'?"

"Someone at my uncle's funeral mentioned it. She said she was very worried about Janet, that she was living on the street and really needed to be put somewhere safe. Or something like that."

"Who was this person?"

"Let me think." Porter nibbled on his top lip for a few seconds, then shook his head. "I really don't remember. It was just a brief comment, not said directly to me, I just heard it in passing. The only reason I remember it at all is because it's uncomfortable knowing an actual relative of yours is living like a bum. Especially a female relative."

"If it was known in the family that Janet

was mentally ill, why didn't Jasper change his will?"

"Maybe he didn't know how ill she really was. I didn't. Or maybe he thought that by leaving her his money, she would get the help she needed. But, you see, it depends on the time frame. I don't know how long Janet was homeless, but Uncle Jasper lived with Alzheimer's for years, so it's possible that he couldn't understand about her, even if someone tried to tell him. And even if someone could make him understand, he probably wouldn't have been competent to make a new will."

"How long was he incompetent before he died?"

"About four years, I'd say. I visited him until he didn't know me anymore."

Malloy nodded. According to his information, Janet had been homeless for about three years, perhaps a little longer. But she'd started slipping from eccentric to crazy before that.

"Do you know when your uncle made the new will?"

"No. But it was before he was diagnosed. I was surprised by it, because he had made that earlier one, the one leaving everything to me. You see, I was the golden-haired boy of my family, supposed to go to medical school, to become a surgeon — and I did, only not for human beings. He was angry with me about that; he'd given me money for medical school and I disappointed him. But I didn't think he'd make a new will." A sour smile pulled at Alec's mouth. "So I guess it was my turn to be disappointed. Ms. Kingsolver said Janet was the heir but I was a 'contingent legatee.' She said she had hired someone to look for Janet, but I guess she died before he could find her." He gave a faint shudder. "Even half of the estate is a lot of money, and I sure could use it, but not at that price. It's awful to think about, a death like that, all alone in the frozen dark." The troubled look in his eyes seemed authentic.

"Yes, a very unpleasant thought," agreed Malloy, writing things down. "One other question: Do you know a Carolyn Carlson?"

"No. Is she mixed up in this somehow?"

"She's the other dead woman."

"Is she? Carolyn Carlson — okay, I guess I did read that name. Maybe this Carlson woman was the one the killer was after, and Janet just got in the way somehow. Or do you think he went after both of them? Did they both die of the same thing?"

"I think so. There are still some tests to be run." No need to tell him the testing was on hold for now.

"Tests — so you're thinking poison?"

"Yes, sir."

Porter nodded, his expression grim. "Well, good luck to you."

As Malloy got in his car for the drive back to Excelsior, he considered the interview he'd just completed. Porter's story hung together and fit with the other pieces he'd gathered so far. On the other hand, he had said himself that he badly needed money.

This was a hell of a case. He could find someone with a motive for killing either Janet or Carrie. But not both. What was he missing?

Betsy was at home, doing the backstitching on a Joseph Hautman counted cross-stitch pattern of a male and female cardinal perched on a blooming apple tree branch. It was coming along really well, and she was beginning to feel competent in the area of counted cross-stitch. The backstitching was giving definition to the male cardinal's head and breast. She paused for a minute to admire it. The pastel blossoms of the tree gave an oriental air to the pattern; the bright colors of the birds were almost shocking in contrast. She liked it so much that perhaps, when she finished using it as a model in her shop, she'd bring it back to her apartment.

Her doorbell rang. She looked at her watch; it was almost bedtime. Who would be calling on her at this hour?

She never had gotten around to installing a two-way speaker system down at the entrance to her building, and this was a reminder that she really must call someone about that soon.

She pressed the door release button and opened the door to her apartment to see who came up the stairs.

It was Margaret Smith, looking very stressed.

"Oh, Betsy, I need to talk to you!" said Margaret, panting a little as she hurried up the last few steps.

"Of course, Margaret, come in."

Betsy led her into the living room and bade her take a seat on the couch, recently upholstered in a deep, browny purple. Margaret had pulled off her silver fox coat to reveal a wool suit the color of a daffodil. She looked like an exotic flower, small and lovely, sitting in the dead center of the dark upholstery. But she was clearly scared.

"Now tell me, what's the matter?" asked Betsy.

"You had lunch with Marty today, he told me about it."

"Yes?"

"Well, he's nervous about your conversation with him." Margaret began entwining her fingers in complicated patterns.

"Why is he nervous?"

"He was surprised, I suppose. You aren't what he expected." Betsy didn't know how to reply to that. "I think he thought you'd be . . . I don't know — diffident, understated, that you'd let him lead the conversation."

"But I did let him lead the conversation. What is it you're trying to say?"

"He thinks you suspect him of murdering Carrie!" Margaret blurted out the words in a defiant rush. "I thought you were going to help us!"

Betsy said as gently as she could, "You asked me to find out what really happened. I warned you that it might not go as you wished, that things might turn up that you would rather be kept secret. I could see at the time you were not pleased, and I wondered what was bothering you, but you said to go ahead, that I should do whatever it took to clear this up. I think both of you are keeping something secret. Do you want to tell me what it is?"

Margaret said, "It has nothing to do with Carrie!"

"I hope you're right about that. Do you want me to stop investigating?" Betsy wasn't sure she'd be able to just stop sleuthing, but she could try to stop doing it on Margaret's behalf, if asked.

Margaret started to say something, then changed her mind. She sat thinking about it for a long minute. Betsy held her tongue.

At last Margaret said, "No, I don't want you to stop. I just wish I could convince you that by looking at us, you're looking in the wrong direction."

NINE

The next day, Betsy took I-94 across the Mississippi and exited on the far side of downtown Saint Paul. She had punched the address into her GPS — a device she had almost immediately come to think of as indispensable — and it took her to a modest stucco building on an obscure side street. The sign announcing its presence in the neighborhood was so set back she nearly missed it.

She parked on the street, went into the small lobby of the building, and stopped at the window to a tiny, cluttered office where a plump woman sat working at a computer.

"May I help you?" the woman asked.

"I have an appointment with Mary Compagne."

"Your name?"

"Betsy Devonshire."

"Just a minute." The woman checked a log on her computer. "Yes, you're right on time." She picked up a phone and punched three numbers into it. "A Ms. Betsy Devonshire is here to see you." She hung up and said, "She'll be right out."

In about a minute, Betsy saw an attractive young woman come toward her. She had flaming red hair cut to just below her jawline, and was wearing a close-fitting brown skirt and long-sleeved green silk blouse.

As she got nearer, Betsy could see that her darkly lashed eyes were gray, and there was a scatter of freckles across her cheeks and nose. She held out her hand and said, "Welcome to the Naomi Women's Shelter."

"Thank you," Betsy replied, taking the hand.

"If you'll follow me, please," Ms. Compagne said, and turned to walk away.

Betsy followed her to a plainly furnished office with stacks of folders covering the desk. "We're reorganizing our files," Ms. Compagne said in apology.

"You have my sympathy," Betsy said with feeling.

The woman smiled and sat down behind the desk. "Please, take a seat. How may we help you?"

Betsy sat on the hard wooden chair indicated. "I'm inquiring into the deaths of two women who I believe had been at this shelter. One's name is Carolyn Marie Carlson, and the other's is Janet Turnquist."

Ms. Compagne stiffened just a little. "I don't believe you told me you are with the police."

"I'm not. Nor am I a licensed private investigator. But I've been asked by Margaret Smith, who is Carrie's cousin, to see if I can find out how she came to die in Excelsior. And since her body and Janet's body were found not far from one another, it is possible the deaths are related."

"And how do you expect me to help you?"

"I want to know when Carrie stayed here, and if Janet did, too; and if while here, Carrie got into some kind of altercation with someone that ended with her suffering bruises. Especially if that someone was Janet."

"I wish you had been more forthcoming when you called to ask for a meeting, because I could have saved you a trip. I can't give you that information. We have very strict confidentiality rules against telling anyone who is or is not a resident."

"But this is a case of murder!"

"Really? Are the police investigating?"

"Yes, of course!"

"Then I think we should let them do their job."

Ms. Compagne could not be moved from that position, so Betsy left, frustrated and upset with herself for wasting so much time on a futile mission.

She had just about reached her car when she heard her name being called.

"Wait up, wait up!" the voice continued.

Betsy turned to see Annie hustling up the walk toward her. She wasn't wearing a coat or boots — and the temperature was about five degrees above zero.

"Annie, what's the matter?"

Annie stopped, her breath smoking in the frigid air. She was hopping from foot to foot — she was wearing only heavy socks — and trying to draw her hands up into the sleeves of her brown sweater. "You're looking for information about Carrie, aren't you?"

"Yes, I am. Do you know something you didn't tell me about?"

"No. But I can find things out for you."

"You can? Here, let's get in my car. You must be freezing."

Betsy pressed the button that made her car honk softly, flash its lights, and unlock its doors. Annie quickly climbed in the passenger side and sat huddled, using both hands to rub her upper arms through the bulky cardigan she wore, while Betsy hustled around to get in on the driver's side. She started the engine and turned the heater up high.

They sat in silence until the air blowing out the vents turned warm. It didn't take long.

"Now," said Betsy, "what do you mean, you can find things out?"

"They sent you away from Naomi without telling you anything, didn't they?"

"Yes, they have a strict confidentiality policy."

"Which is okay and necessary, I suppose. But I'm staying in Naomi! I can go anywhere in there, and talk to anyone! I know people in Naomi who I bet were residents when Carrie was there. I'll talk to them for you — I mean, if you want. Would . . . would that be all right?"

Annie had gone from assertive to tentative in that brief spate of words.

"But what if the people in charge find out what you are doing?"

"So? I'm only talking to people. I can do that. No need to tell them I'm also talking to you, is there?"

"Well . . . no, I guess not."

"So see? I told you I wanted to help, and now here's a way for me to do that! Why are you looking sideways at me?"

"That's a valid question," said Betsy, nodding. "One reason is because I don't want you to get tossed out of the place. The more important reason is, if this is murder, you may find yourself in the line of fire."

"Awww, not to worry! I've done slicker things than this and got away with them! I used to work on the line in a factory until the company moved overseas. The stuff we got away with . . ." Annie shrugged and fell silent for a few moments. "Anyway, I can do it if you want me to."

Betsy thought it over. "All right. Thank you very much. Seriously, thank you."

"Sh— heck, it's all right. What do you want me to find out?"

"I want to know the dates that Carrie Carlson stayed at the shelter. And how she got bruises on her body. It happened days before she died — but we don't have an exact date of her death. Her body was found on January sixth, so it happened before then. I want to know if she fell or if someone hit her, and if the latter, who it was and why it was done."

"Okay, I think I can manage some of that. Maybe all of it. Anything else?"

"Yes, see if you can find out if Janet Turn-quist also stayed there, and when. And if the two of them were talking to one another. Now listen, I want you to be very careful."

"Sure," Annie said cheerfully.

"I mean it."

"Don't worry, don't worry." Annie had a big grin on her face.

"How will you contact me with what you find out?"

"What's your e-mail address and your phone number? I can use the computer at any library, and phone from someplace else. See? I know better than to contact you from Naomi."

"That's good thinking." Betsy went into her purse and brought out a business card. "It's got my business phone and my cell phone numbers on it, as well as my e-mail address."

"Great, thanks. One way or another, I'll be in touch."

"Thank you again — and remember, be careful, all right?"

"Not to worry! Miss Sneaky, that's me! All I'm going to do is talk to people. I do that all the time!" And Annie bailed out of the car to go jittering and shivering her way back up to the shelter.

But all the way home, Betsy worried.

Godwin, depressed by winter, was trying to cheer himself up by pulling a batch of summer-themed counted cross-stitch patterns. He was thinking that perhaps a display of them under a ten percent off sign would be a good thing. He smiled over one that showed a cat on a sunny windowsill, and pulled it off to set on the chosen stack, exposing the next one, a golfer taking a mighty swing under a brilliantly lit sky. That broke his feeble composure and he put the stack down with a heavy sigh.

The door sounded its two notes, announcing the presence of a customer. Forcing a smile, Godwin turned to greet her — virtually all of Crewel World's customers were women.

But standing just inside the door was a very handsome Latino man about Godwin's age. He was fashionably dressed in a dark brown overcoat, a broad knit scarf in shades of dull red and bright yellow, and highly polished boots.

"Rafael!" exclaimed Godwin, his smile broadening. "What brings you out on such a cold day?"

"Gorrion!" replied Rafael, using the nickname he had given Godwin. It meant "sparrow," which he said described a small, brave, determined sort of person. "I had an appointment with my financial advisor. He thinks I shouldn't be selling my municipal bonds just yet, and wants to shift some of

my American stocks into overseas investments. After an hour with him, I want badly to talk to someone about something other than money. So I come here." He looked around. "You have your warm-weather patterns out," he noted. "Are you so tired of winter already?"

"Well, I am, but that's not what's going on," Godwin replied. "These pieces take a long time to complete, so stitchers are usually working a season or two ahead." He looked around. "But also Betsy and I are impatient people, always looking forward to the next project, trip, or holiday, so this business of looking ahead to the coming season suits us very well." He smiled at Rafael. "That's what I like about you. You're always content to be where you are, doing what you are doing."

Mock annoyed, Rafael said, "Is that all? You like me because I am content, like a cow?"

Godwin chuckled. "You're not in the least like a cow, and you know I don't think that. But it's really nice the way you are comfortable no matter where you are; it's a gift you have."

"In that case, I thank you. Where is your boss today?"

"Out sleuthing."

"Is she making good progress?"

"No, things are coming slowly. I think it's because she is trying to solve two murders at the same time, without knowing if they are related. It would be a very big co-incidence if they weren't, but coincidences happen."

Rafael said, "Perhaps it is because she is involved with a different class of people, people she doesn't find familiar, who live by rules different from her own."

Godwin nodded sharply. "I think you're right, that's at least part of the problem. Hey, you want a cup of coffee, or tea?"

"All right. Tea, the strong black kind. No milk or sugar."

Betsy's stomach prodded her as she drove into Excelsior. She often didn't have time for lunch, but today wasn't going to be one of those days. She parked in the small lot behind her building, paused for a moment to look at the big Dumpster placed on its margin. What was it making her think of? She didn't know.

Instead of taking the back way into Crewel World, she took the back way into Sol's, the delicatessen to the left of the store. The kitchen area of the deli smelled delectably of breads, cured meat, cheeses, herring,

140

garlic, pickles, and onions. She walked through to the front, past the glass-fronted counter into the public area.

The owner, whose name was not Sol, offered her a cheery hello.

"Hello," said Betsy. "I want a roast beef sandwich with horseradish sauce, and your biggest dill pickle."

"Potato chips?"

If he hadn't mentioned them, Betsy would not have, either. But since he had, she said, "Sure. Scant me." Meaning fewer than usual.

"Take-away?"

"Yes."

She looked around the store, with its big square floor tiles of black and white, the little wire-legged tables with wire-backed chairs pulled up to them — and at one of them sat Mike Malloy, eating a very large submarine sandwich dribbling shredded lettuce onto the table.

"Hi, Mike," she said, approaching his table and taking the other chair.

"Hey," he said brusquely. "What do you want?"

"How do you know I don't have something to tell you?"

"Do you?"

"Maybe. Have you run into that curtain

of privacy the women's shelters live behind?"

"Sure. Takes a court order to get any
information out of them."

"Have you asked for one?"

"Not yet."

"Are you still looking at Margaret Smith
as a suspect?"

He nodded. "That's right."

"What do you know about her that I
don't?" Betsy asked.

"Why should I tell you anything?"

"Because I tell you when I find things out,
and you like it when I do that. I will tell you
that I have a mole in the Naomi Women's
Shelter who can ask all the questions she
wants of the clients staying there."

"Say, I'm going to want to talk to her."

"As soon as she tells me something, I'll
tell you."

Mike looked at Betsy with respect. "Good
work."

"Your turn."

Mike sighed elaborately. Then he said, "All
right. You probably think of the Smiths as
people of solid respectability, right?"

"Of course."

"Well, there's a shady side to them. Mr.
Smith owns a veterinary medical supply
company, and several years ago it was under

investigation for selling outdated medicines to local animal doctors. He nearly went under until he proved the relabeling of the medicines was not done by him, but by his supplier. Lost a lot of business over that, though he's recovered most of it now."

"But Margaret wasn't involved in that, surely!"

"No, she has her own sad story. Her father came down with cancer a little over twenty years ago and she went into action to see that he was given every treatment, no matter how aggressive, to survive. The old man finally called the parish priest to ask him to talk to her. He'd been ready to give up months before that.

"But she learned the lesson too well. When her mother had a stroke sixteen years ago, she slapped the woman into hospice care almost immediately, where she lived for nine months before dying."

"Nine months isn't very long," said Betsy.

"The average length of stay in a hospice facility before dying is forty-three days. They don't do physical therapy in those places. It's possible that the old woman, with prompt therapy, might have recovered enough to go home."

"Oh," said Betsy, shocked. She hadn't known that.

How wretched it must be for Margaret to live with having made not one but two mistakes in her parents' care!

"Surely she meant well," Betsy said.

"I'm sure she did. But Margaret Smith shows a tendency to think she knows best, even in matters of life and death." He sighed at the abysmal condition of humanity, then remembered something. "Here," he said, reaching into a pocket and pulling out what looked like a light blue bookmark. "What's this?" he asked, handing it to her.

"Ooooh, pretty!" said Betsy. It was a bookmark, done in Hardanger embroidery on even-weave needlepoint canvas with overdyed blue, cream, and pink floss. A closer look showed evidence that this was an early attempt. The tension varied across the piece, and it was clear from the blurring of the floss that it had taken several tries to get the Kloster Blocks properly aligned. Still, the overall effect was attractive.

"What is it?" he asked.

"A bookmark done in Hardanger. Where is it from?"

"It was in Carrie's personal effects, stuck inside a paperback book. Does Margaret Smith do this kind of embroidery?"

"No. She likes needlepoint and counted cross-stitch. If this was with Carrie's things, maybe she did it."

"Before I showed it to Mrs. Smith, I asked her did Carrie do needlework, and she said no. She said she had no idea where this came from, that Carrie must have picked it up someplace."

"It's hand done," said Betsy. "And not by someone experienced in this craft. But no one I know who is involved in this case does Hardanger at all." She handed it back.

"Betsy, here's your sandwich!" called the man from behind the counter.

"I have to go. Talk to you later, Mike."

Still thoughtful, Betsy came into her shop. "Oh, hello, Rafael. Good to see you."

Rafael checked his watch. "You took a long lunch today."

"No, as a matter of fact, I haven't had my lunch yet." She held up the white paper sack.

"Did you find anything out at the shelter?" asked Godwin, emerging from the back room with two mugs.

"No, they have very strict confidentiality rules, and refused to tell me even whether or not Carrie and Janet had stayed there."

"Well, ain't that a kick in the head!" He gave one mug to Rafael, and took a drink from the one in his other hand.

Betsy smiled. "That isn't a very old expression." Godwin was a fan of old-fashioned, even antique, expressions.

"Older than me," retorted Godwin, with a lofty smirk.

"So what will you do now?" asked Rafael.

Betsy hesitated, not willing to admit she'd allowed Annie to help, or to share the shocking news about the Smiths. Instead she shrugged and said, "I don't know."

Rafael said, "You will think of something — you always do." He turned and asked Godwin, "So, how would you like to go to a driving range and hit a bucket of balls?"

Godwin stared at him, at first with delight, then miffed. "Don't tease me about things like that! You know I can't travel to Florida right now."

"I'm not teasing. I know you're itching to play. So I looked up 'indoor golf' on the Internet, and there is a place in Edina which has a putting green and a driving range. Want to go?"

"*Indoor* golf? Godwin was smiling, but doubtfully.

"Yes, it's Braemar Golf Dome."

"Oh, a *dome!* What a *clever* idea! And do I *want* to *go?* How can you even *think* you need to *ask?* Of *course* I want to go!" Godwin was practically dancing with anticipation, but carefully, so he didn't spill the contents of his mug. Then his face fell, and he turned to Betsy. "But you're going to need me here all this week, aren't you?"

"Yes," she said, "but only because all my part-timers came to inventory. You didn't take a day off last week, and you came in for the inventory, too. I've been really unfair to you, Goddy, and I'm ashamed to say I didn't think about it until right this minute."

"It's all right, really it is."

"No, it isn't. Rafael, would you like to show Godwin where this indoor driving range is?"

Rafael's handsome face lit up with a big smile. "When?"

"Monday," declared Betsy. "Godwin, you take Monday off. That'll give you two days in a row, all right?"

Godwin thought it over briefly. But the prospect of hitting a bucket of balls won out. "All right, if you think I should."

"I think you deserve at least that."

"Then hurrah! I will! Rafael, what time do you want to pick me up?" Godwin's little sports car could not take a passenger and two sets of golf clubs at the same time.

"It opens at eight, but how about we go out there around nine?"

"Can we stay all day?"

Rafael smiled fondly at Godwin. "If you like, *mi gorrion.*"

After Rafael left, Godwin did his famous Gene Kelly "Singing in the Rain" arms-out circle of the library table while Betsy stood watching him, a fond smile on her face.

TEN

Mark Turnquist sat in the smallest conference room at work, staring into a cooling cup of coffee as if it were a crystal ball that would give him answers to the questions being asked of him.

Janet Bronson Turnquist was dead. The State of North Dakota, his employer, and lots of people thought she was his ex-wife, but in an important sense she wasn't. They also thought Lindsey Miller was his second wife, but in that same sense she wasn't.

But she was going to be, by heaven, as soon as he could arrange it, as soon as their parish priest was able to find ten minutes free on his calendar. *At last, at last.*

For ten years he'd wanted to be free of Janet. He'd finally gotten a civil divorce, but Lindsey, like him, was a Roman Catholic and, like him, wanted to be married in the eyes of the Church as well.

But Janet wouldn't cooperate. She had

always been a little quirky — that's one reason he fell in love with her. Her ability to look at a situation from a different angle was sometimes useful, sometimes amusing, and okay, once in a while, annoying.

But it became scary sometime around their tenth wedding anniversary. Her suspicion that any government body, whether local, statewide, or national, wasn't always operating to the public good became a belief that they were actively plotting to take her freedom from her.

He could still remember the chill he felt the morning she asked him, "Did you hear that voice coming from our living room last night?" She was even more scared about it than he was, and at first went willingly to a doctor to see if something was the matter.

But the questions asked by the doctor scared her even more, and the mind-altering prescriptions he later ordered had some dreadful side effects, both emotional and physical. A change of doctors didn't bring relief. It was after the fourth doctor's failed attempts to find a medication that both soothed her paranoia and left her personality recognizable, if not intact, that she refused to take any more pills.

Mark didn't blame her, but without medication, she turned slowly into a person he barely recognized, fearful, angry, at times incoherent. She started running away from home. She'd be gone at first just for a day or two, but then for a week or more at a time, coming home dirty and often ill, only long enough to wash and eat before leaving again. He finally had her committed to a hospital, but soon after she was released, she ran away — and this time she didn't come back.

She'd phone now and again, to accuse him of trying to harm her, or tell him the sad story of her life on the street. He moved out of their home so she would feel safe going there, and apparently she did, though she rarely showed up. A niece she long ago took an unaccountable shine to would sometimes phone to report that Aunt Janet had been by, and they'd exchange fearful stories with one another about the unfortunate feral creature she had become.

Sometime during those years, Mark became exhausted; his patience ran out, and Janet's incurable craziness killed his love for her.

Then he met Lindsey Miller. Lindsey was a widow — her husband had been killed in Desert Storm — with two teenaged sons, one in college. He hadn't been looking for female companionship, but when he saw her for the third time at the grocery store, he smiled at her and made some comment about them living parallel lives. She replied with something humorous about hamburger, and before long he had taken her out to dinner, then to the theater — they both liked "difficult" plays — and biking.

They grew closer, and after a few months he realized he had fallen in love with her. That spurred him into disentangling himself legally from Janet.

He hadn't known how to contact her, but had to wait until she phoned him. When that happened, he'd told her he wanted a divorce. "You'll never get me before a judge again," was her immediate response, and she'd hung up and never phoned back.

So he'd set off on a complicated effort to get the divorce without her cooperation. He did his part by filing papers with the court, and they tried to find Janet to serve them. When they gave up, he spent several months trying to find her himself. He knew she occasionally came to the house, but so irregularly that her path never crossed with the server's. Mark finally changed lawyers and the new one told him to find out where she was getting her mail. He sent a registered letter to the house and to the Fargo YWCA Women's Shelter and, at his lawyer's suggestion, in care of General Delivery at the main post office. To his surprise, that last gambit worked — she had applied successfully for SSI and apparently was getting her checks that way. So a server was sent to wait for her to come in when the next Social Security check was to be delivered. When she did, he handed the copy of the Summons and Complaint to her. Mark sent her two registered letters, which she signed for, reminding her of her court date. But when the court date arrived, she didn't show up. He ended up with a default judgment.

Then he had to begin the tedious and difficult process of getting his marriage annulled by the Catholic Church. He'd had to write a long, detailed description of their marriage and explain why he felt it had never really been a marriage. He was convinced now that she had been mentally ill from the start of their marriage, and so unable to give proper consent to the vows they'd taken.

But the Church turned him down. The bishop in charge of the process agreed she was now mentally ill, but there was no indication, no proof, that she was mentally ill when they married. The bishop reminded Mark that those marriage vows included a promise to stick with one another "in sickness and in health."

The decision left him angry and miserable. Lindsey was angry and miserable, too. Two years ago they'd gotten a justice of the peace to take them through a marriage service, in part so she and the son still living at home could be covered by his medical insurance and in part so they felt respectable among their set after moving in together. But Lindsey was uncomfortable, still convinced that they were living in sin.

Then Janet's frozen corpse was found in someone's front yard. Mark surprised himself by mourning her death. But now, at last, he and Lindsey could truly marry.

"Penny for your thoughts?" asked a smooth voice.

He looked up to see the freckled police detective who had called him out of his office show a faint, patient smile at his woolgathering. Mark replied, "Nothing, really. Just thinking how I got where I am today. This was a surprise, having a cop wanting to talk to me."

"You know why I'm here?" Sergeant Malloy asked.

"You're from Excelsior, Minnesota, so it must be because my wife — my ex-wife — was found frozen to death there. You think, I assume, that there was something suspicious about her death."

"That's right. When did you last see Janet?"

He thought about that, a frown forming as he cast his mind further and further back. "I guess when she left home for the last time. That was more than three years ago."

"You haven't seen or heard from her since?"

"Oh, I heard from her. Phone calls, mostly. Once she wrote me a letter." He felt a wry smile pull his mouth sideways. He said, "It rhymed but not very well, and it didn't make much sense."

"When was that?"

"A year ago? Maybe longer."

"Do you have that letter?"

"No, I threw it away. Like I said, it didn't make sense."

"Do you remember anything of what it said?"

Again Mark cast his mind back. "Something about no one's been to the moon, and something about living in the library. I can't remember what else."

"When did she last phone?"

"About eighteen months ago. I told her I wanted a divorce, and she told me she wasn't going to help me do that, and then she hung up."

"And that's the last time you heard from her?"

"Except for that crazy poem, yes."

"When did you get the divorce?"

"Six months after that. It took me that long to find a way to get the summons to her."

"So you had her address?"

"No, no one's living in the house. I offered it to her as part of a settlement, took my name off the deed. I was hoping she'd come back to it. But it's condemned now, there was a flood that came halfway up the walls last spring, and she apparently hadn't been back since then. I managed to contact her by sending her a registered letter care of General Delivery at the Fargo Post Office. I know she got it because she had to sign for it. So that's where the server went, caught her picking up her SSI check, and got the divorce papers into her hands. But she never responded, and didn't come to court."

"Had you had any contact with her since the divorce?"

"No, I didn't see or hear from her after that."

"What if I told you that I have a witness who claims to have seen you talking with her in Saint Paul about three weeks ago?"

Now there was a lame trick. "I don't see

how that's possible."

"So the witness is lying?"

"I think you're lying. I don't believe there is any such witness." Mark hoped to God that was true.

"Where were you between January tenth and January fifteenth?"

Was the gap that large? "I haven't been out of Fargo since before Christmas."

"Can you prove that?"

"Certainly. I haven't missed a day of work, and my evenings and weekends were spent with my wife or my wife and friends. There's no time gap big enough for me to get all the way to the Twin Cities, do the deed, and get back."

Sergeant Malloy took his time writing that down in his notebook. He asked, "Have you ever met a woman named Carolyn, or Carrie, Carlson?"

The question surprised him. Was this man trying to lay another trap? *Tell the truth, tell the truth.* "No. Is she a suspect, too?"

"You're not a suspect, Mr. Turnquist, you're a person of interest."

"I am? I suppose there's a difference, so all right, I guess I'm glad to hear that. Who is this Ms. Carlson?"

"She's dead, too."

Sergeant Malloy was looking at him very

sharply. Mark could not think how to respond to that information, so he said nothing.

Malloy asked, "Do you know if Janet and Carrie were friends?"

"I told you, I've never heard of Carrie Carlson. And I think my wife was too paranoid to have a friend."

Malloy just kept looking at him, until he shifted uncomfortably in his chair.

"I can't sit here talking to you all afternoon," Mark finally said. "If you haven't got anything else to ask me, may I go back to work? I have a lot to do."

"I think that's all for now. If I have more questions, I'll let you know." He stood and put his notebook away.

"Fine. I'll be here."

He watched the detective go out the door, gave him two minutes to get out of sight, then went into the men's room and vomited copiously.

When Betsy turned on her computer up in her apartment that evening, she found an e-mail from Annie.

Hi Betsy! This here is Annie. At the library. I talk ed to 8 weomen who was at the shellter before Jan. 6. 2 of them remmember Jan nette. There nmed Alis an Tameka. Alise sez, Carrie was there till Jan. 4, she thinks, and beatup by a man nomed Paul On jan. 1. Tamica sez, Carrie was there till Jan. 3, maybe, and cou ld sneek liquor in to the shelter without nobody seen her. Alise sez, she saw Carrie talkin to Janet. I will talk to you soon, Bye!

There it was, the link between the two dead women. A resident "saw Carrie talkin to Janet." Betsy could not help feeling a thrill of excitement at that.

And "a man nomed Paul"?

Maybe Alis — Alice? — wasn't remembering correctly. Maybe the name of the man who beat Carrie up wasn't named Paul — but Paulson. As in Dice Paulson.

ELEVEN

On Monday morning, Godwin rode shotgun in Rafael's new Lexus, admiring everything from the car's performance to its red, black, and silver steering wheel. They came east on Highway 7, turned south on Highway 169, and exited at Valley View, and after a few minutes on a winding residential street, found themselves at Braemar Boulevard. They turned right, and the dome appeared around a gentle curve.

It was not as big as the Minneapolis Metrodome, of course, but it was substantial, over a hundred yards long. A modest, cement block, one-story building was attached to the front end, facing a middle-size parking lot. About a dozen cars were already parked there.

After finding a spot for the Lexus, they went around to the trunk and brought out their golf bags.

Godwin chuckled. "It feels weird to be

carrying these bags over a winter coat," he said.

"I am so glad we do not wish to play snow golf," replied Rafael.

Godwin did not want to say that he had actually thought about such a possibility, playing on a snow-covered course with bright orange balls. But he would have had to buy a looser-fitting winter coat and heavier, warmer boots, and his vanity would not allow either.

They went up three steps into the building and found themselves in a seedily furnished room with a counter at the far end and vending machines along one wall. There were two round wooden tables and chairs in front of the machines.

They each paid for a wire bucket generously filled with golf balls and went through the double doors into the dome. It was a little run-down in there, too, and the air smelled dusty. The aisle they were standing in was not carpeted, but out past the long row of stations were what seemed like acres of smooth, green indoor-outdoor carpet under an off-white quilted dome stretched high overhead. Near the far end of this space were three raised greens, complete with flags, and behind them, against the far wall, were giant targets painted on canvas.

Hundreds of golf balls were scattered on the floor, and as Godwin stood looking, a player a couple of stations down hit a beautiful drive that bounced off one of the faraway targets.

The stations were marked by knee-high barriers that looked something like small versions of the ball return in bowling alleys. Rafael chose one near the center of the row, and Godwin took the next one to the left. Rafael selected his eight iron, and Godwin his favorite hybrid.

Rafael's first shot landed on the center green, knocking two balls already there off the far side.

Godwin's first shot went straight but not very near the front edge of the same green.

"Your aim is very good," said Rafael.

"Yes, but my distance sucks. I hit that ball as hard as I could."

"That can be fixed, *gorrion*. It is not strength alone that gives you distance. Let me show you how to arrange your shoulders before you swing."

After a pleasant hour of golfing, the two men took a break. Godwin sat on an uncomfortable chair at a battered wooden table by the vending machines, turned his cell phone on, and found three messages waiting for his attention. One was from Betsy, and it was very brief. Godwin played it on speaker: "Goddy, on your way home from golfing, could you stop by the Sun-Sailor's office and pick up an envelope they're holding for me? Thanks."

"Oh, rats," said Godwin.

"What, 'oh rats'?" asked Rafael. "Is it so far out of our way? What is the Sun-Sailor?"

"No, it's not that. They publish a number of local weekly newspapers, including Excelsior's own. Now I'll be just dying to know what it's about and it will spoil my practice."

It did, too. Until the very last ball. He was so relieved to be finished that he totally focused on getting the thing off the tee, and it went sailing to the far end and bounced off the exact center of the bull's-eye he was aiming at.

He smiled all the way back to Excelsior.

The six-by-nine brown envelope Godwin handed to Betsy the next morning had been torn open.

"Did you peek?" asked Betsy sternly.

"Of course I did! What did you expect?"

Betsy shook her head, defeated by his impudence. "What do you think about what's in it?"

"I'd say they both look down but not beaten."

Betsy pulled out two three-by-five full-color computer printouts of head-and-shoulder jailhouse mug shots. They were both eloquent examples of womanhood gone sour. The tousled hair was gray or growing out gray, the eyes red-rimmed, the faces dirty and in one case bruised.

They were Carolyn Carlson and Janet Turnquist down at the jail, each identified by white letters stuck on a black holder at the bottom of the photo. Since each photo was a copy of a copy, the letters were hard to read, but Janet appeared to have fallen into custody last summer, in June or July; Carrie more recently, in early December.

Janet's eyes were wide and her mouth a grimace of badly contained terror. Carrie, whose cheek was bruised, looked sleepy and sullen, her mouth turned down at the corners.

"It seems sad that these were the photographs accompanying the newspaper story about their being found dead," noted Godwin. "I mean, if you were out to lunch and saw either of them at a table, would you ask if you could join them?"

"Shall we look up your mug shot, Goddy?" asked Betsy gently.

"Tou-*ché*," said Godwin, and he went to continue his earlier task of pulling summertime cross-stitch patterns.

Still, it was a stern reminder to keep an attractive photograph of oneself around just in case it was requested for an appearance in the press.

That evening, Betsy ran the photos through a scanner and printed four copies of each of them. She put one pair in a pocket of her purse, resolving to get them laminated. She picked up another set of the photographs and studied them. She was struck again by how unprepossessing the women were, how pathetic they looked. Who could possibly consider one or both of them a threat that needed to be eliminated?

She was determined to find out.

The next day Emily Hame came in to pick up a counted cross-stitch pattern she'd asked Betsy to set aside for her, of a single, fully open parrot tulip in very deep red, lightly touched with yellow around the tips of its ragged petals. A Nel Whatmore design, it was a fourteen-inch square meant to be framed, but Emily wanted to make a small pillow of it to front the stack of pillows on her bed. Betsy had kitted it up for her, using black Aida fabric and Anchor flosses.

"How are you coming along with the case?" asked Emily, *sotto voce,* glancing

165

around for eavesdroppers.

"I'm afraid not very well. I'm not a police investigator, nor do I have access to their records, and this seems to be the kind of case best solved by police methods. I hate to sound so discouraging, but I don't want to give you false hope."

"I understand," said Emily, but she did sound as if her hopes were shaken.

Betsy asked, "Have you heard anything from Mike about how he's doing?"

"No. He doesn't seem to have much hope, either. He actually called me in to his office to look at the stuff Aunt Janet was carrying around in those dreadful plastic shopping bags, to see if I recognized anything. I think he was wondering if she stole some of it from me."

"Stole some of it? Like what?"

"A can of baked beans, one of those little, one-serving ones, with the lid you pull off instead of using a can opener. A plastic spoon."

Betsy nodded. "What else was there to look at?"

Emily thought. "There was half a box of Handi Wipes, a clean change of underwear. An old pair of socks. And there was some needlework. She liked trying new things, and there was an old book, one of those large-format ones, the size of a sheet of typing paper. It had a cute title: 'Take the Hard Out of Hardanger.' "

"Did she do Hardanger?" Betsy was thinking of the Hardanger bookmark Mike had showed her. But it had come from Carrie's things, not Janet's.

"Not that I know of. There wasn't any Hardanger embroidery work in her stuff."

"And she hadn't stolen anything from you?"

"No, of course not."

"What else was in the bag?"

"Bags, there were three bags. Her knitting, of course. A scarf, barely started, using dark green wool that looked like it had been raveled from something else, and a pair of plastic knitting needles, size eight. There was a plastic box, hard plastic, with a cracked lid. In it was part of a skein of overdyed floss and two or three other partial skeins of DMC floss, two needles stuck in a scrap of felt, a pair of stork scissors, and also a Clover thread cutter. There were some little white buttons, two balls of different sizes of pearl cotton thread, and a spool of white sewing thread. That's all that was in the box." She paused to think, tapping a forefinger on the tip of her nose. "There was a white cotton T-shirt, a bar of soap wrapped in a raggedy pink washcloth, and a Social Security card . . . This is like that children's party game where you look at a group of odd things on a table and then look away and try to remember everything that you saw. I was always really good at that."

Betsy laughed. "I can believe that."

Encouraged, Emily thought some more and then said, "There was half of one of those energy bars, the kind made with peanut butter, a pair of magnifiers with one lens missing, and an old newspaper, all wrinkled but not wadded up. I mean, it was folded up right, but it looked like she had sat on it. In fact, Mike said newspapers are very insulating, that she probably had sat on it or slept under it or used it as a pillow. It made me sad to think of her trying to sleep with a newspaper for a blanket." She frowned, wrinkling up her nose attractively while she thought. "There was more stuff, should I go on?"

"Sure, if you can."

She could, but none of the items gave Betsy any ideas, unless there was something about Carrie having the bookmark. She dutifully wrote down all the items Emily mentioned.

"Well, what's next, then?" asked Emily.

Betsy cudgeled her brain, but all she could come up with was, "I think I'm going to have to go to Fargo to see if I can find out anything there."

"All right, if you think that will help."

"Frankly, I don't know if it will. But it's all I can think of."

Promising to call Betsy with the address of Janet's condemned house in Fargo, Emily picked up the bag with her kitted tulip pattern and left.

Later, Betsy phoned Sergeant Malloy to ask if he had any good news for her. "Did you find Dice Paulson?" she asked.

"No. But I know where he is."

"Where?"

"In prison in Illinois. He had a fake ID on him when he was arrested for bank fraud and attempted murder of a police officer, and was sent to Joliet Penitentiary down there under the fake name. He's going to be there for at least three years."

"Oh," said Betsy, her hopes dashed.

"Where are you in this case?" he asked.

"Not any forwarder. I think I'm going to have to go to Fargo."

"I've been. Bring warm clothes. And good luck."

TWELVE

Betsy called Roz Watnemo, owner of Nordic Needle in Fargo, North Dakota. "Roz, I need to come to Fargo for a couple of days. I'd like to visit you, see your plant, if I may."

"Hi, Betsy! Sure, come on over! What day are you thinking of?"

"I'll be leaving here Wednesday night, so I'll see you Friday around one, if that's all right."

"Certainly. Is it a business trip?"

"Er . . . yes."

"Well, be careful out on the highway. It's slippery, and more snow is likely tonight."

"I'm taking the train."

"The Empire Builder? Oh, good for you! But then how are you going to get around?"

"I've got a rental car reserved. They're even going to bring it to the hotel."

"Where are you staying?"

"At the Radisson. It's just a couple of blocks from the train station."

"Sounds like you've got your bases covered. Good for you! Looking forward to seeing you Friday."

That evening, Betsy was doing some bookkeeping when her cell phone began to play a Beatles song, "With a Little Help From My Friends." She'd been expecting a call and so had it handy on her computer desk. "Hello, Connor!" she said.

"Machree," he said in his pleasant baritone, that being Irish for "my heart."

"Glad you still think so."

"I'll never stop thinking so," he replied.

"How's it going?"

"Well, Peg's lobbying on behalf of her mother for us to get back together."

Betsy's heart sank. "I guess we shouldn't be surprised. What's her argument?"

"The same as her mother's. We broke up because I wouldn't stop going to sea, so now that I've stopped, there's no reason we shouldn't reconcile." Connor was a retired merchant marine captain.

"And your reply?"

"Very simple. I've moved on, and so should she."

"Is she really angry?" Betsy hoped Connor could not detect the hope in her voice.

"No, she's all sweetness and light. Kind of reminds me of back when things were good

171

between us."

"Oh, Connor —"

"Now, darlin', there's nothing to worry about."

But Betsy did, and spent a restless night in bed, worrying with all her might.

Said Godwin the next morning, "Why on earth did you let him go?"

"He's a grown man. I can't order him around like a child!"

"Couples in love can do things like that. He may have been hoping you'd do that."

"So I could be the bad guy with his daughter? Uh-uh, we've been through that already."

"All right, but don't say I didn't warn you this could end badly."

About nine fifteen on Wednesday evening, Betsy took a cab to the Naomi Women's Shelter in Saint Paul. She had the cab pull up and stop, but she didn't get out. A woman was standing inside the door waiting; when she saw the cab, she came hustling out, carrying a small suitcase: Annie, all smiles.

The cabdriver got out to take her suitcase and put it in the trunk. Annie brushed falling snow off her shoulders and got in beside Betsy. "Wow, I can't believe we're really going on a train! I haven't been on a train since I was a little girl!" She was wearing a thick mannish coat, jeans, her shabby boots, and pilled black mittens. "I'm kind of sorry I couldn't get dressed up for the ride, but if I'm gonna pass for homeless, I gotta dress like it."

"The Amtrak Station, please," said Betsy to the driver when he got back in.

The depot was on the west side of Saint Paul, not far off I-94, in a quiet part of town that was mostly warehouses. It was a modest modern building, two stories tall, painted sky blue, with a good-size parking lot in front.

"It don't look much like the train stations in old movies, does it?" said Annie a little wistfully.

"No, though there's a beautiful big old station in Minneapolis and another in Saint Paul. A pity the Empire Builder couldn't be routed through either of them." Both had been converted to other purposes and were no longer available to the railroad.

They got out of the cab and retrieved their suitcases from the driver. Betsy paid and tipped him, and they crossed the broad sidewalk to the front door of the depot.

Annie asked, "Why does this train come in so late? I mean, there's only one train a day, and this is a big city, right? So why can't it come in at a decent hour?"

"It says in their brochure that they want to be passing through 'the spectacular Rocky Mountains' in daylight, so they have to come through here at ten thirty at night."

"But we're not going as far as the Rocky Mountains, right? So maybe they should run more than one train a day, so passengers can choose whether they want to see mountains, or get to their destination at a decent hour."

Betsy chuckled. "You should write a letter."

"Maybe I will," Annie said loftily.

The inside of the train station was as characterless as the exterior, with beige walls and several rows of armless, unstylish chairs with silver legs and thin padding, all linked together. The rows of chairs faced a big map of the United States on one far wall with all the routes covered by Amtrak marked with thick red lines.

On the left was a high check-in counter behind which a man and a woman waited to issue tickets, check baggage, and answer questions. There were about twenty passengers present, but none at the counter.

Betsy, who had called ahead and made reservations, took Annie over and they presented identification. They were each issued a white paper ticket, about three by eight inches, perforated near one end. It had their names, destination, some arcane coding, and a notation that each of them had a "reserved coach seat."

They went with their suitcases to the rows of chairs and took two adjoining ones. Betsy took off her dark blue winter coat, and sat down. She had that mild headache that comes with being up too late, but she stirred herself to look around. There was a glassed-in room off the back of the lobby, which had a coded lock on the door. She watched as a couple approached the door, consulted a scrap of paper, then punched in the numbers. The door obediently opened and they went in, dragging their suitcases behind them.

"What's that for?" asked Annie.

"I think it's for people who have sleeping accommodations," she said.

"Sleeping accommodations," sighed Annie. "If we was going to be on the train till morning, we woulda got sleeping accommodations, right?"

"Yes, of course." Now that she thought about it, perhaps she should have reserved a "roomette."

She looked out of the big windows along

that wall, and could see, through the thin curtain of snow coming down slantwise in a steady breeze, railroad tracks under a roof supported by plain wooden pillars.

She looked at her watch. Twenty minutes until the train was due in. Or was that twenty minutes until the train was due to depart? Probably the latter. Whichever, she had some time to wait. So she dug into her purse — the big one she used for travel — and pulled out the zippered plastic bag that held her latest knitting project, a pink mitten. She got it out, counted her stitches, and set off knitting.

"I wish I knew how to do that," remarked Annie, leaning a little sideways to look at it.

"Maybe I'll teach you how sometime," said Betsy absently.

"Would you? Would you really?"

Betsy looked over at Annie's eager face. "All right, if you like."

"Yes, thanks! Do some more, I want to watch you do it."

Betsy set off again, trying to ignore Annie's flattering but intense scrutiny.

As she sank into the rhythm of the stitches — she was past the thumb and had a few inches of just knit, knit, knit — her mind was freed to contemplate other things. For example, was it such a good idea to travel by train? Airline travel was faster, and if she'd chosen to drive, she wouldn't have had to depart at such an awful hour. On the other hand, it was cheaper than flying, and there was less hassle to it. Plus, she didn't want to drive for six hours, in the dark, on snowy roads after working all day in the shop. The train was a good choice, considering the alternatives. She hadn't been on a train since a summer in Europe, many years ago, and like Annie, she was looking forward to this trip.

Then she heard the deep thunder of an immense engine slowly growing louder and louder, almost as if it had been summoned by her thoughts. She looked up and saw a creeping immensity, a huge locomotive, rolling into the station. It was aerodynamically shaped in silver with blue trim, and its single headlight gleamed brightly in the night.

"That sucker's really *big,* ain't it!" murmured Annie.

Silver and blue passenger cars trailed behind it, their roofs wet with melted snow. They were two stories tall, with half the downstairs and all of the upstairs windowed.

The sound of the engine — engines? — dropped a tone as the train came to a stop. Passengers alighted from two of the cars and straggled sleepily or hurried eagerly through the double doors into the station. Most were greeted warmly by people waiting for them, and they all went out the front doors.

An announcement was made that passengers for the westbound Amtrak Empire Builder should line up at the doors to the platform, tickets in hand. Betsy tucked her knitting away; Annie grabbed her purse and suitcase.

Betsy put her coat back on and, pulling her wheeled suitcase, led Annie to a place in line with the dozen other passengers. Annie nudged Betsy and nodded in amazement at some of them carrying blankets and pillows.

A lectern Betsy had not noticed earlier stood in front of the doors with a man in a white shirt behind it. As they neared the lectern, Betsy could hear the ticket taker ask for tickets, note aloud the destination, then tear off the bigger portion of their ticket and direct each passenger to a specific car. He also gave each of them a slip of paper with a few letters written vertically in bold capitals on it.

Betsy and Annie handed over their tickets. Their slips of paper said F A R. They were told to go to the next to last car. There were only six cars in the train, so it wasn't a really long walk. Another man in a charcoal black uniform stood beside an open door to that car. He asked Betsy her destination.

"Fargo," she replied.

"Me, too," said Annie, holding out her ticket stub.

"This is the right car, then," he said. "You want to go upstairs. And pointing to the slip of paper in Betsy's hand, he added, "You'll want to stick that up over your seats." He helped each of them up onto a little stool and again into the car, which was cramped and not brightly lit. On their right were deep, floor-to-ceiling shelves, almost filled with suitcases. They found a gap on a shoulder-high shelf and stowed their suitcases on it.

The enclosed stairway to the second floor was opposite the shelves. It was narrow, with higher-than-normal risers, and it twisted sharply around on its way up. Betsy climbed up, Annie breathing heavily behind her — whether from excitement or exertion, she couldn't tell — into a dimly lit aisle lined with rows of twin seats. Several of the seats were occupied by sleeping passengers draped with blankets and snuggled deep into pillows — *that's why people are bringing them along,* she thought. Most of the sleepers were taking up both seats. She went down along the aisle and found a pair not occupied. She took her coat off and looked around for a clue as to where she should put the F A R slip of paper.

There was a shelf running the length of the car above the seats and on its outer edge, over each pair of seats, was a metal holder. Above the occupied seats other slips of paper had been tucked into it. She tucked her own in, did the same with Annie's, then sat down by the window.

Annie took off her coat. She was wearing a thick brown sweater under it. She took her own and Betsy's coat and stuffed them into the overhead shelf, then sat down with a satisfied sigh.

The seat was wide and comfortable. Looking around, Betsy saw it could be laid back, and there was even a flat support that came up from under it to rest one's legs on. There was ample space between Betsy's seat and the seat ahead of her, and a little metal footrest. Her seat came up high enough in back that she could rest her head against it.

"This is all right, isn't it?" said Annie, grinning, experimenting with her seat, wriggling her shoulders and settling her bottom. "Better than the old Greyhound."

"Much. Even more comfortable than flying coach, that's for sure," replied Betsy.

She looked out her window, which was on the side away from the station. Back here, the rumble of the locomotive was silenced, and the only sounds were of a pair of passengers several rows forward, talking quietly. There was another set of railroad tracks out there, across another platform, and beyond them some brick buildings — warehouses, by the look of them. Big snowflakes passed into and out of the halos of the platform lights.

Disconcertingly, one of the supports for the roof over the tracks began to drift slowly backward past her window.

No, the train had started moving forward, smoothly and silently.

"We're on our way," said Annie softly, somewhere between excitement and awe.

THIRTEEN

The train made its sedate northwesterly passage through a series of big railroad yards Betsy didn't know existed. A downtown — Saint Paul? Minneapolis? — she couldn't tell, it was from an unfamiliar angle. Whichever, it stood in tall, golden glory, glimpsed fitfully in the distance between nearer buildings, and through filmy curtains of snow.

As they moved faster, the car began to rock gently from side to side.

Now and again they would cross a street, with cars waiting behind barriers guarded with flashing red lights.

These became fewer until, finally, they were out in the country. It was very dark out there. Rarely, a light would appear up on a high pole that marked a farmhouse and barn. The train speeded up and the car's rocking motion increased, causing Annie to sit up straight with an anxious look on her face. But when no one else looked alarmed, she settled back with a little nod, and smiled reassuringly at Betsy.

"Are you nervous about tomorrow?" asked Betsy.

"Naw, why should I be?"

"You've never been to the women's shelter in Fargo."

"Aww, that don't matter. I been to a lot of shelters, they're all pretty much alike, though some are better than others."

There was a stir in the seat in front of them, and a tousle-haired woman rose up to peer at them, with a very disapproving look on her face.

"Oops," said Betsy in a much quieter voice. "We're keeping someone awake."

"She's not the only one," growled a male voice from across the aisle.

Annie hunched her shoulders. "I guess we should be quiet from now on."

"I guess," said Betsy.

The two women sat back in their seats and fell silent.

One of the things that Annie had learned at the Naomi Shelter — and that she'd shared with Betsy — was that there was a good shelter in Fargo, run by the YWCA. Doubtless Janet had stayed there. The plan was for Annie to go to the Fargo shelter tomorrow, where she would apply for two days' refuge, during which time she would, perhaps, learn from the other people staying there something about Janet Turnquist. For example, did anyone hate her?

Meanwhile the late hour, dim lighting, and gentle rocking were making Betsy drowsy.

A movement in the aisle brought her back to full awareness. She looked around, then up, to see a conductor standing like the Statue of Liberty with his lit flashlight pointed at the ceiling. He was peering at the slips of white paper tucked into the silver metal holder over their seats.

Annie was looking up at him with bright curiosity.

Betsy had a sudden inspiration. "Is there a club car or an observation car on this train?" she asked softly.

"Yes, ma'm, the observation car is one car forward," he murmured. "The club car is downstairs from it, but it's closed for the night."

"Thank you."

He touched the bill of his cap and resumed his walk up the aisle.

Annie heard Betsy ask the question she'd been hoping for. "You want to go up there?"

"Sure! Do we take all our stuff?"

"No, just our purses."

Stumbling a little under the impetus of the rocking train, they slowly walked past the sleeping or reading passengers — Annie had noticed that there were individual reading lights over each seat, but she hadn't turned hers on — to the door at the front end of the car. It took a few moments for them to see that there was a push plate on it to make it open.

There was a brief, rackety passage across the plates between cars, then another push plate, and they were in a well-lit car that had luxuriously comfortable swivel chairs looking out the windows at one end, and café-style tables at the other. The windows, larger than in the passenger car, actually stretched up onto the roof. Cool! Annie wished it were daytime, so she could sit and look out.

All the chairs on one side of the car were taken by a group of twenty-somethings, men and women, in ski lodge wear — bright bulky sweaters, skinny leggings, fat boots — talking and laughing, existing in a happy bubble that excluded everyone else on the train, maybe even the train itself.

Annie, after a brief, interested halt to eavesdrop, led the way to the other end, where she scooted into a bench seat at a

Formica table, and smiled at Betsy sitting down across from her.

"What should we talk about?" asked Annie, feeling brightly awake. She was dismayed to see Betsy was looking tired but took care to disguise her disappointment.

Betsy sighed just a little bit and said, "Let's go over in more detail what you learned at the Naomi Shelter."

"Okay. Ask me questions. Otherwise I'll talk your ear off. What do you want to know?"

"All right. How many people did you talk to?"

"About Carrie? Seven or maybe eight — yeah, eight. About ten more didn't want to talk about anything except did I want to go out with them to buy dope or booze, or could I loan them money, or complain about how life treated them bad."

"Did all eight know Carrie Carlson?"

Annie thought about that. "All but two. Carrie was in there a lot, they said. She never stayed long, just long enough to get warm and clean and put on fresh clothes. She usually had some money in her pocket. Five dollars, ten dollars, sometimes even twenty dollars, enough to buy wine, or whatever. But she would hardly ever share it with anyone."

"Did she drink only wine?"

"I don't know. But all the people like her that I know, dedicated drinkers they're called, will drink anything with alcohol in it. But I don't know if she was like an exception." Annie considered the odds to be fantastically against Carrie being an exception, but she didn't say so; she'd already taken too long to answer that one question.

"She was found with a bottle of bourbon."

Annie thought about that. "Maybe someone gave it to her? No, more likely she bought it. She had money almost all the time."

"Yes, that's right." Betsy stopped talking to think. Annie could almost see the wheels turning in her head. "But what if Mike Malloy is right? Someone put something in that bottle, something lethal, and put it where Carrie would be sure to find it."

"Okay, what if," said Annie.

"Who might that be? Why would someone want Carrie dead? It would have to be someone who knew Carrie, who hated her —"

"Or was scared of her," amended Annie.

"Yes." Betsy nodded, flashing an approving look at Annie for her perceptiveness. "Or was scared of her. Because she knew something. Because she had threatened this person, either with physical violence . . ." Betsy trailed off, frowning.

"What? What are you thinking?"

"I'm wondering which of the two, Janet or Carrie, would be more likely to get into that kind of situation. Janet was mentally ill, paranoid, and so more likely to feel threatened. But Carrie was quarrelsome and inclined to react violently. Janet's enemies were mostly imaginary, while Carrie's were more likely real."

Annie felt a stir of excitement. Here was someone thinking like a detective! "So which was the one the killer came after?" she asked.

"I don't know. Did anyone at the shelter know Janet?"

"Four people did. Three of them were the same ones who knew Carrie."

"What did they say?"

"That she was crazy. She looked crazy, she acted crazy. But there are a lot of crazy people who are homeless, us people know how to act around them, we aren't scared of them mostly. They said Janet cried a lot, but wouldn't talk about why." Annie thought that was very sad.

Betsy frowned, as if this fact about Janet was painful. "Did the staff try to help her?" she asked in a sad voice.

"I'm sure they did. But crazy people have crazy rules in their heads, and they're stricter than what anyone standing on the outside can do. Like there was this one woman who had to count her steps, and if she got interrupted or forgot the number, she had to go back to her room and start over. Sometimes she missed supper because she started over too many times. You could tell her and tell her she didn't have to do that, and she'd say, 'Yes I know,' real annoyed, but she'd do it anyway."

"You never met Janet, did you?"

"No, I never did."

"Are you sure? Maybe your paths crossed and you either don't remember or she never told you her name."

Annie thought about that for a moment. "I suppose that's possible. Is there a picture of her somewhere?"

"Actually I have one." Betsy went rummaging in her purse and came up with two color printouts of the photographs that had obviously been taken during a jail booking. They were folded into quarters. She unfolded them and put them on the table for Annie to look at. "This is Carrie, and this is Janet."

Carrie was thin, with heavy bags beneath red-rimmed eyes, and graying dark hair that looked as if it had been cut in the dark with nail scissors. Her expression was angry, her thin lips poised as if to say something.

"Whoa!" said Annie. "Not exactly a beauty queen!"

"Yes, but people tend not to look their best right after being arrested. And Carrie, according to her cousin, was angry a lot of the time. Does she look familiar?"

Annie squinted at the picture, trying to imagine her looking more rested, less angry. "I don't think so," she said.

She turned her attention to the other picture, which was of a woman probably close to Carrie's age, with hair that had once been dyed a dead black but was growing out very gray. Her eyes, looking a little to one side, were wide and wary, her mouth a little crooked, her shoulders hunched. She was wearing a torn black shirt.

"Oh, I know her!" exclaimed Annie. Her nose wrinkled at the memory. "She always wanted fresh clothes but they had to be black — and she didn't wash herself enough. She was sure that someone could sneak up on her in the shower — I think she saw that movie *Psycho* and it scarred her for life. I had to share a room with her, and I got her to use a washcloth instead of taking a shower, but even then she didn't like the water running, she said it made too much noise. She'd turn it on and then right away turn it off again. I felt sorry for her, but at the same time I tried to stay away from her. She was just too weird, and she smelled."

"How long did you share a room?"

"Two — no, three days. That was back in November. She said the FBI was after her, and if anything happened to her, I should contact my senator." Annie hesitated, but decided to ask, "Should I?"

"I don't think so. Someone was after her, but he, or she, wasn't from the government."

"Yeah, but the government's the ones with secret poisons, aren't they?"

She could tell Betsy was trying not to laugh at her, and tried not to be offended. Betsy apparently realized that, and, sobering, said, "Actually, you may be right, but they had no real reason to come after Janet."

"Oh. Yeah, I guess that's so."

"On the other hand, she is dead. Annie, I'm concerned I might have dragged you into a situation that is more trouble than you can handle. So you don't have to check in at the Fargo shelter if you don't want to. You were so clever at getting behind the walls at the Naomi Shelter that I just assumed you'd be willing to go for a stay at the shelter in Fargo."

Annie beamed with pleasure at this praise. "But I do want to!" she said.

"Are you sure?"

"Sure I'm sure! This is important, right?" Annie said this as firmly as she could.

"Well, yes, it is. And I'm grateful that you're willing to do this."

"No problem, honest, no problem." Not a problem she couldn't solve anyway.

"Well, that's all I wanted to know. This bench isn't nearly as comfortable as our seats. Want to go back?"

"I'm not sleepy," hinted Annie. "And there's nuthin' to look at out the windows back in the regular car."

"Well, then, what do you want to talk about?"

"I dunno." Annie looked expectantly at Betsy. Maybe she'd talk about what it was like to run a business.

But Betsy picked the topic Annie was most tired of. "Tell me about yourself. Where are you from?"

"Minneapolis. Born there. I'll probably die there, too, or maybe as far away as in Saint Paul." She tried to change the subject. "What about you?" she asked Betsy, looking genuinely interested.

"I was born in Brown Deer, a suburb of

Milwaukee. My sister Margot started the shop, and I inherited it when she died. How did you come to . . ." Betsy bit her tongue, but her eyes said she really wanted to know.

Annie surrendered. "Be homeless? It wasn't hard. All I had to do was make some easy mistakes."

"Like what?"

Annie sighed. "First, drop out of school. My parents warned me, but I was seventeen and knew everything." Annie was sure that many homeless people were high school dropouts — some didn't even get that far. Though if the economy was bad, even rich people could end up homeless if they didn't have rich relatives.

"But that's just to start with," said Annie. "It didn't help to pick a bad man for a husband."

"Bad how? Was he cruel to you?"

"Not on purpose. He was fun actually. We laughed a whole lot. But he was lazy and he drank too much. Couldn't keep a job. Smoked marijuana a lot — I think it was the marijuana that made him lazy. It was making me stupid, so I quit. I thought he'd stop all that stuff once we were married, but he stayed like a kid when he should have been like a grown-up."

"I had a boyfriend like that once," said

Betsy. "I was young and thoughtless, and I almost married him. I'm really glad I didn't."

"Why didn't you?"

"I had a good friend who got me into a conversation about where we wanted to be in ten years, and I suddenly realized Gary wasn't going to help me get there." She smiled. "I think she did that on purpose!"

Annie said wistfully, "I wish I'd had a friend like that."

"So go on, then what happened?"

Annie sighed, but obediently went on. "Then I had an even stupider idea. I thought having a baby would force him to grow up, but it made him worse. His jokes weren't funny anymore, we fought all the time, and he finally walked out."

"But didn't he pay child support?" Betsy asked, the soul of naïveté.

Annie gave a high-pitched sound, almost like a bark. "Ha! Every time the law found him, and started to close in to make him pay child support, he'd quit his job and move to a new address."

Betsy gave a sympathetic sigh. "The pig!"

"I thought so. I worked two jobs to support my son and myself, but without that diploma, they were crappy jobs and we lived hand to mouth. Plus, I was a crappy mom, because I wasn't home much and too tired when I was."

"But what else could you do?"

Annie paused to think, though it was a familiar question. She shrugged. "I don't know. Dick Junior was a wild kid, and he grew into an irresponsible man, a lot like his father, only without the charm."

"Did he ever straighten up?" Betsy asked hopefully.

"Last I heard, he was living in his car somewhere in Arkansas — but that was two years ago. I don't know where he is now."

"You don't ever hear from him?"

"He wouldn't know how to get in touch with me even if he wanted to. And vice versa." This conversation was really getting her down.

"You said you had a good job at a factory."

Annie looked out the window into the darkness. "Yeah, that was the best job I ever had, workin' on the line at that auto parts factory. But they moved overseas, and I'm too old to get another factory job." Annie pulled her shoulders up. That *had* been a good job.

Betsy said, "Oh, Annie . . ."

Annie looked at her and saw tears forming in her eyes.

"Now don't you go getting all sympathetic on me, okay?" she scolded. "It's not a pretty story, but it's not unusual. There are an awful lot of women with a story just like mine. If I think about it too much, I get depressed, so I just stay . . ." She searched her brain for the word she wanted, then brightened on finding it: "Assertive."

Betsy was one of those people who looked for solutions. "What about the factory? Didn't they offer a pension?"

"Sure, but I didn't work there long enough to earn one. They gave us six months' pay when they let us go, but a year later, I still got no job so I can't pay my rent, so . . ." She shrugged again. "That's how come I'm homeless."

"But what about welfare?"

"Oh, I'm on welfare. But welfare doesn't pay enough for me to rent an apartment, even in a bad neighborhood. I'm on a waiting list for a subsidized place. It'll happen. Once I get a place to live, I can really start over. I can find some kind of a job maybe. At least I'll have a real address, and I can open a bank account." The familiar dream made her voice turn quiet. "Save up and buy a TV. Yeah, that'll be nice."

This time the tears spilled over. "Oh, Annie . . ."

"Say, I told you, don't feel sad for me! I'm alive and kickin'. Things'll work out, they generally do. I'll be fine!" She'd really had enough of this conversation, so she faked a big yawn. "Well, I guess I'm tired after all. How about you?"

She could tell that Betsy recognized the ploy for what it was, but that was all right, because she said, "Yes, me, too. Let's go back."

Betsy led the way back to their seats, finding them in the dim light when she recognized their coats on the rack above them. They sat down with identical sighs, and in a few minutes both women were sound asleep.

They were awakened by the conductor. "Ladies, we're coming into Fargo," he said quietly. "You'll need to gather up your things and come down the stairs. Be sure to check the overhead."

"Gotcha," murmured Annie.

"Thank you," mumbled Betsy.

He moved up two rows and bent over a figure wrapped in blankets.

They got their coats down from the shelf, shrugged their way into them, picked up their purses from the floor, and made their way to the steep, narrow stairway going down. After the dimness upstairs, the lights now seemed bright down there, and Betsy found their suitcases with no trouble. It felt even more crowded down there with four other people, also waiting to get off. There was a sliding, slow, thumping sound from behind them and two more people appeared. The others rearranged themselves so the new arrivals could get their luggage. Then they all stood quietly, with legs well apart, trying not to stagger as the train rocked ever more slowly, coming into Fargo.

It was the soul-deadening hour of half past three in the morning and nobody was saying much.

There were no windows where they stood, so Betsy felt, rather than saw, the train gliding to a gentle stop. A conductor opened a door around from the luggage shelves and a current of icy air came drifting in.

When Betsy got to the front of the line, the conductor, now standing on the platform, took her suitcase from her with one hand and helped her down with the other. Betsy took a few steps, then turned to wait for Annie.

"Which way to the Radisson Hotel?" Betsy asked the conductor.

"I don't know, I'm from Portland," he replied, helping the last passenger down.

The modest, one-story, brick train station

was lit up, but nobody seemed to be in there. Betsy went around to the west side of the building, where two of the passengers were putting their luggage into the trunk of a waiting car. It was snowing, but the parking lot was clear except for a thin coating of fresh snow.

"Which way to the Radisson, do any of you know?" Betsy asked loudly.

The nearer of the two women pointed down the street perpendicular to the parking lot. "That way, about two blocks," she said and stepped back while the other closed the trunk.

Betsy turned around to ask Annie if she could walk that far in the snow and cold.

"Piece o' cake," said Annie before Betsy opened her mouth.

The streets and sidewalks were piled with four or five inches of snow. They waited while the two cars picking up passengers went out into the snow-clogged street and disappeared quickly from sight. Betsy, glad she had worn her boots, waded through the snow as she crossed the street and began walking down the sidewalk, Annie behind her. Not a single building showed a light, and now there was no traffic at all. It was so quiet that when she stopped to listen, all she could hear was the faint whisper of the snow falling all around her.

Midnight, she mused, was not the dead of night. At midnight, bars are still open, people are still out and around. But at three, the late-nighters have gone to bed and the early-risers have not yet awakened.

There was an icy patch under the next few steps of snow, and the snow itself was a weightless powder. "Ooo-ups!" exclaimed Betsy as her feet came out from under her. But she regained her balance after a fast dance and didn't fall. "Watch it right here," she said in warning to Annie.

Annie dutifully did the snow-country shuffle and got across the patch with no trouble.

Then they both heard a deep scraping sound, and looked up to see an immense snowplow coming up a side street.

"Hey, lookit that! Aren't you glad to see that big ol' plow?" asked Annie. " 'Cause I am." Cheered, they hastened their steps.

They crossed another street, and saw light coming from a building on the far corner. It marked the corner entrance of the Radisson Hotel. They stopped inside the vestibule to stamp snow off their feet.

They went through the second set of thick glass doors, into the large, shining, marble-walled lobby. It appeared abandoned at first

— but then Betsy saw a young man rising from behind the check-in counter. He'd evidently been stooping to pick something up.

They checked in, and while waiting for their magnetic room keys, Betsy asked for a wake-up call at nine thirty. Then they took the elevator to their room on the ninth floor.

It was big and tastefully decorated, with two queen-size beds, heavy drapes, and a lush, thick carpet. "This is *nice!*" said Annie, flipping the lights on and off in the large bathroom.

"Yes, it is," said Betsy, mindful of the far more modest hotels and motels of her youth, and aware that Annie had likely never been in a room this fine.

They changed quickly into pajamas, brushed their teeth, and fell gratefully into bed.

FOURTEEN

The shrill ring of the phone was loud in the silent room. It rang again and Betsy groaned.

"What? Stop it!" grumbled Annie, rolling away from the sound.

Betsy, desperate to hush the noise, lifted the receiver. "This is your nine thirty wake-up call," said the recording of a bright and chipper male voice.

"Okay, thanks." Betsy grinned at herself answering a recording and dropped the receiver back into its cradle. "Time to get up," she sighed.

"Uff da," said Annie, but she obediently rolled out of bed.

"Wow, five hours of sleep just isn't enough," said Betsy, following suit. She rubbed the top of her head with her fingers and yawned prodigiously. "You want to shower first?"

"Sure!" Annie headed eagerly into the

bathroom and in a minute Betsy heard the sound of running water.

Later, over breakfast in the hotel's second-floor restaurant, Betsy, resplendent in a bright red pantsuit, nibbled at a soft-boiled egg, toast, and coffee. "Will you be able to call me today from the shelter?" she asked Annie.

"I'm sure I can find a way — they prob'ly have a phone that residents can use. If they don't, I can walk to a place with a pay phone." Annie was eating an omelet made with selections from a big Texas vegetable garden, with bacon and hash browns on the side. Her eyebrows were signaling that she found the meal delicious.

"I hope you don't have to do that; pay phones are becoming rarer and rarer these days."

"Tell me about it." Annie sighed, but another bite of omelet cheered her back up.

"Here, before I forget," said Betsy, reaching for her purse. She took out her wallet and removed four five-dollar bills from it. "Take this with you. You might need it."

Annie started to refuse, but changed her mind. "All right, you're right. Thank you." The money went into her shabby black purse.

Shortly after ten, they were down in the

lobby waiting for Betsy's rental car to arrive.

"Don't be nervous," Annie said to Betsy,
who was unconsciously drumming her
fingers on the arm of her chair.

"Who's nervous?"

"You are," said Annie with a nod toward
the drumming, which Betsy immediately
halted. "I keep tellin' you, this is a piece o'
cake. I been going to shelters for a long
enough time, I know how they work. I'm
not gonna do something stupid, I'm not
even gonna be brave. I'm just gonna drink a
little coffee or play cards and talk with
people. Gossip. Everybody does that."

"All right, you're right. I should have more
confidence in you. After all, you did very
well at Naomi."

"That's right. Hey, lookit that; I wish that
was our car."

It was. A midnight blue two-door Chrys-
ler of recent vintage, freshly washed, it even
had a full tank of gas. Betsy signed for it,
and she and Annie set off for the YWCA.

The Y was just short of an exit from I-94,
on University. The building was new-looking
and attractive, two stories of clean red brick
with steeply slanting gray roofs. A good-size
parking lot was in front.

"You want to go in first?" asked Betsy.

"No, they probably have a camera watching the parking lot," replied Annie. "They'll see me getting out of the car, so we might as well go in together. We'll say you saw me outside the hotel and gave me a ride."

"All right."

Though Annie would not have admitted it for any reason, she was nervous as she walked with Betsy into the shelter. This was a really important job, and she had volunteered for it. People could go to prison if she found the answers to the questions Betsy wanted asked. So she had to do her very best, and part of that was looking and acting like she wasn't being sneaky. But she also couldn't act different from usual. She'd done a real good job of that at Naomi, but she'd never been in Fargo before, much less in a shelter here. She'd told Betsy all shelters were alike, but that wasn't really true. She'd only said it because she didn't want Betsy to get even more nervous.

She took a deep breath. *Okay, lady, here we go.*

The Y was a really nice building; everything inside looked both clean and new.

As at Naomi, there was a tiny receptionist's office with a window into the lobby. They both stopped there.

Annie said, pitching her voice low and humble, "Hi, I'm Annie Summerhill, and I need a place to stay for just a couple of days. This here lady gave me a ride." She glanced at Betsy.

"Welcome," replied the receptionist, a very attractive brunette sitting at a small, paper-clogged desk with a computer on it. "If you'll wait just a minute, I'll have someone come out to get your paperwork started."

"Thank you," said Annie, letting the tension she'd had no trouble allowing to show on her face relax just a little, and offering a grateful smile.

She stepped aside so Betsy could have her turn. "Hello, I'm Betsy Devonshire, and I have an appointment with Fran Coleman."

"Welcome," said the receptionist. "Just a minute, I'll let her know you're here."

A pretty young woman in a gray wool suit came out first. She wore gold jewelry and maroon shoes. Her brown hair was long, and tied up on top of her head.

She held her hand out to Betsy, who was looking good in that red pantsuit. "Hello," she said with a smile. "I'm Fran Coleman."

Betsy shook her hand. "Thank you for agreeing to see me on such short notice," she said. Then she turned to Annie. "This is Annie Summerhill," she said. "I saw her outside my hotel. She needed a ride to a shelter; I hope it was all right to bring her here."

"Yes, of course. Welcome, Ms. Summerhill."

"Thank you," said Annie.

"Now, if you'll come with me," said Fran, and she led Betsy away.

Annie stood awhile, her battered secondhand suitcase at her feet, her secondhand black purse hanging off her arm. Then she watched as a woman approached. She was plump, with short, curly black hair liberally streaked with gray, kind eyes, and a little too much nose. She was wearing a dark green skirt, and what used to be called a sweater set in light green. She even had a two-strand pearl necklace — how old-fashioned could you get? She walked up to Annie and held her hand out. "Welcome to the YWCA women's shelter," she said. "I'm Shelly Wisniewski. Why don't you come with me, and we'll get you signed in."

"Thank you," said Annie. As she walked beside Shelly, she gave the story she and Betsy had made up together. "I don't need to stay long, I have a cousin in Saint Paul who is going to take me in. She even made a reservation for me on the train for Friday.

But meantime, I don't have money for a hotel."

"I understand. In here, this is my office."

The office was fairly large, carpeted, and very neat, no loose folders or papers strewn around. There were no windows. Gray metal file cabinets and wooden cabinets, like the ones you might find in a kitchen, lined one wall, and a shelf was filled with both books and loose-leaf binders. A stack of shallow, gray metal boxes was on a corner of the desk, each box half filled with forms. The inevitable computer station was on an adjoining wooden shelf, its screen saver of a snowcapped mountain rising from a calm, tree-lined lake, really pretty.

"Have a seat, this won't take long," said Shelly, by which Annie knew it was going to take a while. Shelly began pulling out forms, one from each tray.

"Um, I don't spell so good," announced Annie before Shelly could hand her the sheaf of forms. It was more that she couldn't read those tiny words on the forms, but never mind.

"All right, I'll ask the questions and fill in the answers for you, okay?"

"Thanks." Annie unbuttoned her old coat and pulled it open — it was warm in the office.

The first form was meant to collect what Shelly called basic information: full name, date of birth, *and* age, which Annie always thought was, what was the word? Oh, yeah, *redundant.* And her Social Security number, whether or not she was a citizen, what race she claimed to be — once, annoyed by the numerous choices, Annie had said she was an earthling. But they didn't think that was funny.

Shelly wanted to know whether she had any little children with her, whether she had children at all and where they might be, whether or not she was pregnant, the address and phone number of an emergency contact person. It always pained Annie to be asked that last question, because she had nobody. Then she remembered her imaginary cousin and made up a name and address.

"We're almost done with the front of this form," said Shelly cheerfully. "How did you find out about this shelter?"

"Someone in Saint Paul told me."

"Have you ever been here before?"

"No."

Out of a list of ten possible reasons for coming to the shelter, Annie picked "Traveler" because it sounded better than "Homeless."

Shelly turned to the back of the form and asked where she had been staying before she came here. "Naomi Shelter in Saint Paul," murmured Annie — but at least it wasn't in a place not meant for human habitation, like a car or in a doorway.

"How long were you there?" asked Shelly.

"Two weeks."

"Why did you come to Fargo?"

"I have this friend, her name is Janet Turnquist, she's from Fargo, and she's homeless like me. I thought maybe the two of us could get a room together. But I can't find her. Is she here in this shelter maybe?"

"I don't know. You can have a look around after we get through here."

"Okay. What's next?"

"Income sources."

"I got GAMC and food stamps, that's all." Annie wasn't old enough for Social Security, or disabled enough for SSI; her income was barely over two hundred dollars a month.

Shelly read the last question on that page: "Are there any physical or mental health concerns we should be aware of?"

"No, ma'm." Annie put it firmly. She did not want to waste any time talking to a shrink or a nurse.

Page three asked about specific health issues, such as HIV status, or problems relating to drug abuse. "No, all I got is type two diabetes and glaucoma — and I have my pills and eyedrops with me."

"Are you on parole or probation?"

"No, and I never have been. Though it's because I been lucky so far not to be arrested for vagrancy or begging."

"Last question: Are you able to give us a dollar per day for your stay?"

Annie started to say no, then remembered the money Betsy had given her. "Yes, ma'm! In fact, I can give you five dollars!" Annie reached for her purse, smiling proudly.

"Well, that's fine. Are you sure you can spare it?"

"Yes, all I need when I get to Saint Paul is bus fare to my cousin's house, and I got that, too." Annie handed over the money with a warm feeling in her heart. Bless Betsy!

There were other forms, but they were much easier than that big first one. Shelly made her sign a release for medical treatment, if she needed it, and to say she'd been given a copy of the rules of the place, and that she wouldn't sue if she got hurt or sick while she was here, and that she understood they'd call the cops on her if she got out of line — all standard stuff.

She was taken to a small but very clean

room that had both a bed and a mattress on the floor. The mattress was to be hers; it seemed she had a roommate with a prior claim to the bed, though she wasn't currently present.

She was given sheets, a pillowcase, and a nice, thick blanket, and shown the tiny closet and bottom two drawers of the little dresser, which were more than adequate for the few articles of clothing she'd brought with her. She hung her coat in the closet, put her suitcase on the bed, and continued the tour.

The place was bigger, a lot bigger, than she'd thought. There was a room where a few clients were "shopping" for nice clothing, even shoes and purses. A special smaller room had even nicer clothing, and perfume, jewelry, and makeup for clients going to work or out on job interviews. There was a little hair salon and a medical clinic — very few of the residents had any kind of insurance. There was a half-size gym equipped with everything from Wii — two women and a toddler were exercising in front of a flat-screen TV, and Shelly explained a little bit how it worked — to hula hoops. There was a big kitchen with several refrigerators, where meals were served and clients took turns cleaning up and cooking. There were classrooms — one with up-to-date computers.

There was even a coffee lounge for adults needing a space where no children were around. Annie made a special mental note of its location.

There was a free Laundromat.

There was a locked back door for clients to use if they needed to slip in or out, away from prying or lurking eyes. Seeing that, Annie thanked her lucky stars that her ex-husband was a bum, not a violent stalker.

There were all kinds of counseling and classes, from effective parenting to getting a GED to developing good work habits. Residents were each assigned a case manager and were expected to take advantage of these offerings.

For residents with jobs, there was no-cost child care. There were a lot of kids staying here, but most of them were in school at present.

And for clients who failed an alcohol test, there was a banishment of twenty hours — and even then there was a shelter in town with, okay, more humble, mat-on-the-floor spaces — but still, spaces for people drunk or drugged.

Fargo was all right.

There was sleeping space for sixty-five —

in a pinch, sixty-six — residents.

Back in her room, Annie combed her hair and took off her boots; the place was warm enough for stocking feet. She went to the coffee lounge. Three women playing 500 rummy welcomed her as a fourth. She sat down, waited till it was her turn to deal, and said, "Is everyone here from Fargo? I'm from Saint Paul, just passing through."

Two of the other women were locals, and the third was from Moorhead, right across the Red River into Minnesota.

"I know someone from Fargo. Maybe one of you does, too," continued Annie, shuffling the cards expertly. "Her name is Janet Turnquist. I met her in Saint Paul, but she's from here."

One of the Fargo women, a very slender blonde with a sad face further marred by a black eye and a big bruise on her jaw, said, "I don't know anyone with that name." She was wearing the kind of clothes generally worn by people who worked in hospitals or doctors' offices.

But the other local, a larger woman in an orange sweater, with badly dyed red hair growing out brown, said, "I remember her. She was here a couple weeks ago."

Annie said, "Do you know if she's still around? I'm hoping we can get a place together." She began dealing the cards.

"I don't know where she is now. She said she was going to the Twin Cities, she said . . . I don't remember who she said it was, but she heard from someone, I don't know how, someone like a cousin or an uncle or a brother-in-law, someone like that, a relative, who wanted her to come to the Twin Cities. I think to live with him. I think it was a man, but it might've been a woman."

"That's too bad, I really would like to connect with someone interested in being a roommate."

"You probably wouldn't have liked it with her," said the pseudo-redhead. "She was very strange."

"I can put up with strange — I'm a little strange myself." Annie smiled to show she was exaggerating.

"I might be interested," said the third woman, who was dressed in purple jeans and a lavender shirt.

"Are you willing to relocate?" asked Annie.

"No, I can't. I'm not even supposed to be over here in Fargo."

Adding another lie to her story, Annie said, "I got a cousin who wants me to come to the Cities. She don't have room for me

215

to live with her — she's got kids and a husband. But she says she's got a job lined up for me. It ain't much of a job, but it's the real deal, with a paycheck and FICA and ever'thing. She even bought me a train ticket; it'll be waiting for me at the train station Friday night. But I'll have to work out of a shelter there, and that's a big hassle."

"Tell me about it," said the bruised woman in hospital scrubs — Annie remembered now what they were called. "Especially working nights."

"Yeah, you really got it tough," said Annie. "So if I can get one, I need a roommate, an' last time I talked with Janet, she sounded interested. I mean, here's my chance, thanks to my cousin. Ain't it great to have relatives?"

"Not if they're husbands," said the woman with the black eye sadly.

"Yeah, ain't *that* the truth?" agreed Annie sincerely. "But if I could link up with Janet, we could maybe afford to get a little place together, and I could start digging my way out of the hole I'm in." She looked at her cards and smiled, because she had two pairs and three hearts in sequence.

But she made sure not to win.

With that very promising start to her

inquiries, Annie sat with another set of women in the kitchen at lunchtime and yet another in the TV room afterward. But no one else she talked to had ever met or even heard of Janet Turnquist.

At supper, a very tall woman with broad Indian features and sloping shoulders came up to where Annie sat and said in a thin, light voice, "You the one looking for Janet Turnquist?"

"Yes," said Annie eagerly. "Do you know her?"

"I know something about her you won't like to hear."

"What's that?"

"She's dead."

Annie's heart sank, and she let it show on her face. "Are . . . are you sure?"

The woman nodded emphatically. "Yes. She died over there in Minnesota. It was weeks ago. Froze to death right on the street in some little town."

The other women still sitting at the table offered expressions of shock, dismay, and sorrow. "That's so awful!" said one. "I'm sorry for you, Annie, losing a friend like that."

"Gosh, I can't believe it!" said Annie. "I thought . . . well, it don't matter what I thought, I guess. But this is real bad news, and I'm sorry to hear it." Mostly because it meant Annie couldn't ask any more questions about Janet without rousing suspicions about why she wanted to know.

She finished her meal in a depressed silence.

Later, she took her metformin pill, put drops in her eyes, and went to the TV room to watch a G-rated movie with some women who said "Awwwwww" every time a puppy or kitten turned up, and who wept real tears when the family had to move out of its home. Annie herself got moist around the edges at that part. Losing one's home was not an imaginary problem for these people.

After the happy ending, Annie went to her room, where she found her roommate already in her nightgown, sitting on her bed, painting her toenails purple. Wads of Kleenex were stuck between her toes to separate them.

"Hello," said the woman shyly. She was thin and blond, and looked awfully young, like maybe sixteen, and she had a pimpled complexion.

"Hi, I'm Annie."

"I'm Alex."

"Sorry to be taking up a hunk of your floor, Alex."

"That's all right. It happens around here.

They don't like to turn people away."

"This is a real nice place. I won't be here long, just a couple of days."

"Yeah, Shelly told me that. Is it true a friend of yours named Janet froze to death just recently?"

Annie sighed at the efficiency of the grapevine. "Yeah. I mean, she wasn't a real close friend, but I was hoping we could be roommates. One reason I stopped in Fargo was to see if I could find her."

"I knew her. For what it's worth, it probably wouldn't have worked out for you with her."

"No? Why not?"

" 'Cause she was crazy."

"No, she was a little offbeat —"

"No, I mean she was insane. She heard voices."

"Not all the time."

"Yes, all the time. Just sometimes she could ignore them."

"Wow. Are you telling me she was dangerous?"

"No, she wasn't dangerous. Poor thing, she was scared — scared of *herself,* isn't that horrible? She hated being crazy, hated hearing voices, hated that people were scared of her. She woke me up one night crying and yelling, 'Shut up, shut up! Stop it, stop it!' So I sat with her for two hours and we talked. She was real intelligent about some things, but just insane about others, like her husband gave her pills that made her crazy. All mixed together."

"She was your roommate, then?"

"Yeah, just like you, sleeping on the floor."

"She didn't talk real crazy when I was with her."

"She could hide it when she had to, like when she needed to check in here. I just caught her on a bad night, I guess. She left the next day, said she had a bus ticket to Minneapolis."

"You mean Saint Paul."

"Does it make a difference?" asked Alex.

"I don't know. But suppose it does."

"Well, I remember for sure she said Minneapolis."

Annie wondered if that was just Janet being crazy, or if she really wanted to go to Minneapolis, and if that meant anything.

FIFTEEN

As at Naomi, the Fargo YWCA had very strict rules about disclosing who was or was not staying at their shelter. The same applied to former residents. During Betsy's interview with Fran Coleman, she learned some facts about the shelter, including that YWCAs were independent organizations, each of which could determine its own mission, whether it was advancing the health of the female community, helping women by educating them in classes, or offering shelter to those who were abused or homeless. After they'd spoken, Betsy wrote a check as a donation to the shelter and departed.

She went back to the room at the Radisson. There, she got out the local phone book and looked up the names *Bronson* and *Turnquist.* She found a Mark and Lindsey Turnquist — Janet's ex-husband and his second wife. Progress! She took a deep, encouraging breath and dialed the number. After four rings the answering machine picked up.

"You have reached the home of Mark and Lindsey Turnquist and Jack Walton," said a man's voice. "No one is available to take your call. Please leave a message."

At the beep, Betsy said, "This is Betsy Devonshire of Excelsior, Minnesota. I would like to talk with Mark Turnquist. I am staying at the Fargo Radisson." She gave her cell phone number, repeated it, and hung up.

Durn.

So what else could she do while she waited to hear from Annie? She wasn't going to see Roz at Nordic Needle until tomorrow.

Maybe she should try to find the condemned house Mark had given to Janet. She liked seeing locations — it helped to clarify her thinking — though the house was not the scene of any crime that she knew of.

She checked her notebook — it was a tall, narrow reporter's tablet — for the address, and reached for her coat. Just then her cell phone rang.

Was Annie calling with a report already?

No, the number was Crewel World's. She punched the "Talk" button, and said, "This is Betsy."

"It's Godwin. We have a little — well, not-so-little *problem* here!"

Oh, Lord. "What is it, Goddy?"

"ISBN's front window is broken, really *smashed!*" ISBN's was a used-book store next door to Crewel World in Betsy's building.

"Oh, no! How did that happen?"

"A city snowplow was coming down Lake Street, and just as it was passing our building, a big chunk of ice or frozen snow *flew* up and *smash!* Right through Paulie's window! Scared her half to death, of course." Paulie Johnson was ISBN's third proprietor since Betsy had bought the building. All of them liked the original name ISBN's and had kept it on taking over.

"You're sure it was a snowplow?"

"Are they dark blue with a big silver blade and a door that says CITY OF EXCELSIOR on it? Anyway, the driver pulled over and went in to see if anyone was hurt. I think he was driving too fast."

"Did he damage anything else?"

"Nothing in the store, or on the street. Remember, they issued an order that no one was to park on our side of the street today so they could plow right up to the curb. We're under a winter storm warning for tonight and tomorrow, and they want to clear some of the old snow out to make room for the new."

"You need to get that opening boarded up right away," said Betsy.

"I *know* that! That's part two of the problem! When I called Wally Middleton, he said the order had to come from *you!* When I told him you were in Fargo, he said, 'Haven't the telephone wires reached as far as Fargo yet?' " Godwin did a good imitation of Wally's nasal drawl.

"Very funny. Give me his number."

Wally was a glazier who also turned out at any time to board up broken windows. As landlady, Betsy was responsible for the building. She needed to get the window repaired not only because it was a dangerous eyesore, but because heat was gushing out the opening. It wasn't as if the cost of fuel for heating wasn't high enough . . .

She dialed the number Godwin gave her. It was answered on the second ring.

"Wally's Windows."

"Wally, this is Betsy Devonshire —"

"About time you called."

"What do you mean? I only this minute heard about your refusal to go board up ISBN's window for me."

"Who's refusing? Okay with you if I go right over?"

"Please do."

"I'll leave my bill in your store."

"Thank you. Also please leave an estimate to replace the glass."

"I hope the City of Excelsior doesn't raise a fuss about reimbursing you for all this."

Betsy sighed. "Oh, they probably will."

Well, at least that was settled. After she and Wally hung up, Betsy called Paulie Johnson at ISBN's.

"No, we're all fine," Paulie said to her. "I took a picture with my phone of the chunk of ice that came through the window. And I got the name and address of the driver of the truck, and the truck's license plate, too."

"Well done, Paulie. I've called Wally's Windows and he should be there very soon to put a piece of plywood over the hole in your window. I also asked him to leave an estimate for a replacement. Was your sign damaged?"

"No, just the posters on the window. Thanks for being so prompt about this — it's getting really cold in here."

"If he's not there within the next half hour, tell Godwin, and he'll raise hob with Wally."

"Will do. Thanks, Betsy."

After they hung up, Betsy put her coat and boots on, made sure her notebook was in her purse, and left the hotel.

Blessing the inventor of in-car GPS, she followed its directions to an address on Southwood, near the river. The attractive forest green ranch-style house was set diagonally on a corner lot, with a white brick fireplace chimney in front. But Betsy had been told that the house Mark gave to Janet was condemned and abandoned. This house looked fine — and there was a cranberry-colored late-model car parked on the plowed driveway. Had her GPS failed her and taken her to the wrong address?

She parked on the street and went up to the front door. The white-painted metal numbers going vertically down the frame of the door were correct. She opened the screen door to knock on the wooden one. She had to knock twice before it opened. A man, improbably wearing his winter coat, looked out at her.

"Yes?" he said, sounding like a busy man needlessly interrupted.

"Who're you?" blurted Betsy.

"No, lady, who are *you?*"

"Yes, of course, you have the right to ask that. I'm Betsy Devonshire, and I'm looking for the house that Janet Turnquist used to live in."

"She's not here anymore."

"I know. She's deceased."

226

"So why do you want to see her house?" His voice suddenly warmed. "Are you interested in buying it?"

"No. But now that I've answered your questions, will you answer mine?"

"I'm Mark Turnquist, her husband. Ex-husband."

Now Betsy's voice warmed. "Are you really? Well, I'm very pleased to meet you!" Betsy held out her hand.

Mark looked down at it but didn't take it. "Why are you pleased to meet me?" he asked.

"I've been trying to think how I might get in touch with you. I'm looking into Janet's death."

"Are you a cop?" His voice was definitely not pleased now.

"No, I'm a private citizen. I'm trying to help two friends who are related to two dead women, one of them Janet Turnquist. Both of them have asked me to look into this. The police are thinking that perhaps one or the other of the relatives murdered Janet, as well as Carrie Carlson." Seeing an incredulous expression forming, she said, "I *have* done this sort of thing before."

"Did you ever do this sort of thing *successfully?*"

"Yes, often. Enough times that our local

227

police investigator, Sergeant Mike Malloy, takes me very seriously."

"Maybe he should; he could hardly do worse than depend on his own talents."

Betsy smiled; she couldn't help it. "You've talked with him? Be aware, he's a lot brighter than he acts."

There was a pause while Mark studied her face. Betsy held her tongue while he thought things over.

"All right, what do you want to know?"

"May I come in? It's awfully cold out here."

"It's awfully cold in here, too. There's no heat."

So that explained why he was wearing his coat indoors. As Mark stepped back, Betsy came into a living room that looked okay at first glance. There was gray carpet on the floor, green couches and chairs, a coffee table, end tables, a flat-screen TV against one wall. Then Betsy noticed that what she thought were two shades of blue paint dividing the walls horizontally was actually a high-water mark with a dark line of grime dividing the two colors like a chair rail. And then she realized the upholstered furniture wasn't a deliberately muddy shade of green, but marred by having been soaked in dirty water.

"Gosh, when did this happen?" she asked.

"It'll be two years ago this spring," he said. "I gave the house to Janet as part of the divorce — it was all paid for — but she rarely lived in it, and didn't even try to restore it after the Red River flood. The city condemned it, but she ignored the notices." He held out a fistful of red and yellow documents. "Even when they nailed them to the door."

"So what are you going to do about the house?"

"Nothing. The house was hers, and now it will go to some woman in Excelsior."

"You mean that holographic will she embroidered is good?"

He nodded grimly. "Apparently so."

"So they have decided she died after her Uncle Jasper."

He looked at her with respect. "You've been doing your homework, I see. No, they're still waiting for an official decision."

"If it goes the other way, then what?"

"The house will still go to her niece in Minnesota — which is as it should be, she's been paying the taxes on it for years. I called her and told her I'd take a look at the house, to see if I thought it might be worth something."

"Is it?" Betsy looked around. There was

no moldy smell, but that was probably because everything was frozen.

"No, the foundation is unstable, the plumbing is shot, the wiring is dangerous, the downstairs furnishings are destroyed. The land is all right, it's a nice corner lot in a decent neighborhood, but the house will have to come down."

"What will you recommend?"

"That she sells it 'as is,' takes the money, and walks away."

"Are you thinking of buying it?"

"Hell, no, I don't need the hassle of tearing down and then building a new house. Anyway, I've moved into my wife Lindsey's house. I just don't like loose ends, so I'm doing her this favor." He looked around. "Too bad, this might have been salvaged if it had been taken care of right away."

"It is too bad, I agree. This is a very attractive house." Betsy turned completely around, taking in details. When she faced Mark again, she said, "May I ask you a hard question?"

"I didn't murder Janet."

"I wasn't going to ask you that — at least not right away. I was going to ask you who you think might have wanted her dead?" Betsy was reaching into her shoulder bag for her notebook and pen.

"You know, I've been thinking about that. Sergeant Malloy thinks he has a motive for me, but I think I know someone with a better one."

"Who is that?"

"His name is Alec Porter, and he's a veterinarian at the Small Animal Medical Center in Saint Paul. He is also the one who gets the money left to Janet if it turns out that she predeceased Jasper."

Betsy thought that over while she took down Porter's name, and the name of his clinic in Saint Paul.

"What else do you know about him?"

"Nothing, except he seems to think very well of himself as a surgeon. He may be, who knows, but he's very unfriendly."

"Strange trait for someone dealing with the pet-owning public." She made another note, then asked, "How do you know him?"

"I don't. I met him one time, at a funeral, and he was damn rude. Someone told me he was like that most of the time."

"I see." Betsy thought for a few moments, then said, "You know, if I wanted to ensure an inheritance and it was based on who died first, I'd try not to blur the line."

"Dr. Porter didn't know Jasper was that close to dying."

"Are you sure? I mean, was there anything

suspicious about Jasper's death?"

"I assume there wasn't. Sergeant Malloy didn't ask me anything about it."

"He wouldn't, would he? Jasper died far outside Mike's jurisdiction. But has anyone from around here come to talk to you about it?"

Mark shook his head. "No."

"Is there anyone you know of who could talk to me about Jasper Bronson?"

"He died right here in Fargo. Maybe someone at the nursing home knows the name of his doctor. Or you could talk to the cops about it."

"Were they called when he died?"

"I have no idea."

"Do you know which nursing home he was in?"

Mark screwed up his face and thought. "I used to, but it's gone into the memory hole now."

"Did you ever wish your wife was dead?"

He hesitated before replying, with an air of resignation, "Often. But I wouldn't kill her. And strangely enough, I was sad to hear she had died — and I was *shocked* to hear she froze to death on the street of a small town. That's a terrible way to go. What kind of a town are they running over there? Sergeant Malloy thinks she was murdered, but he has no proof. Surely it's bad enough she couldn't get back up when she fell, and worse that no one saw her fall."

"Yes, that is a scary idea, isn't it? To fall and lie helpless while the cold seeps into your bones . . ." Betsy shuddered.

"Anyway," she continued in a stronger voice, "thank you for talking with me. Would it be all right if I contacted you again? It would likely be long-distance, since I'm from Excelsior."

His eyes widened. "Oh, from the town where it happened — of course, you would be, I suppose. All right, sure." He went into a trouser pocket and pulled out a small leather case from which he took a business card.

"Thanks," said Betsy, and she gave him one of her own, "in case you think of something that might help."

Betsy went back to the Radisson. Annie hadn't called yet, and she was starting to get a little worried. She had a late lunch in the hotel restaurant, then went up to her room. As she often did when stressed, she got out her knitting. She turned a comfortable chair so it was under the light coming through the window, and set to work on the pink mitten.

After a while she became aware that the

light was fading from the winter sky. She still hadn't heard from Annie. She pulled her cell phone out of her purse to make sure it was turned on. It was.

She was about to put it back, when it began to play "With a Little Help From My Friends." She didn't recognize the number but quickly pressed "Talk" and put it up to her ear.

"Hello?"

"Hi, this is Annie."

"Hello, Annie, where are you?"

"At the Y, only out in the backyard. I borrowed a cell phone from my new friend Alex — Alexandra, I guess her real name is, but she wants to be called Alex. But talk fast, it's cold out here."

"Fine. What have you learned?"

"That's the sad part: nuthin' much. What happened was, someone told me in front of everyone that poor Janet was dead, so that put a chill on me asking about her. I mean, I was already supposed to be her friend, so how could I ask people what she was like? All I could do was act sad she was dead. But some people who knew her came up to me and said a few little things about her. I'll tell you about them when we get back together."

"Do you want me to come and get you?"

"No, I better stay till tomorrow. Maybe someone will tell me something else. It's okay here, really. I got a place to sleep and the food isn't bad. Oh, and someone from the Y is gonna give me a ride to the train depot after supper tomorrow, so I'll meet you there. That should be around six, maybe a little before or a little after. Okay?"

"Yes, that's fine. I'll come by there around six thirty."

"Gotcha. Bye."

Betsy was finishing her supper in the hotel restaurant when her cell phone began its merry little summons. She hastily swallowed the last bite of chocolate pie, dug in her purse for the phone, saw it was an unfamiliar number, and murmured, "Hello?"

"Betsy?"

"Oh, hello, Connor! Good to hear from you!"

"How's it going?"

"Slow, I'm afraid. I'm in Fargo until tomorrow night when we take the train back to the Cities. It's snowy and cold here. How are things in New York?"

"We're doing fine here. Going out to a Broadway play in a couple of minutes. It's an exciting city, and we're having an exciting time." The phone was taken away from his ear. "Yes, yes, I'm coming right now," she heard him say.

"I won't keep you then," she said.

"I'll be home soon. Good-bye, sweet-heart."

"Good-bye. I love you."

But she was speaking into a dead phone.

SIXTEEN

The next day, after breakfast, Betsy sat down with the phone book in her room and began to call nursing homes. She had decided that the best way to try to solve this case was not to figure the two deaths were both deliberate, but to consider one first with the other as collateral, then the other. Since she was in Fargo, today she'd try thinking the murderer was after Janet.

By putting on a hurried and slightly officious voice, she got the information she wanted with hardly any lying. It was at the third nursing home that the administrator conceded that Jasper Bronson had been a patient, and said that his doctor's name was Christopher Marland.

Dr. Marland's receptionist said he was with a patient. Betsy, at her most officious, said it was important and she'd wait. But after five minutes she started to become concerned about the state of her cell phone battery. Finally —

"Yes?" said a voice every bit as officious as her own.

"Hello, Dr. Marland," said Betsy. "My name is Betsy Devonshire and I've been hired to look into the death of Janet Turnquist. She was a niece of Jasper Bronson, who is also deceased."

"And?"

"I understand that you were Mr. Bronson's physician. I'm sorry to interrupt your busy day, sir, but I need to know if there was anything suspicious about Mr. Bronson's death."

"For God's *sake* —" began the doctor, but he cut himself off as abruptly as an ax chops a piece of wood. "Who are you in this matter?"

"A private investigator." That was sort of true. "I came here to Fargo from Excelsior, Minnesota, where Janet died."

"Jasper Bronson was in the last stages of Alzheimer's. There was nothing more likely than his death. Why would you think otherwise?"

"I didn't say I thought anything about it. But do the police, for example, also think otherwise?"

"That is an outrageous question."

"I guess it is. I take it they have not

involved themselves in investigating this death?"

"Of course not! There was nothing to indicate there was anything suspicious or improper about Jasper Bronson's decease, nothing whatsoever."

"I am very glad to hear that."

"Good-bye!" The doctor hung up.

Betsy sat back in the comfortable chair in her room. *Might have died at any time:* Did Alec Porter know that? If so, that might have made him very anxious to see Janet dead before that happened.

She got out the phone book again and looked up the number for Regina Kingsolver, attorney-at-law.

"Radner and Kingsolver, how may I direct your call?"

"Is Ms. Kingsolver available for a short interview?"

"I can check. Who's calling, please?"

"Betsy Devonshire, of Excelsior, Minnesota."

"May I ask what this is in regard to?"

"I am conducting a private investigation into the death of Janet Turnquist, who was Jasper Bronson's niece."

It took half a minute of waiting before Betsy heard another woman's voice say, "This is Regina Kingsolver. How may I help you?" Her voice was quiet and reassuring.

"Good morning, Ms. Kingsolver. I understand you were Jasper Bronson's attorney."

"Yes, that's correct."

"Were you the one who advised Dr. Alec Porter of the terms of Mr. Bronson's will?"

"I talked to him about it, but as he had Mr. Bronson's power of attorney, he already knew the terms."

"Are you sure about that?"

"Yes, quite. Have you talked with Detective Sergeant Michael Malloy on this case?"

"Yes, ma'm. Thank you very much for that information, you've been very useful. Have a nice day." Betsy disconnected before Ms. Kingsolver could ask any more questions.

Power of attorney, wow. So Dr. Porter had access to all of Jasper's papers. That was a damning piece of information. Betsy was relatively sure Dr. Porter had not told this to Mike.

She sat back in her chair to think.

On the other hand: Marty Smith was very protective of his wife. And his own reputation. If it became generally known that Marty was sued by some of his customers for selling them outdated medications — even though it turned out not to be his fault — it might have destroyed his company. Or if someone spread the word that Margaret, in her usual officious way, had made her father suffer months longer than he wished to, and didn't offer her mother the therapy that might have prolonged her life — her reputation, of which she was both proud and protective, would have been destroyed. Did Carrie know any of this? Was that why they gave her money whenever she came asking for it? If Carrie was becoming less and less stable as her alcoholism advanced, might not Marty have taken action to protect himself and his wife?

After a light lunch, Betsy got in her rental car and used her GPS again, this time to get to Gateway Avenue South, where a newer and larger-than-expected brick building sat near the back of a parking lot. The lot was freshly plowed, with great piles of snow along its border and heaped up around the big stand-alone sign reading NORDIC NEEDLE at the entry to the lot. Betsy pulled in between an SUV and a little Saturn so coated with dried salt its color could not be determined.

The center entryway led past the checkout counter, with its shelves of small kits, cards, and souvenirs, to slanted counters filled with books of patterns. The shop was large, well lit, and open, and the walls were covered with framed models of different kinds of needlework.

Betsy had barely begun to look around when an employee, a nice-looking young woman with blond hair just reaching her shoulders, came over to her. "May I help you?" she asked.

"Yes, I'm Betsy Devonshire and I'm here to talk to Roz." Roz was the owner of Nordic Needle.

"Oh, hello, Ms. Devonshire! I'm Zoe. Roz told us you were stopping in. Just a minute, I'll go get her." She hurried away.

Betsy wandered around the rest of the store. It was neat, clean, and extremely well organized, nothing out of place or awkwardly situated.

She paused by the instruction manuals and pattern books on Hardanger, wondering if perhaps she should give the craft another chance — she had taken a class on Hardanger a few years ago and had been surprised to find herself a dismal failure at it. It wasn't that complex, really, but every stitch had to be placed exactly right, and Betsy was more creative than accurate.

She shouldn't have been surprised; there were other needle arts she seemed to have no talent for, either. It used to bother her, before she discovered there were very few needle artists who could do *everything*.

Still . . . She picked up one of the books and was pleased to see it had been written by Roz and Sue, founders of Nordic Needle. *Beginner's Charted Hardanger Embroidery* was the title, and on the cover was a simple (ha!) chart of the little squares and weavings that formed the base of Hardanger patterns.

She knew Roz and Sue's story, how they both fell in love with the Norwegian needle art back when supplies and patterns were hard to find. They started out ordering them just for themselves and a few friends — and before long ended up with a small shop in downtown Fargo. They expanded into other kinds of needlework, and moved to a bigger shop. Then they got into catalog sales and then into wholesale, and now their company was housed in a building they had designed themselves.

Sue had retired recently, but Roz was as busy as ever with the business.

"Hello, Betsy!" came a cheerful voice, and Betsy, startled, turned to see Roz smiling at her. She was an attractive middle-aged woman, a little above medium height, with short, dark hair and brown eyes.

"Oh, hello, Roz! Thanks for taking time to talk with me."

"No problem for someone who is a good, steady customer. But I suspect you didn't come to Fargo just to pass the time of day with me. May I ask what did bring you out here?"

Betsy hesitated. But she would leave no stone — however unlikely — unturned. "All right. A customer of mine is a suspect in the suspicious death of her cousin, a homeless woman named Carrie Carlson. Carrie was found frozen to death in Excelsior earlier this month. And now another homeless woman has been found frozen to death in Excelsior."

Shocked, Roz said, "What in the world is going on in your town?"

"That's what we would like to know. The Excelsior police investigator on the case is Sergeant Mike Malloy. He thinks the two deaths are related, and therefore it's a case of murder, but while he discounts the notion of two murderers, so far he can't find any reason why any one person would want to murder both of them.

"And there's this weird link to my shop: Both dead women have relatives who are customers of mine. And Mike is looking sideways at both of them as suspects. But neither of the dead women has ever been in my shop — or at least none of us remembers

244

seeing them."

"What motive could either of your customers have for murder?"

"Well, one customer is Margaret Smith. She's Carrie Carlson's cousin — Carrie is one of the victims. Margaret had been harassed by Carrie, who actually broke a window in Margaret's house when Margaret wouldn't give her some money. And the other victim is Janet Turnquist. She is my customer Emily Hame's aunt. Emily is the beneficiary of a will Janet wrote, leaving her a small fortune."

"Wait a minute: a fortune? I thought you said both dead women were homeless."

"They are. But a great deal of money was left to Janet by her uncle on his death. He died very shortly before Janet."

"And you're in Fargo because . . ."

"Janet is from Fargo. Her uncle, Jasper Bronson, is, too, and he also died here. I'm here to see what I can find out about both or either of them."

"So the stories I've heard about you are true! You *are* a sleuth!"

"Only once in a while. I'm looking into this because I've been asked to by both Margaret and Emily."

"Is there anything I can do to help?"

"Did you know Jasper Bronson?"

"No," Roz said. "I've never even heard of him."

"Well, perhaps it's just as well," Betsy said. "I'm here in your shop to talk about my real job, selling needlework supplies. I have a friend working on the murder mystery at a place I have no access to. Meanwhile, I've always wanted to see your operation."

Roz proudly gave Betsy the "grand tour," which in addition to the display room included a big back room where orders were taken and billing and other accounts were kept. Betsy had brought along an order for stock for her own shop. She handed it over to another employee, Chris, and the tour went on. A shipping room was next, and it had a side door through which mail and delivery people could drop off and pick up shipments. The basement was very large, with shelf upon shelf of stock, each item with its own identifying number. The mail-order business had caught up with and surpassed the brick-and-mortar shop's business some time ago.

"Very efficient," said Betsy, with real envy in her voice — she had thought of and discarded an idea for going into catalog sales. "You seem to have just about everything figured out."

"We do our best," said Roz with a smile.

"There's even a nice restaurant right across the street."

Betsy showed Roz the manual on Hardanger she had chosen. "Ring this one up for me. I thought maybe I'd give it another try. I'll need a square of fabric, thread, and a needle, too — I can start working on it on the train ride home."

Roz gathered the materials, and put them on the manual at the computerized cash register. Then she seemed to think of something, and frowned. "What did you say the dead woman's name was? The one from Fargo?"

"Janet Turnquist. You couldn't possibly know her, could you?"

"Was she, um, sort of crazy?"

"She had a mild form of schizophrenia. Why?"

"Because I think she came here to take a class on Hardanger."

Betsy went into her purse for her personal credit card and also brought out the color print of Janet's mug shot. "Is this her?"

"What an awful picture!" Roz held it out at arm's length, tilting her head a little from side to side. "But yes, that's her. So we *are* talking about the same person. But now she's dead? That's very sad, I'm sorry to hear that."

"How did she manage to afford the class?" Betsy asked. "She was very poor, living in shelters."

"Yes, I thought that was the case. It was very clear that she *couldn't* afford the class, so I let her come for free — which, mind you, I almost never do. She had come in before, several times, very shy and rather strange. She couldn't afford to buy much, usually just floss and then only when it was on sale. Once or twice I gave her some odd fabric ends. My employees kept an eye on her, afraid she was a thief, but if she was, they never caught her at it. She'd gotten hold of an old book on Hardanger and was trying to teach herself how to do it. She was asking questions about it, and finally I said I was teaching a class and she could sit in if she wanted to. She'd come in as early as an hour before the class started to be sure to be on time — I don't think she had a watch — and I think sometimes she walked a considerable distance to get here."

"Was she a good student?"

"Well, if you had asked me that early in the class sessions, I would have said she was more interested than talented, very determined but pretty impatient with herself. I finally realized she couldn't see very well and loaned her a pair of magnifying glasses.

And all of sudden she could do much better. The next time she came in, she had the money to buy them. But the class ended before she finished her bookmark, and I never saw her again."

"How long ago was this?"

"The class started the second Friday in August, and went for four weeks. She seemed to really enjoy the stitching."

Betsy thought. "You know, I got an inventory of everything that was in her possession when she died, and there wasn't a Hardanger bookmark listed. Maybe she lost it, or gave it away. And her magnifying glasses were missing a lens."

"Oh, how sad," said Roz. "I'm sure she made some serious compromises to buy them, so that must have hurt. It would be like you or me losing half our inventory."

"Ouch, there's a horrible thought!" said Betsy with a wince. "But I think you're right. She used to visit her niece in Excelsior a couple of times a year, and on the winter visit, Emily would buy her a new coat or a pair of boots. Maybe she came to Excelsior this year hoping Emily would also buy her a new pair of magnifiers."

Roz fell silent. "I don't know why that makes me even angrier on her behalf, but it does. You said Sergeant — what's his name?

Malloy? — thinks it's murder. Do you?"

"Well, it's a huge coincidence that two homeless women died a few blocks from each other in the same small town. Neither of them lived there, but they both came to see relatives who did."

"Did they die on the same day?"

"They were found a few days apart, but it's possible they died at the same time, or close to it. Janet's body was on somebody's front lawn, but the home owners were out of town and the body was covered up by snow."

"So it happened after the home owners went out of town, right?"

"It must have."

"Did they leave before the other woman's body was found, or after?"

Betsy looked sideways at Roz. "You ask very good questions. Maybe you should try out for detective work, too."

"Yes, in my copious free time."

Betsy laughed. "I'm lucky to have a store manager who is willing to cover for me."

Roz repeated her question. "So, did they go out of town after the first woman's body was found?"

"No, they'd been gone almost a week when Carrie's body was discovered. So it's possible that even though Janet's body was found later, she might actually have died before Carrie. Knowing which of the two women died first would really be helpful."

"Why is there a question about whether or not it's murder?"

"Because they weren't shot or stabbed, and there was no trace of poison in their systems."

"So what do you think happened?"

"I don't know. I think they traveled together out to Excelsior — a Minneapolis city bus only comes that far out of town a few times a day, so that's not unlikely — and that one of them was targeted and the other killed because she knew something or saw someone she could name."

"But how? If not shot, stabbed, or poisoned, how?"

"That's one of the really big questions I'm trying to answer."

"Well," Roz said after a moment, "good luck with it." She started to turn away, then saw something on the checkout counter and picked it up. "Here's the bookmark we made in class."

Betsy stared at it, then reached slowly for it. It was the same pattern as the Hardanger bookmark Mike Malloy had found among Carrie's possessions.

■ ■ ■ ■

Around five thirty, Betsy went to the restaurant on the second floor of the Radisson and had supper — just a salad; she wasn't very hungry. Then she went down to get her suitcase out of their storeroom. She had checked out that morning, but the hotel agreed to store it for her while she went about her business in town.

By ten after six she climbed into her rental and drove through a light snow to the train depot.

There were no cars in the lot, and the building was dark. Betsy parked and went to the door. It was locked. And Annie was nowhere to be seen.

Her concern increasing by the second, she hurriedly walked around the building, seeking but not finding a light on inside, or an unlocked door.

Of course, she thought; there are only two trains a day through here, both late at night, so why should they keep the station open all day?

But where was Annie?

"Maybe she's not here yet," Betsy muttered to herself. She waited in her car until nearly seven.

But no one drove up to let Annie off.
And Betsy had no idea where she might
be.

SEVENTEEN

Betsy put her car in gear. But where was she to go to look for her friend? She had given Annie four five-dollar bills this morning. Twenty dollars wouldn't take her far — if she hadn't already spent it.

If Annie had been here and found the depot locked, why didn't she call Betsy?

Ah. Because she didn't have a cell phone. And because she was on foot at night in the cold and snowy weather, and in an unfamiliar neighborhood, she didn't know where to go to find a pay phone.

Wait a minute.

Betsy drove out of the lot and two blocks up the street to the Radisson. She parked and ran into the hotel. There were eight or ten people in the beautiful marble lobby, but none was Annie.

She hurried over to the check-in counter, where she had to wait while a couple ahead of her finished. At the counter, she didn't recognize the clerk.

"I stayed here the last two nights," she said rapidly. "The night before last, I had someone with me, a woman about my age, with graying dark hair and brown eyes, poorly dressed. I think she may have come back here within the last half hour, but I can't find her. Have you seen her?"

The clerk stared at Betsy as if she were speaking in a language he couldn't identify.

"I beg your pardon?"

Betsy took a breath, and spoke more slowly. "I am wondering if a woman who I was supposed to meet at the train station came here instead. She was a guest here the night before last. Her name is Annie Summerhill. She has dark, graying hair, and is probably wearing a dark brown coat, a green knit hat, and black mittens."

"Has she got a reservation for here tonight?"

"No, she has a train ticket — but the train doesn't leave until two in the morning, and meanwhile the train depot is closed. Someone was supposed to drop her off there around six, so she's on foot, and this hotel is close to the depot, so she may have come here."

"Oh, I see. What does she look like again?"

Betsy gritted her teeth. "She's about my

age and size," she said slowly, "but she wears mismatched clothes, brown coat, green knit hat, black mittens — she looks like she's homeless. I'm hoping none of your staff made her leave."

The clerk looked shocked. "I'm sure that wouldn't happen, unless she was bothering people."

Betsy bit down hard on her first retort, and said firmly but politely, "She wouldn't do that."

"Well, I'm sorry, but I haven't seen a person such as you describe. Still, as you can see, I've been busy."

Betsy turned a little bit to see that two guests had lined up behind her to check in. "Yes, I do see that. Thank you anyway."

"You're welcome."

Both frantic and despairing, Betsy forced herself to walk slowly around the big lobby, looking at every face present, making sure she hadn't missed Annie playing her invisibility game. She would have looked in the restroom, but there wasn't a restroom on the ground floor.

And Annie wasn't anywhere in sight.

She checked her watch: quarter past seven.

She went back to her car. The snow was thickening, coming down in huge, feathery flakes. She thought a little while, then said a prayer that was part penitential — for being careless about the arrangements for meeting Annie — and part petitionary — asking God's angels to watch over Annie and guide Betsy to her. Then she started the engine, put her car in gear, and pulled away to begin a widening circle of the neighborhood.

Half an hour later, she pulled over to sit behind the wheel, with the engine still running. The wind had come up, and the snowflakes were smaller now, but falling faster and harder. The only other open store in the area was a drugstore, and Annie wasn't in there, either. It was now nearly eight o'clock. Where could she be?

In Betsy's imagination, Annie was wandering the bitter cold streets, unable to find anywhere to get warm. What if she, in desperation, had tucked herself into a doorway imperceptible from the street?

This was all Betsy's fault. She should have planned this more carefully, she should have arranged to pick Annie up at the shelter.

What if Annie had said something at the Y shelter that brought a murderer after her? There was a sickening thought! Betsy shouldn't have gotten Annie into this in the first place, no matter how fervently she had volunteered.

Betsy thumped her hand on the steering

wheel, her mouth set in a thin line. Should she check back at the YWCA? The shelter was miles from here, she would need the GPS to find it — so how could Annie have found her way back there on foot? She had no idea what to do now.

It occurred to Annie that hiding in the restroom meant she wouldn't see Betsy, and Betsy wouldn't be able to find her if she came looking for her here at the Radisson. Which of course she would, once she saw the train depot was closed.

So she came out and looked around for stairs or the elevator — the restroom was on the second floor, around enough corners that she had to think for a few moments which way was out.

She went back downstairs and over to one of the tall windows to peer out into the darkness for the beautiful car Betsy had rented. The snow was coming down so thickly it was hard to see all the way to the curb. And the wind was making it swirl and dance. When had that happened? Some while ago, seeing how deep it was on the sidewalk. What time was it anyway?

Because she was a little nearsighted, she had to go halfway across the lobby, and toward the front desk, to see the clock on the back wall. It was ten after seven. Whoa, that was later than she thought! She went back to the window. What if —

"Miss? Miss?" Annie looked around. The man behind the check-in counter was gesturing at her. Annie looked around, in case he meant someone else. But no, it was she he was summoning.

Oh, damn, thought Annie. *I'm about to get kicked out.*

Rather than hear a lecture, she began to walk to the door.

"No, no, don't leave! Come over here!"

What, were they going to have her arrested? Annie looked, but there wasn't a cop in sight.

"Please, miss, it's all right. Could you come here for a minute?"

Very warily, Annie walked over to the check-in counter.

But the man was smiling. "Are you Annie?" he asked.

"Maybe. Who wants to know?"

"There was a woman here a little while ago looking for a woman named Annie, and I think that might be you."

"Who was it?"

"I didn't get her name, but she was about your height, blond hair, wearing a long, dark blue coat and dark blue hat."

Betsy.

Annie's heart sank. "You mean she's already come and gone?"

"I'm afraid so. She walked all around the lobby but couldn't find you."

"That's 'cause I was upstairs in the ladies' room. Well, this is a fine how-dee-do."

"I don't suppose you have her cell phone number?"

Annie grinned at him. She'd forgotten all about the phone number. "You suppose wrong!" It took a search through several pockets to find Betsy's business card. "Here it is."

She handed the card to the man, who went to the phone on his side of the counter and punched in some numbers. Reading the name off the card, he said into the phone, "Ms. Devonshire? This is Wayne Murchison at the Radisson Hotel. The party you were looking for is here." He paused while Betsy said something. "Yes, I'll have her wait right here. You're welcome."

He hung up the phone and said, "She sounded happy to hear that. She'll be here in a few minutes."

"Thank you very much."

"You're very welcome."

Betsy was so relieved that she had to just sit

still while her heart slowed and she got her breathing under control. After a few minutes, the tears quit rolling down her cheeks.

Safe! Annie was safe; there wasn't going to be yet another frozen corpse.

She drove as fast as she dared to the Radisson. But the streets were snow-covered and slippery; this snowstorm was becoming serious.

Annie saw a car drive up, a dark shape behind the veils of falling snow. It was Betsy's car, all right; she watched as a Betsy-shaped figure climbed out and came tottering, arms out for balance, across the icy sidewalk toward the entrance to the hotel.

Annie turned to greet her, but Betsy surprised her by running up and throwing her arms around her. "Oh, I am *so glad* to find you! I was worried *sick* about you!"

"It's okay, I'm okay," said Annie, breaking free of the embrace, embarrassed at this public show of emotion. "It's my fault, I was hangin' out in the ladies' room the first time you came through here."

"You *were?*" said Betsy, drawing out the word, suddenly narrow-eyed and sharp-tongued. "Why did you do that?"

"Old habit," said Annie, a little ashamed. "Plus, you said you wouldn't get to the depot till half past six, an' I got there early, an' it was closed up tight, an' what was I gonna do if you got there later than you said you would? So I walked down here. Everyone else in here was dressed so nice, I got nervous. But I asked the woman mopping the floor where was the ladies' room and she told me upstairs. So I went. It's a nice ladies' room, I got kind of comfortable in there. I guess I lost track of time, huh. I'm sorry."

"No, no, of course it's not your fault! I arrived at the train station early, not late. When I saw it was closed, I wondered if you might have walked down here. I got here probably just a few minutes after you did. If it's anyone's fault, it's the desk clerk's, because he didn't remember seeing you."

"It's the desk clerk's fault?" queried Annie doubtfully.

"Okay, it's everyone's fault!"

"Oh, I getcha, if it's everybody's fault, it's nobody's fault." Annie did get it; Betsy had been scared half to death, and was having a relief conniption. She said, "Anyway, here I am, safe and sound, and here you are, you found me. I'm sorry you were scared. But somebody told me once, a good scare every now and then is healthy."

"Whoever said that is crazy!"

Annie smiled and said, "Come to think of it . . ."

Betsy laughed a little too loudly. Then she sobered.

"I want to talk to you about what you learned today, if anything."

"Well, I did hear a few things."

"But first, we have a problem. Where are we going to stay until the train depot opens?"

EIGHTEEN

The problem solved itself when Betsy gassed up and headed for the car rental headquarters out at the airport. By the time they got there, it was snowing even harder and the wind was blowing a gale.

"The airport! Of course!" said Betsy as they drove slowly up the slick road toward the terminal. "It's open all night, and there are cabs waiting right outside the door. We'll just sit out here."

"That's a good idea," said Annie. After a moment she said softly, "Someday maybe I'll get to ride in an airplane."

Betsy, still feeling pleased that Annie was safe, said impulsively, "You know, that's an idea. How about we see if there are seats on a flight to Minneapolis? I mean, if we can fly home now, we don't have to sit up until two in the morning waiting for the train."

"Wow," said Annie in an awed voice. "Wow, are you serious?"

"Certainly. Come on, let's turn this car in, and see about a pair of tickets."

"Wow."

But as they entered the new-looking terminal with its slanted, glass-fronted façade, a woman's hollow voice was echoing through the area. ". . . the ticket agent at your airline counter for reticketing information. Again, because of blizzard conditions, all flights are canceled until further notice. See the ticket agent at your airline counter for reticketing information."

The very large space was full of people burdened with luggage and heavy winter coats. A chorus of groans rose from them, and there was a collective movement as they all lumbered toward the ticket counters.

"What does that mean?" asked Annie anxiously. "Are they going to close? Do we have to leave?"

"No, they'll stay open until the weather clears. But it does mean we won't be flying anywhere for hours and hours, probably till morning. Let's look for a place to sit down, because soon there will be a rush for seating."

The ticketing area didn't have many places to sit. Betsy started up the shining floor, as Annie trailed behind, looking up and all around. "Hey!" she said. "Lookit that!"

"That" was a full-size biplane suspended from the ceiling.

"I wonder what it would be like to ride in one of those rickety old things," said Betsy. "It might be nice, flying low and slow, the wind in your hair . . ."

"You go ahead and find out, why doncha," said Annie. "An' tell me about it when you get back. Me, when I fly, I want it to be in a big plane made of . . . of *steel,* with a roof and four jet engines and two pilots, and stewardesses, and, and *seat belts.*"

"I think a plane made of aluminum would be better," noted Betsy.

"Whatever. Speaking of seats, look, over there, a place to sit down!"

It was a bench with a thick pad, hidden in the shadow cast by a tall electronic board that listed airplane arrivals and departures. As they hurried past the board, the schedule was changing to indicate the cancellations of both incoming and outgoing flights.

Annie reached the bench ahead of Betsy. She sat down on it, with her back very straight and an "I have every right to be here" smile on her face. She placed her suitcase at her feet. Betsy sat down beside her, and put hers under the bench.

"I guess we take the train after all," said Annie.

"It's just as well, probably. I was speaking off the top of my head. I don't like flying in bad weather. When that plane starts sliding and bouncing all over the sky, I get scared."

Annie nodded. "I seen that in movies lots of times. Is it really like that, flying in a storm, tipping and jumping? Did you ever get hurt in a plane?"

Betsy said, "Louis Armstrong said something one time that I've never forgotten. He said he wasn't afraid to fly because 'they might kill you, but they ain't likely to hurt you.'"

Betsy smiled, but Annie said, "Hey, that's not funny!"

"Sure it is, because it's mostly true. Listen, you stay here and hold our place, I'm going to go find us something to eat and drink."

"Are you hungry?" Annie sounded surprised.

"No, but I may be before we get home. Remember, the club car was closed on the train, so no snacks were available."

"Betsy, what if when it's time to head for the train station, the roads are closed, too? What if the *railroad* is closed?"

"I don't think the railroad will cancel, but

you may have a point about the roads. I'll detour to the cab stand to see what the status is on my way to look for food. Sit tight."

"I will."

Betsy came back about twenty minutes later with a white plastic bag, which she put down on the bench beside Annie.

"What did the taxi driver say?" asked Annie, pulling the top of the bag apart and peering in. She saw an apple, an orange, a banana, a package of six Oreos, a bag of corn chips, and two diet Pepsis.

Betsy said, "Funny mix of food, right? But there were lines everywhere, and I had to take what I could get at the end of the shortest line. About the cab: I bribed a driver with fifty dollars. He called it an advance on the fare, but it's a bribe; it can't possibly cost fifty dollars to take a cab from here to the train depot. Look around, people are leaving now, so there are plenty of fares, but he says that will stop soon, and when it does, he wants to go home. But for fifty dollars, he'll either stay or come back. He said the train depot opens an hour before the train comes in." She checked her watch. "That's a little under five hours from now. We'll go out to the cab at half past midnight. While we wait, how about you tell me what you learned at the YWCA shelter."

"Okay." Annie paused to gather her thoughts. "Janet was crazy but not the kind of crazy that scares people. She was the one who was scared — of herself, mostly. And here's something interesting: Putting together what two different women told me, Janet was contacted by a relative of some kind who wanted her to come to Minneapolis. The woman was sure it was Minneapolis, not Saint Paul. The relative bought her a bus ticket."

"How did that happen? I thought no one there would tell a visitor or even someone asking on the phone the name of a person staying there."

"That's true, but there are ways. Like, there's a bulletin board near the back door, and a resident or staff member can pin up a message for someone. And there's no way to prevent someone from talking to a resident outside the shelter, is there? An' givin' her a message to pin up. Plus I think the people running the place will put a message up, too. They won't admit the resident is staying there, but they'll put up a message. Then it's up to the resident, if she's there, to get in touch or not. But what I don't understand is why Janet would reply to any message. She thought everyone was out to get her."

"Not everyone. She liked her niece in Excelsior, for example. And she called her ex-husband every so often, too. When did she receive this offer of a bus ticket?"

"About three weeks ago." Betsy frowned over that for a while. It just about fit the timeline of the murder. But who sent it to her? Emily would want Janet to come to her hometown — wouldn't she? But Emily wasn't a suspect. Why would Janet's ex-husband want to get her out of town? So he wouldn't be linked to her death? And what about that cranky veterinarian, Alec Porter? Could it have been the one person Janet trusted: Emily Hame?

"What are you thinking?" Annie asked.

"Oh, a whole lot of things, none of which I really understand. Not yet anyway."

"Ohhhh-kay. So what do we do next?"

"We wait until we can go to the train depot and start for home." Betsy went into her big purse for the instruction book on Hardanger, but quickly decided it had been too long a day for her to begin again to learn it. She put it away and got out her knitting instead. But she was also too worried to concentrate on decreasing on the three double-ended needles of the pink mitten, and so she went into her suitcase and brought out a scarf she was knitting in heavily slubbed purple yarn on fat, size ten needles.

"Can I see that?" asked Annie.

"What, the knitting?" It would be easier to see how the stitches were formed on needles this size.

"No, that other stuff, whadja call it?"

"Hardanger. Sure, take a look. Maybe you'll come to understand it and can teach me."

"Maybe I will," Annie declared. She opened the book — so thin it was almost a booklet — and read in silence for several minutes, turning back a page then going forward again several times. "You know, this doesn't look hard at all," she said at last.

"I know. That's the cruel thing about Hardanger. It doesn't look hard. In fact, some people I know don't find it hard. But for some reason, I do. Have you done needlework before?"

"No, but I can sew on buttons. This doesn't look much harder than that."

Betsy smiled. "Next time you come to the shop, I'll give you some floss, a needle, and some fabric and let you sit down and show me how it's done."

"Just maybe I'll do that!" declared Annie, and she went back to studying the instructions with even more enthusiasm, now and again making stitching motions with one hand.

Betsy counted her stitches in the scarf and resumed knitting. Really, she thought, it would be much more useful for Annie to learn to knit, especially scarves and mittens, than to do the esoteric Hardanger. On the other hand, Hardanger was beautiful, and it was possible there wasn't much beauty in Annie's life.

Betsy settled into the rhythm of knit two, purl two. As often happened, she got lost in the repeating stitches and her thoughts began to slow their anxious rush, her mind cleared, and she began to consider the case calmly.

What did she know? The puzzle had started with two homeless women found dead in Excelsior. The first, Carrie Carlson, was an alcoholic from Excelsior; the second, Janet Turnquist, was a schizophrenic from Fargo. They weren't sisters or cousins or in any other way related, though they were not far apart in age. They knew one another, too, but probably were not friends. They both had stayed at the Naomi Women's Shelter in Saint Paul.

In addition to being homeless, they were unhappy people. Carrie was a bitter and self-centered woman, a permanent adolescent suffering the physical ravages of long-term alcoholism, who also used drugs when she could get them. Long ago, as a teen, she had had a relationship with a criminal named Dice Paulson. She had no children.

Janet heard voices and thought the United States government was after her. She was divorced, also with no children.

Carrie had once been a beautiful woman, much admired by her older brother. By the end of her life, she'd become a ravaged petty thief, a window-breaking vandal. She'd also been the cousin of Crewel World customer Margaret Smith. She had a Hardanger bookmark very probably made by Janet in her possession. She was a thief; had she stolen it? When?

Janet liked needlework and had been learning to do Hardanger. She had embroidered a holographic last will and testament on the shirt she'd been found wearing, leaving all her worldly goods to her niece. She drank to quiet the voices, but was not an alcoholic. She was the aunt of Monday Bunch regular Emily Hame.

So there was another link between the two dead women: Crewel World.

Carrie's frozen body had been found behind Excelsior's only movie theater, the

Dock. About a week later, Janet's frozen body was found a few blocks away, on a front lawn, buried under snow.

Interesting, Betsy thought in a kind of sidebar, how close together the incidents of this case were. Emily's home and Margaret's home were not even three blocks apart. And the lawn on which Janet's body was found was between them. And the movie theater was less than three blocks from there.

It was possible that Janet had fallen or been put on that lawn at the same time — or even a day or two before — Carrie. Therefore, it was impossible to know for sure whether or not the two deaths were related.

Sergeant Mike Malloy was sure poison was the cause of both deaths, but the autopsy didn't find any evidence of poison in either body — or in the trace of liquor in the bottle that was found with Carrie's body.

What, besides poison, might have caused the deaths?

A warm weight came gently onto Betsy's shoulder. Startled, she nearly moved away from it, then realized it was Annie's head. Poor thing, she had fallen asleep.

Betsy checked her watch. It was a little past eleven. Might as well let her sleep a little longer. It had been a long day, a tiring three days. Moving as little as possible, Betsy continued knitting and thinking.

"Annie. Annie, wake up."

Annie woke, alarmed and confused. "What's going on?" she asked. She realized she was leaning on someone and jerked herself upright. "Oh, sorry, sorry!"

"It's all right."

Oh, heck, she'd been sleeping on Betsy. "My gosh, why did you let me do that?"

"It's all right, but come on, it's time we headed for the train depot."

They gathered their things. Annie paused and looked carefully around before she followed Betsy to the exit. She had a lot of her good things with her and didn't want to lose any of them. No, nothing was left behind.

They went out into the wind and cold. Snow filled the air, but it was hard to tell how much was falling and how much was being lifted off the ground by the wind. A lone vehicle was at the cab stand a little up the way.

"That don't look like a cab," said Annie. "It don't have that little light on the roof."

Indeed it didn't. Betsy's heart sank. But the headlights came on and it pulled forward. It was a big car, bright blue in color

— a Subaru Outback, sitting high off the ground on big tires with lots of tread, its windshield wipers briskly throwing snow off the windshield. And behind the wheel, waving at them, was the taxi driver.

Betsy opened the passenger side door and laid her suitcase down on the leather seat, then turned and took Annie's suitcase and put it on top of hers. Betsy and Annie took their places in the backseat.

"Whew!" said Betsy. "What a terrible night this is!"

"I hope the train can get through," said Annie.

"The old Empire Builder generally does get through," said the taxi driver, a burly man in a leather jacket and matching pinch-brim hat. "But I tell you what. I'll wait at the station for one of you to run in and see what this storm has done to the timetable. If the train's going to be really late, I'll take you to a hotel, all right?"

"Thank you very much," said Betsy. "That's really nice of you."

"It's my pleasure," said the man. He switched to a high-pitched drawl. " 'Taint a fit night out for man or beast."

Betsy, recognizing the line from an old W. C. Fields movie, chuckled.

"What?" said Annie, and Betsy distracted

herself and Annie from the slippery ride to the depot by telling her about the infamous comic of the thirties. She wound up with one of his most famous quotes, as the driver made a controlled slide into the snow-clogged parking lot. " 'A man who hates dogs and children can't be all bad.' " Annie laughed.

Another car, some dark color, had apparently just arrived ahead of them; its roof and hood had barely started to accumulate snow.

"See?" said the driver, nodding toward the other car. "I'm not the only one with faith in Amtrak."

"Wait here," Betsy said to Annie and bailed out to move at a careful trot into the depot.

The little waiting room smelled of freshly heated air, dust, and faintly, humanity. There was a young couple with a wailing baby in the man's arms. Betsy went to the counter, behind which stood a seriously obese middle-aged woman in an ill-fitting black cardigan.

"Is the eastbound Empire Builder on time?" Betsy asked.

"Right now she's half an hour late," said the woman.

Betsy smiled in relief. "Wow, I was afraid

it might be canceled."

"Never happens," said the woman proudly. "She might run late, but she won't be canceled."

"Terrific." Betsy hurried back out to the taxi, where she collected her change from the fifty she'd given him earlier, not neglecting a generous tip. As she and Annie went back to the depot, Betsy noticed someone sitting in the car she'd seen earlier. It was, she noted, a dark cranberry color.

She and Annie took their suitcases into the warm depot. A back-to-back row of fabric-covered, metal-rimmed chairs filled the center of the room and they sat down with identical weary sighs to wait.

Wait a minute, Betsy thought. *Where have I seen that car before?*

Mark sat up straighter in his seat. There she was, and she had someone very shabbily dressed with her. He just wanted to be sure she got out of town, not hanging around to waylay him again with her questions.

NINETEEN

The train lost more time traveling through the blizzard raging out on the prairie west of Fargo, and pulled into the station two hours behind schedule, rumbling deeply and shedding great chunks of snow off its nose.

Betsy and Annie climbed on board, stowed their suitcases, staggered to their seats, and fell asleep almost as soon as they sat down.

Four hours later, Betsy was wakened by daylight coming through the window. She looked out on a world an improbable pale apricot under an intensely blue sky. As she stared at it, the apricot grew paler and paler until, smitten by the rising sun, it turned dazzling white, with blue shadows marking oceanic waves of snow. The land went gently rolling away to the distant horizon, a vista broken only by the occasional tree lifting its naked black limbs to the sky.

The train seemed to be moving at a great

clip, probably trying to make up some time. She looked at her watch. Nearly half past seven. Breakfast time.

And she was hungry. She thought about the snacks she'd bought at the Fargo airport, but she didn't want a snack, she wanted a meal. She'd heard the food was very good on Amtrak trains. She looked over at Annie, her head canted toward the aisle, peacefully asleep. Should she wake her? Could she get past her into the aisle without waking her?

Then Annie's head came around to look at Betsy; she was not asleep after all. "Oh, good, you're awake," Annie said. "They been announcing that the dining car is open for breakfast, and it's making me hungry. Where are those snacks you bought?"

"I didn't hear any announcements."

"Yeah, you're a pretty good sleeper."

"The snacks are in my suitcase. But would you like to go to the dining car instead?"

"Could we?"

The two rose and went swaying up the aisle, through the club car and another passenger car, to find themselves in the dining car, with its booth seating on both sides of the aisle, interrupted by a very small kitchen in the middle. Breakfast smells filled the air.

The place was full of people and there was

another couple waiting ahead of them, but it was only a few minutes before they were seated side by side, facing a slender man and woman, both with silver hair and great tans.

And British accents, revealed when the man said, "Good morning, ladies," and his partner added, "Lovely morning, innit?"

A waitress came by with menus for Annie and Betsy — the British couple was finishing up, each of them having a second cup of coffee. The prices were reasonable, and the choices varied. Impulsively, Betsy ordered the corned beef hash. Annie went with scrambled eggs and toast with a side of fresh fruit.

The British couple explained that they were spending their retirement traveling the world. They came to America frequently and always traveled by train. They were tanned because they'd just spent a week in San Diego.

"Brilliant country you have here, smashing mountains," said the woman.

"And so many climates, all in one nation," agreed the man.

"Where are you going now?" asked Betsy.

"Chicago, and then New York," said the woman.

They wished Betsy and Annie good traveling and left the dining car. Because they had booked a room, they explained, their breakfast had been free.

"Gosh, isn't traveling by train great?" said Annie as their coffee arrived. She doctored hers generously with milk and sugar. Stirring, she said, "Can I ask you a question?"

"Of course. What is it?"

"Are you rich? I mean, really rich? Like a millionaire?"

Betsy was nonplussed for a moment. "Well, yes, I suppose I am, sort of. That is, if I sold everything I own, it might make a pile of money. But I don't know how big a pile. And anyway, a million dollars isn't the big money it used to be."

"Of course it is! Gosh, I never thought I'd meet a real millionaire! And you're so nice and everything. Not snooty at all. But it makes me feel kind of funny, me traveling with you and starting to think we're friends, all the while me being about as far as I can be from rich."

"Don't let it get to you. We are becoming friends, and why not? I think rich is a state of mind. There was a time not so long ago when I was homeless and didn't have any money, either. My sister took me in and gave me a job in the shop I now own. I didn't earn my fortune, I inherited it. And right now it's all tied up in investments, so it isn't as if I could write a humongous check or buy anything I want. Why are you asking?" Betsy hoped Annie wasn't going to ask for a handout.

"I just sort of wondered. You said we could fly home from Fargo, and that would of meant we just threw our return train tickets away, and only really rich people can do stu — uh, things like that." Annie hid her face behind her coffee cup, ashamed she'd almost accused Betsy of doing something stupid.

"You're right, it would have been a foolish waste to throw the tickets away. But I was impatient to get home, and you really wanted to fly, so I figured a little foolishness would be all right this time."

"For a rich person, you're all right, you know that?"

Betsy laughed. "Thank you."

The corned beef hash was the best Betsy had ever eaten.

They'd barely gotten back to their seats when the conductor came through to announce their arrival in Saint Paul.

Betsy spent two minutes combing her hair and putting on lipstick, then smoothing and brushing her suit coat with the palms of her hands before she put on her coat.

"Who's meeting us?" asked Annie.

"Connor Sullivan, I hope."

"Boyfriend, I guess."

"Yes — that's right, you haven't met him."

"Is he really good-looking?"

"I think so."

"Another millionaire?"

"I haven't looked at his bank accounts, but probably not."

"You be careful he's not after your money."

"I will keep that in mind." Betsy turned her head away to hide her smile.

Connor, a man of Betsy's age, reasonably tall and athletic, good-looking rather than handsome, with a grin she found bewitching and laughing sea gray eyes, stood inside the depot waiting for them. He wore a tan overcoat over a tan wool suit, and had pulled off his old-fashioned fedora to expose his curling salt-and-pepper hair. *"Machree!"* he called on seeing them. "Hello, Connor!" replied Betsy, hurrying to him, and dropping her suitcase to give him a hug. He smelled wonderfully male, of cold, wool, and a hint of aftershave.

Annie stood politely silent while greetings were exchanged.

"Connor, this is Annie Summerhill, whom I've told you about."

"Hello, Annie," said Connor, holding out his hand.

"Hello," said Annie, suddenly shy, taking it tentatively. When he released her hand, she put it in her pocket. But as Connor took up Betsy's suitcase and they started for the door, Betsy noticed Annie giving him a pretty sharp look-over.

"Anything happen while I was gone?" Betsy asked after they were in the car and on their way to take Annie to the Naomi Shelter.

"Nothing important. Sergeant Malloy called to ask that you call him when you get home. They had some interesting video on the news last night of a locomotive with a big snow-plow on its front end clearing the tracks west of Fargo."

"That must be why they didn't shut the line down," said Betsy. "It was snowing like crazy in Fargo last night."

"I'm glad you're home safe."

"We had a good time and learned some important facts," asserted Annie from the backseat.

"She really was helpful, Connor," said Betsy.

"Anytime you need more help, I'm available," said Annie.

A few minutes later, "Thank you for coming along, Annie," said Betsy as the car rolled to a stop in front of the Naomi Shelter. "Your assistance was extremely valuable."

"Will you let me know how this turns out?" asked Annie. She had one hand on the backseat door handle.

"Okay, if you like. But that means you have to stay in touch."

"I'd like to do that."

"Good. I'd like you to do that, too."

"Oh, you're just so *nice!*" Annie stooped forward and put her arms around Betsy's shoulders.

Betsy stroked her arms with both hands. "Thank you, you're nice, too."

"Thanks. Bye." Annie grabbed her shabby suitcase and went out into the cold.

As they pulled away, Connor asked, "Was she really helpful?"

"Yes, she was. And very brave, too, poor thing. I wish . . ."

"What?"

"That there was something I could do for her. But the problem is, if you give them anything, the government deducts the value of it from their dole. If you give them enough, they can become cut off altogether. And while I could probably manage to pay her rent for an apartment, I certainly couldn't afford to pay for her medical care — and considering what rents are running these days, she'd likely end up getting nothing from the government."

"That can't be true!" protested Connor.

"That's what I've been told."

"Let me do a little sleuthing of my own in that regard."

"That would be great. I hope you can find out some good news in there somewhere." Betsy hesitated. "Connor . . ." she began.

"Suzanna has gone back to Ireland. She promised she'd write to me, but she's not much of a letter writer."

"Are you going to visit her there?"

"No. I made no promise to do that, and I have no intention of going over there."

"Oh, dear."

"What?"

"I think I'm going to cry."

"You were that worried?"

"I was. Very foolishly, I was."

"You want to know something? So was I."

There was no time for even a brief nap. Betsy put her suitcase in her apartment, washed her hands and face, and went down to open the shop. She found Godwin already there, making coffee. He was wearing a pale ivory sweater with a faintly raised checker pattern, something he'd knit himself.

"Lord, that smells good!" she said.

He greeted her with a smile that turned shocked. "Wow, I hope you don't feel as awful as you look!" he blurted out, surprised.

Betsy looked down at the deep red pantsuit she was wearing. It had looked so great only yesterday. "I'll go up and change in a little while, as soon as we get things started down here."

"You look like you slept in that outfit," Godwin said as he came toward her with the first mug of coffee out of the urn. Crewel World offered free coffee to paying customers.

Betsy took the mug and sipped from it. "I did. The train got held up in Montana and North Dakota by a blizzard, and when we finally got on in Fargo, we went to sleep. I got a whole four hours' worth before the sun woke me up, and not enough time to nap or even change before I had to come down to get us opened up."

"Well, you just sit down and drink that coffee, while I shovel the front walk."

"Thank you, I will. How much snow did we get here?" Looking out the front window, it certainly didn't look as if a blizzard had struck Excelsior.

"Only five inches. The worst of the storm

went north of us. I hear Duluth is up to its eyebrows in drifts this morning." Godwin had been putting his coat back on while he talked. He went in back and returned with an ergonomically designed snow shovel. "Be right back."

Betsy sat at the library table and, between tired sighs, drank her coffee, which was extra-strong but not really bitter. In a few minutes, Godwin had finished his task. He opened the door and stood for a few moments, kicking snow off his good shoes. Coming in, he said, "Look, I'm here now. Why don't you go upstairs and get some rest?"

"No, I'll stay till Vicki Sue gets here. She's scheduled to work just this morning — in fact, where is she?" Betsy checked her watch; it was nearly twenty past ten.

Godwin checked his own watch. "I don't think she's ever been this late — in fact, she's always on time."

"Yes, that's been my experience with her, too." Betsy finished her coffee and felt the caffeine start its goodly work. She wanted badly to go upstairs and take a shower, put on something more presentable, but now she was as worried about Vicki Sue as she had been miffed at her a few minutes ago.

She tried phoning her, but there was no answer.

She had scarcely hung up when the door sounded its two notes and Vicki Sue came in. A medium-size young woman with brown hair and eyes, usually she was a lively creature, full of little gestures, good-natured and pleasant. She made Betsy think of a tame finch when it sees someone coming with a box of seeds.

But not today. Today she came in slowly, head down, feet dragging.

"Vicki Sue, whatever is the matter?" asked Betsy.

"Oh, Betsy, I'm so upset! It's Penny! I don't know what to do!" And she burst into tears.

"Oh, Vicki Sue, my *dear!* Here, sit down and tell us what the *problem* is!" Godwin, all sympathy and concern, came to help her take her blue winter coat off, unwrapping her purple knit scarf and touching her gently on her shoulders.

Betsy came to hug her. "Would a cup of tea help?" she asked.

With an obvious effort, Vicki stopped crying enough to say, "Nothing will help!" But then her sobs became even more furious. "Penny has to die, and there's nothing I can do to prevent it!"

TWENTY

"Here now, you'd better tell just what this is all about," said Betsy. She took the girl's elbow in a firm grip and led her to the back half of the shop, where there was a small round table covered with a tablecloth printed with hearts and cherubs. "Please sit down and explain it to us. First, who is Penny?"

Godwin produced a handkerchief from somewhere — how like him to have one, thought Betsy irrelevantly.

Vicki Sue wiped her eyes and nose. "She's my little dog, a Chihuahua mix. She's got a coat that's the color of a penny, that's why I named her that. I took her out for her afternoon walk yesterday and there was this big dog coming the other way. Before I could pick her up, Penny panicked and pulled back and her collar came off over her head. She ran out into the street and there was this car coming by and it hit her. I screamed but it didn't stop. Penny was going 'Yi, yi, yi' really loud and holding up her front leg, and I could see it was crooked."

Godwin made a shocked sound and took Vicki Sue's hand.

Tears spilled from her eyes as Vicki Sue continued bravely. "I took her to the vet. He took an X-ray and he says the leg is so bad it can't be fixed, so he wants to cut it off!"

"That's *horrible!*" said Betsy.

"I hate it, but he says it's too damaged to fix. And worse, the cost is seven hundred dollars. I said could he maybe just put a cast on it, and he said no, it'll never heal properly and so will never stop hurting. I can't afford seven hundred dollars, of course, and he said she was suffering, and if I couldn't afford an operation, I should take her to the Humane Society and *tell them to put her to sleep.*"

"Oh, my *God!*" said Godwin.

"This is so awful, I can't make up my mind what to do!" Tears ran down Vicki Sue's cheeks so copiously they dripped into her lap.

Betsy sat down on the other chair and reached for Vicki Sue's other hand. "Here now, here now, slow down. There must be something that can fix this."

"But what? What else can I do? She's almost just a puppy, she won't be two until April!"

"Just a *baby!*" mourned Godwin, who had a heart so tender he was nearly crying himself.

"Surely there's a vet who would be willing to take payments," said Betsy.

"I've been calling and calling, but the ones who will do it at all, they want a lot of money down, and they want payments higher than I can afford."

Vicki Sue was a full-time student at the university, and worked two part-time jobs to pay some of her college expenses. Betsy knew that if it weren't for student loans, Vicki Sue would have to drop out. A sudden expense of this magnitude must be devastating.

"Where is the dog now?" Betsy asked.

"She's at home in her little kennel. She can't put her broken leg down or lay on it or let me touch it, and she makes this crying sound all the time. I had to get out of the apartment, I can't stand to stay and listen to her, it breaks my heart. My roommates are both gone — one to school and one to work — so she's there alone. But what can I do? I don't know what to do!"

"When did this happen?" asked Godwin.

"Yesterday afternoon, around four o'clock. I'd just gotten home from class."

"Maybe if I called your vet, talked to him," suggested Betsy.

"Oh, don't call him, he's no good. I want to know if the leg can be fixed, it's just broken, for God's sake, but he won't even try to fix it, he just wants to cut it off. He said her bones are too tiny to be put back together. I had to dip into my student loan account to pay for the X-ray, and there's not enough in there to pay for the operation." Vicki slammed both fists on the table. "It isn't *fair!* Penny's been the sweetest dog I've ever known! I can't have her put to sleep!" She wiped her eyes with both hands.

A look of determination came over her ravaged face. "It's wrong for me to let her suffer, it's wrong! I guess the next stop is the Humane Society."

But Betsy was appalled at the deadly solution, and sick at the thought of the hurting animal all alone and crying. "Didn't he even give you a painkiller for Penny?"

"He gave her an injection, but it's worn off. She woke me up this morning with her crying. My roommates are upset, of course, but they can't help, they're as poor as I am." Vicki blew her nose on Godwin's handkerchief, and pushed herself to her feet. "I'm sorry. I shouldn't have come in. This isn't helping any of us, is it? Burdening you with this mess. I might as well go back home, I can't stand being there, but abandoning her is even worse. I'll do what I have to do."

Betsy said, "Just hold on for two minutes, okay? Godwin, get Vicki a cup of coffee or tea. I'll be right back."

She went to the desktop computer at the checkout desk in the front of the shop, pulled up Google, and typed, *Dr. Alec Porter, Veterinarian, Saint Paul, MN.* Immediately the name of a veterinary clinic came up — Small Animal Medical Center — with a notation that Dr. Porter was the veterinarian there. She wrote down the phone number printed on the screen.

Then she picked up the cordless phone and dialed. "Dr. Porter?" she asked when a man answered.

"Yes, how may I help you?"

"I have a friend who has a small dog with a badly broken foreleg. Her own vet took an X-ray and suggested the leg be amputated. But her owner is hoping there's another way, perhaps an operation to put the bones back into place. Complicating all this, she's a poor college student, with very little money. I'm willing to help her, if I can. May we bring the dog to you?"

"Yes, of course. How did you get my name?"

"Someone told me about you, said you were a very clever surgeon."

Dr. Porter's voice warmed suddenly. "Yes, I do have good hands for surgery. This is an emergency, obviously. Bring her in right now. How far away are you?"

"Excelsior — but the dog is in Orono." Betsy held her breath. Both were a very long way from the eastern side of Saint Paul, and he might be wondering why they wanted to travel so far.

"Hmmmm. All right, I'll be standing by."

"Thank you."

Orono wasn't far from Excelsior. Betsy followed Vicki's rusty and dilapidated old car to the little town up along the shore of Lake Minnetonka. They pulled into a freshly plowed parking lot in front of an elderly gray stucco fourplex.

Vicki piled out of her car and ran to the front entrance of the place, thrust her key into the lock, and opened the door. She froze in place, turning a white face to Betsy, who was hurrying to catch up. As she approached, Betsy could hear the lamentations of a small dog.

"Oh, my God, oh, my God!" Vicki whimpered.

"Go on, get her and we'll get her to a doctor."

"Yes, yes!" Vicki hurried halfway down a short hall and unlocked the door on the left. Suddenly the dog's cries were louder.

The blue plastic kennel was in the little kitchen, and small enough that it fit easily into the backseat of Betsy's Buick.

The dog's cries did not cease the whole fifty minutes of the trip to Dr. Porter's clinic.

Dr. Porter sedated Penny with an injection — the swiftly fallen silence was a relief — and took the animal away to the X-ray lab. While they waited for his assistant to develop the films, Betsy tried to make conversation with him.

"You must see a lot of animals in pain," she said.

"Quite a few." Perhaps his short tone was because he was thinking about what might be shown on the X-rays.

"How long did you have to study to learn animal surgery?"

"Long enough."

Undaunted by his brusque tone, Betsy continued, "I'm glad you were willing to take a look at this animal. I hope you can save her leg."

"You say this happened yesterday," he said in an accusing voice.

"Yes," said Vicki Sue humbly. "I didn't know who to ask for help. They said I should take her to be put to sleep, but I couldn't! I just *couldn't!*"

The back door to the examination room opened and a young woman dressed in blue scrubs, with very fair hair and an air of competence, came in with three large X-ray films in one hand. "Here they are, Doctor," she said in a quiet voice.

"Let's see what they can tell us," said Dr. Porter. He took the films from her and put them up on a light board hanging on the wall.

It showed a limb not merely broken, but shattered into several small pieces. Betsy winced when she saw the awful state of the bone, and Vicki Sue started to cry.

"Hush," said Dr. Porter absently, studying the X-rays.

Betsy put a comforting arm around Vicki Sue's waist, and the young woman sniffled into silence. Betsy let go of Vicki Sue long enough to pull a Kleenex from her purse and hand it to her.

"Thanks," murmured the wretched girl.

"I said, hush," said Dr. Porter, now standing very close to the light board and looking intently at the damaged limb on first one film, then another, then the third, then going back to repeat the examination.

The women fell silent, though Betsy could feel Vicki Sue trembling.

"All right," said Dr. Porter at last, turning toward them. "I think I can save your dog's leg. It'll be tricky — and expensive. You may want to go with amputation. It's quicker to heal, and less costly. On the other hand, I think I can give your dog back its leg, maybe even in a state to be walked on." He turned away from the women and began studying the X-rays again. Betsy could sense his eagerness to go for the tricky save.

On the other hand . . . "When you say expensive, how much are we talking about?" Betsy asked.

Dr. Porter turned back. "Something in the neighborhood of three thousand dollars for the surgery, then there will be a fairly long recovery time, with further X-rays and physical therapy, which may total another six hundred dollars. Perhaps more."

"Holy Mary, Mother of God," said Vicki Sue in a low voice.

"Amen," said Betsy, her voice equally awed. She'd had no idea!

Vicki drew herself up and asked, "Can she

get along on three legs?"

"Ah . . . yes," said Dr. Porter. "She'll do a funny-looking hop when she walks, but she'll run just fine." A light in his eyes had gone out.

"But . . . will she be *happy?*" asked Vicki Sue desperately.

The light came back on. "Yes," he said, and for the first time there was compassion in his voice. "She'll be just as happy as she was before the accident."

"Well then . . . all right, let's go with amputation," said Vicki.

"How much will it cost?" asked Betsy. "And when can you do it?"

"It will cost six hundred and fifty dollars, plus kennel care of twenty dollars a day for as long as she remains here. And it should be done as soon as possible. The dog is in a lot of pain, and pain causes stress, which can send a little dog like yours downhill in a hurry. I can do it today, if you like. Then I'll want to keep her for at least three days afterward, to make sure she's healing properly."

"All right," said Vicki with a slight note of query in her voice.

She looked at Betsy, who obediently asked, "How do you want to be paid?"

"I'll want three hundred now, and the balance when you pick her up in three or four days."

"All right," said Betsy, glad she hadn't been able to opt for the airplane ride home from Fargo. "Do you want a check or credit card?"

Vicki began to cry again, murmuring between sobs, "Thank you, thank you, thank you. I'll pay you back, every dollar, every dime."

She was allowed to visit Penny, who was still heavily sedated.

Meanwhile, Betsy asked, "Do you think Penny knows her mistress is in there with her?"

"Probably not, but it's hard to tell the level of awareness in an unconscious animal. They can't come back and tell us what it was like."

"But humans can. I mean, aren't you using the same medication on the dog as gets used on people?"

Dr. Porter looked faintly shocked. "No. The sedation I used on Penny is not used on human beings."

"But —"

The door opened and the assistant was back with Vicki Sue, who was trying to smile through her tears.

And she wept all the way back to

301

Excelsior.

Vicki Sue insisted on staying at work when they arrived back at Crewel World and told Godwin the good — and bad — news. "I'd go crazy at home, and besides, I need the money."

"All right," said Godwin. "That means we'll be here to hear from Dr. Porter that your little Penny sailed through the surgery and is going to be just fine!" he said.

"I'll give you a ride home after work," said Betsy.

"Thank you, so much, for everything, Betsy," Vicki Sue said. "You know you are an angel!"

"I don't know what else I could have done," said Betsy.

Betsy went upstairs, took a one-hour nap, then a shower, and put on her bright pink knit dress. Just looking at it was a wake-up shock to the system. Back downstairs, she called Margaret Smith and asked her if she could come to Antiquity Rose's combination antique shop and restaurant for lunch.

"All right," said Margaret.

Betsy looked up the phone number and then called her veterinarian.

"Dr. Marsden, do you know if animal medicines work the same way on humans as they do on animals?" Betsy asked.

Dr. Marsden replied, "Some do, some don't. Why do you want to know?"

"I was just wondering."

"Uh-huh. But all right, most mammal medicines work on humans as well as cats, dogs, and horses, though not always in the same way. But there's significant crossover. For example, glucosamine, a medicine that improves joint function, was first used exclusively on animals. For another, there is currently a problem with an animal anesthetic called ketamine, or 'Special K' as it's known on the street. Thieves break into veterinary clinics to steal it."

"Anesthetic? Is it an opiate?"

"No. It's used as an anesthetic in combination with another drug. It is a mind-altering drug, detaching the mind from the body."

"But it knocks you out."

"Not exactly. Used recreationally by humans, it's like LSD combined with alcohol and marijuana. Users claim it gives you an out-of-body experience and puts you in touch with spirits and sometimes a higher power. But it also temporarily paralyzes the users' limbs and has an aftereffect of at least partial amnesia, along with an energetic feeling of well-being."

"Sounds like fun," said Betsy, disappointed.

" 'Fun'? What are you looking for?"

"Something that's not an opiate that will knock you out."

"Why not an opiate?"

"Because it has to pass a drug-screening test."

"What *are* you mixed up in?" Dr. Marsden asked.

"I'm sleuthing for a friend. Please, it's important."

"All right. Hmmmm, something non-narcotic, nonbarbiturate, that will knock you out."

"And doesn't leave symptoms that turn up on autopsy."

"I'm afraid I'm going to have to insist you tell me what this is about."

"Those two women who froze to death in Excelsior a few weeks ago. Our local police detective thinks it might be murder. He was thinking the murder weapon was an opiate dissolved in alcohol, but they screened for that and didn't find anything. A cousin of one of the women is a suspect, and she asked me to help her clear her name."

"I see. I guess." A pause for thought. "All right, there's Telazol."

"What's Telazol?"

"It's an anesthetic that's used on cats and dogs."

"How is it used? I mean, is it a gas?"

"No, a liquid. You inject it. But injections leave a mark most medical examiners notice."

"Could you mix it with alcohol and drink it?"

Another pause. "Yes, I suppose you could."

"That's very interesting. Telazol, eh? Thanks, Dr. Marsden."

The problem was, of course, why Dr. Porter — if he was the murderer — would want to kill Carrie. After all, Carrie was the one in possession of the bottle of liquor.

And then, how did Janet get a share? Betsy remembered Annie holding up her last shortbread cookie. *Then here comes Janet, talking trash, telling stories, and next thing you know, she's eaten my cookie her own self.*

Was that how it happened? Janet insisting on a share of the bourbon? What a cruel trick for Janet to play — on herself!

So then, not Dr. Porter, but someone else, someone who wanted Carrie dead. Someone who knew how to contact her, knew her weakness for liquor, knew where she was that fatal evening. And who had access to Telazol or some similar drug.

Marty Smith had extensive medical knowledge, probably. Did he know his choice of poison would not be detectable in a standard lab test? No, wait. Why would he have to know that? A known alcoholic found frozen to death in an obscure back alley would not rouse suspicion. Of course, Mike Malloy didn't buy it, and demanded a screening test — and even though it was negative, he was sure, now that there were two of them, that the deaths were suspicious. Had Mike found out about Telazol?

She'd better call him right now.

TWENTY-ONE

Antiquity Rose was in a converted house on Second Street, on the opposite side of the block from Crewel World. Though it was bitter cold out, Betsy felt it would be foolish to drive. She wore her warmly lined boots and wrapped a big hand-knit shawl over her head and lower face before setting out. Her mittens were felted wool with suede leather palms.

The sun was shining brightly, dazzling the eye where it struck on the snow piled on lawns, along the curbs, and on the roofs of houses. It might have been beautiful if one were not so weary of the effect.

Margaret had already arrived when Betsy got there. She looked tired and depressed. Though her eyes were bright, Betsy suspected it was from unshed tears. She wore a very subdued brown wool dress with a pattern of black leaves on it. Her mink coat was draped over one arm.

The main room of the shop was crowded with tables and display cabinets full of porcelain, silver, costume and real jewelry, books, and even a few antique dolls and other collectibles.

"I haven't been in here in a while," said Margaret, looking around. "But I like this place. I hope the food is still as good as it used to be."

They were greeted by young and pretty hazel-eyed Bonnie, whose blond hair tumbled attractively around her shoulders. "Hello, Betsy," she said. "I have a table waiting for you." Bonnie led them to a corner table in a small room off the main display room. The adjoining tables were empty, though from the sounds of conversation coming from other rooms, the rest of the café was crowded.

"Hot Russian tea to start," said Betsy.

"I'll have coffee," said Margaret.

The two opened their menus. Betsy saw the listed special — old-fashioned salmon loaf with creamed peas. Then she remembered her extra-hearty breakfast and decided on a salad.

"Margaret, tell me about Carrie's last visit to your house. What time of day was it?"

Margaret put her menu aside. "I don't remember the exact time," she said. "It was dark out, so it must have been after five. Probably around seven. She must have taken the last bus out from the city."

"Was she drunk?"

"Not staggering, but I could smell alcohol on her breath — but I always could smell it on her the last few years, always. She was very rude and demanding, already angry —" She cut herself off as the waitress arrived with their drinks.

"What have you found out?" asked Margaret after the waitress went away with their order.

"Margaret, remember how I warned you when you asked me to look into this that I might find out some family secrets you'd rather I didn't uncover?"

Margaret's mouth pulled into a pained thin line. Two spots of pink appeared on her cheeks. But "Yes?" was all she said.

"Well, I didn't find anything — but Mike Malloy has, and he told me about your secret and Marty's. I'm so sorry to haul them out now, but there are some things I need to ask you about them."

"Oh, my God. Who else has he told?"

"No one," said a man's voice, and when the two women looked up, there was the detective in person.

"Hello, Sergeant Malloy," said Margaret

with icy politeness.

"Hi, Mike," said Betsy. "What's up?"

"I would like to interview Mrs. Smith. Your husband told me you were here," he added.

"I'll want my attorney to be present," said Margaret.

"That's fine, if you like. But you're not under arrest."

"I don't care. I'll call Mr. Frank Whistler and have him come to your office, because I am not saying another word until he is sitting beside me." Margaret sat back in her chair and folded her hands in her lap in a very determined manner.

"All right, have it your way," said Malloy. "If you'll come with me."

Margaret stood and Betsy helped her on with her coat, and then Margaret used her cell to call Mr. Whistler.

Then Margaret's composure broke and she reached for Betsy's hands to say weakly, "Will you come and sit with me, too?"

"I'd love to, but I don't think Mike will allow that."

"Why not?" said Malloy. "I have some questions for you, too."

"Would it be okay if we had our lunch first?" asked Betsy.

"Sure. I'll see you there."

Neither of them did justice to the meal. Margaret was so upset that Betsy offered to drive her to the police station. Margaret gratefully accepted.

Betsy stopped by Crewel World and explained the situation. "Are you two going to be all right without me?"

"I think we'll have to be," said Vicki Sue. "I mean, when the police want to talk to you, you have to go. Right?"

"Yes," said Godwin, "even if it's only dopey old Mike Malloy."

"Now, Godwin," said Betsy, but she was smiling. "I'll come back as soon as we're finished."

When Betsy drove up to the brick and stone police building out on Excelsior Boulevard — which was actually the logical terminus of a street in Minneapolis — she pulled in beside a new-looking bright yellow Mercedes.

In the lobby of the station was a handsome black man in a dark blue suit just this side of too fabulous. He stood poised in a confident way, holding a heavy mug of coffee in one hand, his black overcoat hanging from his shoulders. He greeted Margaret in a gentle, reassuring voice. "Ms. Devonshire?" he said next. He studied her curiously. "Have we met before?"

TWENTY-TWO

"What an extraordinary memory you have!" said Betsy. "I interviewed you a few years ago when I was seeking representation for Godwin DuLac."

"Ah, yes, but you went with someone else."

"Yes, but it was a difficult choice. I'm glad to see Mrs. Smith has retained someone with as good a reputation as you have."

"Thank you." He bowed very slightly, then turned to the police officer behind the reception desk in the room. He checked his watch and said, "Could you tell Sergeant Malloy that we're all here now?"

Betsy knew Whistler's office was in Wayzata, on the other side of the lake, and she wondered how he got here so fast from there — did he take a shortcut directly across the ice?

He smiled at Betsy as if he were reading her mind. "I was in town for a meeting."

Malloy appeared then, and signed for them to follow him back to his cramped office, which had two desks pushed together head-to-head. The second desk was unoccupied. "Take a seat," he said to Whistler, gesturing at the office chair behind the empty desk. "Mrs. Smith, if you'll sit here," he added, pulling out a wooden chair so it sat a little beyond the end of his desk, and slightly turned so it faced his chair.

There was only one other chair in the room, another wooden one alongside the other desk.

"Everyone comfortable?" asked Malloy. "Mrs. Smith, Ms. Devonshire, may I get either of you a cup of coffee?"

"Yes, please," said Betsy, who hadn't finished her Russian tea at Antiquity Rose and was feeling the lack of a good night's sleep. "Plastic sugar and cream," she added.

"Nothing for me," said Margaret, hanging her coat over the back of the wooden chair and throwing a pleading look at Whistler before sitting down.

Malloy brought Betsy a mug identical to Whistler's, and sat down at his desk.

"Mrs. Smith, do you know why I've asked you to come down here to talk with me?" he said.

"Yes, it's about the death of my cousin,

Carrie Carlson."

"Very good."

Whistler interrupted. "I want to instruct Mrs. Smith not to volunteer any information; to answer only the questions asked; and to look at me before making any answer."

"This isn't an interrogation," objected Malloy.

"Still," said Whistler, unperturbed.

"All right," said Margaret.

Mike opened his notebook and paged back and forth until he found the page he wanted.

"Could you please tell me about the last time you saw your cousin?"

Margaret obediently looked at Whistler, who nodded sagely.

"It was on a Saturday. Marty was at work, and I was doing some housecleaning. The front doorbell rang, and when I answered it, there stood Carrie. She smelled of wine, but she didn't seem particularly drunk. I let her in and asked if she wanted a cup of coffee. She said no, but could I give her fifty dollars toward a bus ticket to Jacksonville, Florida? I said no, I couldn't. She started to cry, but she's done that sort of thing before, and I could see she was making crying noises, but there was not one tear. I told her she had to leave, and she got angry and called me names, but I just said she had to leave, now. So she did, looking all broken-hearted. About two minutes later, I heard a crash from down in the basement. When I went to take a look, there were two chunks of ice on the floor — it looked to me like one chunk of ice that had broken in half when it went through the window — and a mess of broken glass. I heard Carrie's voice yelling, 'Serves you right, serves you right, you —' Well, never mind what she called me, it was just more of the same. I never saw her again."

Margaret went into her purse and pulled out a handkerchief, which she used to wipe her nose.

"You're sure it was Carrie who broke the window?"

"Well, there was the sound of breaking glass and I recognized her voice . . ." Margaret looked around at Betsy, who smiled reassuringly. "Who else could it have been?"

Mike nodded and went forward a few pages in his notebook. "I understand you used to work at your husband's business . . ." Malloy had to check his notes again to make sure he had the name right. "Din-Din, Incorporated."

"That's right." Margaret smiled.

"Interesting name."

Margaret looked at Whistler, who nodded. "I invented it. It started as a joke, just among the employees, but pretty soon our customers started calling it that, too. You see, in the beginning we just sold pet food."

"But then you expanded into animal medicines?"

"Yes."

"How long did you work in your husband's business?"

"About five years, until I got pregnant with Teddy. It was a difficult pregnancy and I had to spend a lot of time in bed."

"I understand you've been beating yourself up for certain decisions you made about end-of-life care for your parents."

Margaret looked at Whistler, who nodded again. She looked back at Malloy and said humbly, "I think I made some mistakes."

Malloy smiled. "I've made a few in my life — who hasn't? But what I want to know is, did your cousin, Carrie Carlson, know about these 'mistakes'?"

Margaret swallowed but said bravely, "She knew about my father's cancer and my mother's stroke, and that I made the decisions about caring for them. I don't know if she thought I made any wrong decisions."

"Did she know about the problems your

husband had at his company, with expired medications he sold to veterinarians?"

Margaret bit her lower lip, which had begun trembling, then shook her head without looking at Whistler. "No."

"Was she blackmailing you?"

Margaret looked surprised, then frightened. "Is that what you think?"

Whistler said sharply, "Do you have any reason to believe she was, Sergeant?"

"Only the fact that she's been murdered."

"I didn't murder her!" declared Margaret.

"Any idea who else had a motive to murder her?" asked Malloy.

"I don't think that's an appropriate question to ask Mrs. Smith," said Whistler. "You're asking her to do your job for you."

"Nobody had any reason to murder her," said Margaret. "She was a difficult person, but quite unable to hold a grudge or do anything that would cause anyone to be so angry with her they'd resort to murder. I don't think she was able to come up with so outrageous an idea as blackmail, given the state she'd gotten herself into with her drinking. And anyway, who would she threaten to tell? Her fellow homeless women? How could that possibly harm me?"

"Mrs. Smith —" remonstrated Whistler.

Malloy spoke over him. "Good point. The problem is, they have found traces of Telazol in the bottle of bourbon that was found with her body."

That was fast, thought Betsy.

"Telazol? What's that?"

"It's an animal anesthetic."

Every trace of color fled from Margaret's face. "Oh, my God," she murmured.

Betsy stood and went to put her hands on Margaret's shoulders. They were stiff as stone. "You're all right, you're all right," she murmured.

"Please sit down, Ms. Devonshire," said Malloy, and Betsy obeyed. But her heart was thumping.

"Do you know if Din-Din, Incorporated, carries Telazol?"

Hope bloomed in her eyes. "I think we don't. I've never heard of it."

"It's not a rare drug," said Malloy.

"I know a great deal about my husband's business, and I'm telling you I've never heard of it," insisted Margaret.

"All right. Was your husband angry at Carrie?"

Margaret glanced at Whistler.

"Maybe you should ask Mr. Smith that question," said the attorney.

"I will," promised Malloy. "But I'd like

318

Mrs. Smith's opinion, too."

"We were both angry at Carrie," Margaret said. "She was a very annoying person. But we didn't hate her, and we never were so angry that any thought of murdering her crossed our minds."

Malloy, who had been taking notes throughout this interview, took his time writing something down. Then he closed his notebook. "I think that's all for now. Thank you, Mrs. Smith, for agreeing to speak with me."

"You're welcome, Sergeant." She stood, and so did Whistler and Betsy.

"Come on, I'll give you a ride back to your car," Betsy said.

"All right, thank you."

Margaret shook Whistler's hand and thanked him. "I assume it will cost your usual hourly rate for this?" she asked.

"Yes, ma'm," said Whistler cheerfully. He checked his watch.

"Now hold on a minute," said Malloy. "I want to talk briefly with Ms. Devonshire."

"I'm going now," said Whistler. "Want to ride with me?"

"No, I'll wait out in the lobby for Betsy," said Margaret, not wanting to hire the most expensive cabdriver in the world.

When they had gone, Betsy said, "Well?"

"That's what I was gonna ask you: Well? What do you think?"

"I think you ask good questions," said Betsy. "But I'm not convinced she had anything to do with the death of her cousin. After all, Alec Porter is a veterinarian, he's as likely as Marty to have Telazol in stock. And did you know that Dr. Porter had Jasper Bronson's power of attorney?"

"Where did you learn that?"

"Regina Kingsolver told me."

"Bronson's attorney?"

Betsy nodded.

Malloy paged back in his notebook, frowning, found a place, and started writing. "Can a person with power of attorney go rummaging through the other person's papers?"

"I'm sure he can. Dr. Porter had the responsibility to manage Jasper's affairs, and the only way he could do that, since Jasper was beyond consulting, was to go look at his records for himself. If Jasper had a copy of his will in his home, then Alec had access to it."

Malloy let out a low whistle. "So it is likely that he did know about the second will — and therefore, he must have realized that it was necessary for Janet to die first, before Jasper did."

"He said he didn't?"

"He said he was told the terms of the will by Regina Kingsolver." Malloy smiled. "That's probably true, just not the whole truth."

"Maybe he was scared or nervous of being interviewed by the police."

"No more so, as I recall, than any ordinary citizen is made nervous by a police interview."

"The problem is," said Betsy, "how did he find her? And having found her, how did he persuade her to come to meet him so he could give her the poisoned bottle?"

"Tell me that, and I'll make an arrest." He turned the pages in his notebook to find a fresh sheet of paper. "Tell me about your trip to Fargo. I hear you took someone with you."

"Yes." She nodded. "A homeless woman named Annie Summerhill. I used her to find information about Janet Turnquist. Janet stayed at the Fargo YWCA, which functions as a women's emergency shelter."

"What did you find out?"

"Janet was truly insane, heard voices all the time, according to a young woman who sat up with her one night when she got the greebles."

" 'Greebles'?"

"A scared disconnect from reality. Like, crying, 'No, no, no!' and 'Shut up, shut up!' till her roommate at the Y woke up and sat with her and listened sympathetically to her ranting. Janet could apparently manage to ignore the racket in her head when she wanted something badly enough, such as a place to stay."

"Anything else?"

"She talked her way into a Hardanger class — that's a kind of needlework — at Nordic Needle, a needlework shop in Fargo. Very likely the bookmark you found in Carrie's possession is the fruit of that class. I wonder how Carrie came to own it."

"Maybe Janet gave it to her."

"Stitchers give away their work all the time," said Betsy with a nod. "But the bookmark wasn't finished, and anyway, Carrie wasn't a friend. She went to an awful lot of trouble to learn how to make it. The teacher of that class, Roz Watnemo, had to loan Janet a pair of magnifying glasses in order for Janet to succeed. Janet later scraped together the money to buy a pair for herself."

Mike was taking notes, writing swiftly. "Okay, needlework was important enough to her to suppress the voices. Anything else?"

"Someone — possibly a relative — bought her a bus ticket from Fargo to Minneapolis."

"Is that a generic Minneapolis, meaning the Cities, or even Saint Paul?"

"The witness said Minneapolis."

"Hmmmmm," said Mike.

"Yes, it made me go 'hmmmm,' too. But what does it mean?"

"Somebody either wanted her out of the town he's operating in, or wanted her to come within his reach."

"Alec Porter or Mark Turnquist. Okay, which one?"

"Maybe neither. Neither of them is from Excelsior — or Minneapolis, for that matter. On the other hand, Margaret Smith is from Excelsior, which is where Carrie's body was found. And it appears that Mrs. Smith was the last person to see Carrie alive."

"I know, I know. But I think Marty's motive is thin, and I am as sure as I can be that Margaret is innocent. Were there a pair of reading glasses in Janet's belongings, by the way?"

Mike checked his notebook. "Yes. Not in the box with her other embroidery stuff, but loose in one bag. It was the one tipped over, with stuff spilling out."

"Did you notice the little scissors? They

had the tip of one of the blades broken off."

"What does that mean — and how do you know that?"

"Emily Hame. You showed her the things from Janet's plastic bags, and she has an excellent memory for detail. And I don't know if it means anything, except that when you're carrying all your worldly possessions around in plastic bags, things happen."

"Hmmmm. Anything else?"

Betsy pictured a street map of Excelsior, and in her mind she traced a walking pattern from the Fiedlers' house to the Dock. "The two bodies were found what, a little less than three blocks from each other? I wonder if they were poisoned in the same place, and one of them walked away."

"When I talked with another veterinarian, she said Telazol is very fast acting, and one of its first effects is to paralyze the extremities."

Betsy threw up her hands. "Then I don't know what happened!" she exclaimed, exasperated.

Back in her car, with Margaret beside her, Betsy said, "There is another possible suspect who had access to Telazol. He's a veterinarian."

"Veterinarian? I don't think there's a veterinarian in our family."

"This person had a motive to kill Janet, not Carrie."

Margaret blinked three times, then relief brought color flooding into her face. "Well, there, then! You see? There, then!"

There was a silence that lasted a few moments.

"Who is he?" asked Margaret. "Does Sergeant Malloy know about him?"

"Yes."

"What's his name?"

"I don't think Mike would want me to tell you that."

TWENTY-THREE

It was getting near to closing, and Betsy was beyond tired, too tired to be hungry. And okay, happy — there had been a steady stream of customers all afternoon. It was a good thing there was an extra pair of hands in the shop as Betsy, in her fog of exhaustion, became increasingly clumsy and forgetful.

Another reason she was happy was that Connor had called a few minutes ago to ask if she wanted to go out to dinner. "I know you're probably very tired, *machree,* but I don't feel like eating alone."

"Yes, so long as it's right after I close. And if you'll take me home early. I'm really tired."

"See you in half an hour, then," he'd replied.

So when the door went "bing-bong" as someone came in, it wasn't as much of an effort for her to turn with a smile to greet the customer.

But her smile didn't fool Connor. "Oh, my dear!" he exclaimed, coming to take her into his lovely strong arms. "I can't believe you agreed to go out to dinner when you are obviously in no shape to go anywhere but up to your apartment — and then only with me pushing from behind!"

"Oh, Connor, I love you," she murmured.

Connor sat at the library table until the closing-up business was finished. Then he took Betsy by the arm and led her up the stairs to his apartment. He fixed a nice omelet and fed her like a very young child.

Then he took her to her apartment and put her to bed. He even remembered to feed the cat before returning to his own lonesome bed.

Betsy slept for twelve hours. She woke feeling only a little sluggish, and two cups of black English tea washed away the last of the vapors and brightened her outlook. She phoned Connor to thank him tenderly for taking care of her last night, then toasted an English muffin for breakfast and went downstairs a little before ten to open the shop.

Godwin was pleased to see how quickly Betsy had bounced back from her exhaustion of the day before. But he had already called part-timer Mindy to help them out.

"No, don't send her home," said Betsy. "I have an idea I need to explore." She waited until midmorning, when things slowed in the shop. She announced she had an errand to run and would be back in less than an hour.

She went out into the dazzlingly bright but very cold day, up Lake Street, across Water Street, and into the alley that ran between a small parking lot and the back of the movie theater.

She found nothing but bare concrete scattered with a gritty mix of salt and sand. Evidently the theater owner was out to discourage anyone else from dying back there and lying unseen. Betsy cast about, but couldn't determine for sure where Carrie's body had lain.

She made a grimace of annoyance and set off, up to Second Street, then past Trinity Episcopal Church, around the corner, and two more blocks to the Fiedlers' residence halfway along Maple Street. Theirs was an attractive Tudor-style, brick-and-timber house with a steep swoop of roof over the entrance and mullioned windows marking the living room. The house was set near the back of the lot, and the broad yard's snow cover was unbroken except for the curving sidewalk leading to the front door.

And the small area at the front of the yard, which was more than knee-deep in much-trampled snow. Betsy stood awhile, absorbing details. It had snowed three or four times since Janet's body had been recovered from the scene, so the choppy surface was smoothed into soft lumps.

Toward the back of the disturbed area was a cliff-like structure where the snow had been sliced, probably marking the farthest limit where the body lay. As she looked, Betsy saw that there were horizontal pale gray stripes at irregular heights in the snow. She frowned at the stripes, wondering where they had come from.

And where had she seen that effect before?

She looked around, at the houses on either side of the Fiedler residence. One of them had a big stone fireplace chimney on its side.

Of course.

She went up the walk of the house next door and rang the doorbell. A very elderly man in blue summer-weight trousers and a long-sleeved gray dress shirt answered, an equally elderly woman standing behind him. "Yes?" he inquired, in a strong if age-roughened voice.

"Good morning, sir," said Betsy. "May I

talk to you about your fireplace?"

A few minutes later, Betsy was seated on a comfortable red plaid chair in a very neat and clean living room, drinking a cup of cocoa, while Mr. and Mrs. Holt sat side by side on a green plaid couch, also drinking cocoa. The room was stifling.

She noticed a lot of smoke stains on the upper front of the fireplace and said, "You must build a lot of fires in there."

"Every night since the first snowfall," said Mr. Holt proudly.

"From seven until nine," said his wife. "Sometimes longer."

"What a pleasant thing to do," said Betsy.

"Well, we're getting past going out dancing," said Mr. Holt.

Mrs. Holt said, "Especially in winter. We each gave up driving in bad weather when we turned eighty. That meant Robbie quit three years ago and I stopped on my birthday in April last year."

"Do you miss it?" asked Betsy.

"You know, I thought I would, but once I quit, I realized I'd been scared behind the wheel for at least six months prior. Our daughter gives us a ride to church and takes us grocery shopping and out to a movie once a month."

"Or to the dinner theater in Chanhassen

back in December," amended Robbie. "She's a real sweetie, isn't she, Darla?"

"Yes, she is. That was the one night we didn't build a fire."

"Are you sure there wasn't another?"

They were sure.

"Why did you want to talk to us about our fireplace?" asked Robbie.

"I remember from when I was a little child staying with a great-aunt and -uncle out in the country over Christmas. I saw beside their sidewalk that the snow had two stripes in the middle. I asked Uncle Henry why the snow had stripes, and he said the fireplace sent soot and smoke up the chimney and it fell down on the snow. Then new snow covered the soot and it looked like a layer cake when he shoveled it. Today I saw the stripes in the Fiedlers' yard and I saw your fireplace chimney, and it kind of made me nostalgic. I hope you don't mind."

"Not at all," said Darla. "I think that's sort of sweet, you seeing the striped snow and remembering your great-aunt and -uncle."

"Thank you. Now I must go. Thank you for the cocoa, it was delicious."

Back outdoors, on the sidewalk, Betsy used her cell phone to call Mike Malloy.

He drove up a few minutes later, and

when he got out of his car, she noticed he had a camera in one gloved hand.

"I'm not sure I understand what you meant by striped snow," he said as he approached.

She explained about the senior couple and their habit of lighting a fire every night, then pointed to the effect exposed by whoever had cleared an area around where Janet's body had been found.

"If you clear the snow in front of that part, just down to the level where Janet lay," she said, "and look up the number of snowfalls since her death, it should give you solid information about how long her body was there before it was found."

Malloy thought about it, then nodded slowly. "I think you've got something there," he said. He stooped on the sidewalk and took three pictures of the layered snowbank. "But we'll have to be very careful about it. There was already snow on the ground under her body. I think we'd better get a forensics team out here to do this right." He straightened. "You can be damn clever sometimes, you know that?"

"Thank you, Mike." She looked at her watch. "Oh, boy, I'd better get back to the shop! Let me know if it works, okay?"

■ ■ ■

A few hours later, Betsy was checking a customer out. Mrs. White had bought the counted cross-stitch pattern "Fjord Ponies," a sampler-like design based on a Scandinavian sweater pattern by Cindy Wasner. It was worked in seven shades of blue on ivory fabric. The pattern was only eighteen dollars, but Mrs. White had elected to use silk flosses rather than DMC, which brought the price up to a nice profitable level.

"I hope you'll bring this in to show it off when it's done," said Betsy, who was thinking she might like to borrow it to use as a model for the shop. But she hadn't seen any of Mrs. White's needlework and so didn't want to ask until she saw how skilled Mrs. White was.

Betsy was putting the pattern and flosses into the paper bag with a flowered design that Crewel World was currently using when the phone rang.

"Got it!" sang out Mindy, hurrying to the library table to scoop up the wireless phone from the basket in the table's center. "Crewel World, Mindy speaking, how may I help you?" she said.

She listened for a few moments, then said,

"She's right here if you want to talk to her." She turned to Betsy. "It's Sergeant Malloy. He says he has good news."

"I'll be with him in a moment." Betsy added to Mrs. White, "Here's your change. Thank you for stopping in. I hope you find the pattern satisfactory."

"Oh, I'm sure I will. And I'll be back with the finished piece in about a month."

As Mrs. White headed for the door, Betsy came to take the receiver from Mindy. "Hi, Mike, what's the verdict?"

"Well, it was a little more complicated than we thought, but the experiment seems to have worked. If we're right, then Janet Turnquist died the night before Carrie Carlson's body was found — and according to the medical examiner, Carrie died the night before her body was found."

"So they died the same night."

"Looks like it."

"And that means Janet did die before Jasper Bronson. That means Emily Hame does not inherit."

"Yes, and so that clears her. I think I'm going to go have another talk with Dr. Porter."

Betsy agreed that was a good idea and hung up. But she couldn't help remembering the curiously guilty behavior of Marty

Smith over lunch at Biella's two weeks ago.

It was about three when, on her way to the back room for her roll of tea-dyed linen, she passed Godwin with Madelyn Foreman, who was holding four skeins of hand-spun and -dyed wool and a book of knitting patterns. After Madelyn left, Godwin came over to the library table, where Betsy was cutting the canvas into different-size pieces. "Can I ask your advice?" he asked.

"Sure," said Betsy, putting down her scissors, because the tone of Godwin's voice was serious. "Is something the matter?"

"Yes — but not here at Crewel World. Rafael and I have these get-togethers, usually the same little group of friends, every few weeks. Each one has a theme: Halloween, Christmas, New Year's Eve, Valentine's Day, like that."

Betsy nodded.

"Well, one of the guests is a thief. Only we don't know which one he is."

"What has he taken?"

"That's where the problem is. If it was big things, we'd raise a fuss and try to find out who he is. But it's little things: a jar of curry powder, a bottle of shampoo, my favorite ballpoint pen, a brand-new toothbrush Rafael hadn't even taken out of the package yet. What do you think we should do?"

"I don't know," Betsy acknowledged. "It sounds more like a prankster, or maybe a kleptomaniac, than someone who really needs those things. Maybe it will escalate, so you should put your good things out of his reach."

"Well, we can't lock up everything in the place!" said Godwin, exasperated. "Who knows what he'll take next? This guy would steal the pennies off a dead man's eyes!"

"Goddy! Where did you get an expression like that?"

"Oh, Margaret Smith said it to me when she was talking about Carrie."

"What does it mean? Where did such an expression come from?"

"It just means a person who takes anything that's not nailed down, and has no respect for the decencies."

"Yes, I see what you mean." An idea was forming in Betsy's head, taking shape so quickly and firmly that she didn't hear much of Godwin's discourse on antique funeral customs.

Of course! Why hadn't she thought of it before?

"Mike, it's really very simple," said Betsy over the phone a few minutes later.

"Oh, yeah? Who did it?"

She told him and explained her reasoning.

"Okay, you're making a good case," he said at last. "But there's not enough evidence in what you say to make an arrest, much less get a conviction in court."

"Then maybe you'll consider another idea I have."

At about four o'clock, Vicki Sue came into the shop, bright-eyed and excited. "Can we go soon?" she asked Betsy. She had a small blue plastic and wire kennel hanging by its handle in one hand.

"Yes, right away," Betsy replied.

Godwin said, "You'll have to bring Penny in sometime so we can meet her."

"Yes, of course," said Vicki Sue.

They put the kennel into the backseat of Betsy's Buick and set off for the east side of Saint Paul.

"I want to thank you again," said Vicki Sue, "for saving my little dog's life."

Betsy gave the standard Minnesota reply, "No problem." She touched her chest with one hand — there was a little itch in there she couldn't assuage through the layers of cloth she was wearing.

Vicki Sue said, "I talked with Dr. Porter this morning between classes, and he said that Penny behaved perfectly all through her stay, but seemed to be missing her mistress."

"It's interesting how animals have so many emotions we think of as human," said Betsy, and they talked about that, exchanging anecdotes about pets for the rest of the journey.

Dr. Porter greeted them warmly and said they should wait here while he went and got Penny.

The little dog began to wriggle wildly in his hands when she saw Vicki Sue, whining and struggling to be put down. Porter put the animal on the floor and it immediately hurried to Vicki Sue, using the three-legged hop Dr. Porter had spoken of when they first brought her in.

While Vicki Sue communed with her happy little dog, Betsy went to the counter to make out a check for the balance, asking for and getting a receipt.

Then she turned and said to the young woman, "Vicki Sue, can you take Penny out to the car? I want to speak with Dr. Porter for a few minutes."

"All right."

After the door closed behind Vicki Sue, Dr. Porter asked, "What did you want to talk to me about?" Betsy noticed, now that the excited dog had been removed from the office, how haggard and tired the veterinarian was looking. She felt a stir of pity and was moved to begin by talking about her own pet.

"I have this cat. Her name is Sophie, and she's really overweight. I only feed her Iams Less Active, a small scoop twice a day, but she currently weighs twenty-one pounds. She's otherwise healthy, my own vet says so. I own a needlework shop, and she spends the day there with me. The problem is, my customers sneak food to her."

"Why don't you leave her at home?" Dr. Porter asked sensibly.

"Because she cries when I go out and leave her behind," said Betsy. "She really wants to be around people."

"Especially people who feed her," Dr. Porter said.

"Well, yes, that's true. But at least down in the shop she moves around; at home she just sleeps. I know that because when I leave her at home for even just a long weekend, when I get back, she's gained half a pound. I've bought her any number of toys, but all she does is watch me show her how to use them. I think it amuses her to see me chase a ball around the place."

"Maybe if she had a playmate," suggested

Dr. Porter.

"I hadn't thought of that. You may be right. Of course, my customers would miss her. And I would, too."

"Well, you mustn't always think of yourself. An obese animal is in danger of contracting any number of diseases, such as cancer, heart disease, or diabetes."

"You're right, of course."

There was a pause in the conversation. Dr. Porter said, "You and your friend Vicki came a long way to bring that dog to me."

"Yes, we did. You know what happened in Excelsior, I believe?"

This time the pause was longer. "You mean about those two women who froze to death?" he asked, frowning.

"Yes. One of them was related to you."

His eyebrows lifted, and his eyes shifted away and then back. "Only distantly."

"But her death meant that you would inherit a great deal of money. Money" — Betsy looked around the waiting room with its shabby furnishings — "you were badly in need of."

His gaze sharpened. "How dare — Who *are* you?" he demanded.

"My name is Betsy Devonshire, and I was asked by a cousin of Carrie Carlson to help her avoid a charge of murder."

340

"And your plan is to find someone else to accuse."

"No, my plan was to find out who really murdered Janet."

"You mean Carrie."

"No, Carrie's death was accidental. You took aim at Janet with a bottle of bourbon you had doctored with an animal anesthetic called Telazol. Carrie came along, saw Janet on the ground unconscious or already dead, her belongings spilling out of the bags she was carrying, and stole the bottle and a pretty, handmade bookmark. She went away to lurk behind the movie theater, a dark and private place, and quickly drank the rest of the bottle. Soon she was on the ground, helpless, dying. A snowstorm covered her and Janet's bodies. Carrie was found first, but Janet actually died first."

"Why are you telling me this? I mean, you can't prove that it's true."

"The police know all about it. They've had the bottle tested and they found Telazol in the dregs."

"Absurd," he scoffed, but he was taken aback. "If they think this is what happened, why haven't they arrested me?"

"Because Carrie's cousin's husband owns a veterinary wholesale business, and he has access to Telazol, too."

341

"So why aren't you over at his business, accusing him?"

"Because of the bookmark. Carrie didn't do needlework, but Janet had taken a class in Hardanger, the product of which was a bookmark exactly like the one in Carrie's possession. Carrie had the bottle and the bookmark; she got them both from Janet. And Janet wouldn't have given up either of them willingly."

She suddenly realized he was standing very close to her — too close.

He grabbed her around her neck. "Bitch!"

She kicked him in the shin as hard as she could. He jumped back with a cry of pain. "Mike!" she yelled. "Help!"

She whirled and ran for the door but Porter was faster. He took her by the hair, pulling back sharply and she fell. "Mike! Help, help!"

The door to the clinic slammed open and Mike Malloy stood in the entrance, a gun in his hand.

"Freeze!" he shouted, just like on television. There were more people behind him. Mike sidestepped out of their way, and they hustled in. There were two men in uniform, and a woman in civilian clothes. Saint Paul police, they all had guns in their hands.

They made Dr. Porter step back and then

lie facedown on the floor. One of the uniformed officers came and put handcuffs on him.

Mike went down on one knee to check on Betsy who, stunned and scared, had elected to stay on the floor herself.

"I told you you could get hurt," Mike scolded.

"I'm sorry. Did you hear everything he said?"

"Yes. That was good advice he gave you, about your cat. But he didn't admit anything."

"Well, he attacked me."

"Yes, and that means a lot. But it's a hell of a way to do business."

"I know. Listen, when can I take this microphone thing off? It itches."

STATEMENT OF ALEC THOMAS PORTER, TAKEN AT EXCELSIOR POLICE STATION IN HENNEPIN COUNTY, MINNESOTA

I was warned by police investigator Sergeant Michael G. Malloy, the person to whom I am making this statement, of these rights prior to any questioning of me by the police while I was under arrest:

1. That I have the right to remain silent and not make any statement at all, and that any statement I make may and probably will be used against me in a court of law;
2. That I have the right to terminate the interview at any time;
3. That I have the right to have a lawyer present to advise me either prior to any questioning or during my questioning;
4. That if I am unable to employ a

344

lawyer, I have the right to have a lawyer appointed to counsel with me prior to or during any questioning.

I do not want to consult with a lawyer before I make this statement, and I do not want to remain silent and I now freely and voluntarily waive my right to a lawyer and to remain silent and make the following voluntary statement:

Let's get what I'm sure you think are the important parts out of the way first. Yes, I put the animal anesthetic Telazol in a bottle of Top Marks Bourbon, a lethal dose, and yes, I gave it to Janet Turnquist with the intent that she should drink it and die. Okay? But I didn't know someone else would get into that bottle and die, too. That was not my intent, not at all.

But let's go back a few months. You're taking all this down, right? Making it all in my own words? Good. Somewhere around Christmas last year I visited my uncle, Jasper Bronson, in Fargo, North Dakota, and saw he was in very bad shape. He wasn't walking or talking, and he didn't recognize me and he didn't understand anything I said to him. The nurse in charge of his care said he was near the end. He had Alzheimer's and he'd had it for years — I don't know how many, probably eight or nine. I went to see him because I was very angry with him. You see, I had gone to his house to look at his bills and see if there was any mail that needed answering — stuff was still being sent to his home, though he'd been in a nursing home for a long time, and it didn't always get forwarded to me. I have his power of attorney, so doing that was all legal. While I was there, I looked through his other papers, and I found a last will and testament that I didn't know about. He had an earlier one where he left everything to me. This new one said he left everything to his niece, Janet Turnquist, if she survived him. But if not, he divided everything left after he died between me and the American Cancer Society, which is kind of a joke, since it was Alzheimer's, not cancer, that was killing him. Now he had never told me about this new will, even though he made it ten or twelve years ago, probably shortly after I came to my Small Animal Medical Center, and a little before he was diagnosed with Alzheimer's. I thought that the new will stank. I was his favorite nephew, he always told me that, and he trusted me with a lot of his business affairs when he started losing it. And before, he told me he was leaving everything to me.

Okay, I knew he was disappointed in me because he wanted me to become a doctor — and I DID become a doctor, dammit, just not for people! But he was angry with me about that because he gave me a big chunk of money to go to medical school. I went through premed, and I did go to medical school, for about a year, but I liked animals better than people, so I switched and studied to become a veterinarian and animal surgeon. I've never regretted that decision. But even if he was disappointed, he still wanted me to be the one to handle his affairs when he started to be incompetent to do it himself. The bastard.

So I went to see him about the new will. I knew there was nothing to be done about it, since he was past understanding how badly he was treating me, but I just had to vent about how I'd been taking care of business for him for all this time and it was mean of him to disinherit me without telling me, or at least leaving me something. You know, like the house, so I could sell it and maybe get back some of what I'd spent seeing he was taken care of properly. But like I said, he was too far gone to know I was even there, so all I got to do was vent.

Anyway, I had heard at a funeral that Janet

was hopelessly insane and living in misery on the street. Her husband had divorced her and married someone else. And there weren't any kids. So there was nobody to care, you see?

You know, when a dog or a cat gets sick or starts behaving like it's crazy, and medicine can't fix it, we put it to sleep, to end its suffering. So why we don't do that favor for people I don't know.

I know, I know, in this culture killing a human being is wrong. I should be ashamed for killing Janet, and I am, deep inside. But I was desperate and she was . . . she was not like a human being anymore. You understand that, right? It was like 'Hello? No one home.' Like Uncle Jasper, except he was not walking around, like she was. Like him, she wasn't like a real human being anymore. She was angry and unhappy and suffering from an incurable disease. She didn't suffer from what I did to her. She drank the bourbon I prepared and laid down and died. Should that be 'lay down and died'? Never mind, grammar was never my strong point. I met someone outside the YWCA in Fargo and gave her a note to hand to Janet with a phone card in it and my phone number. She called, and I told her I had some really good news about some money coming to her, and sent her a bus ticket care of General Delivery at the main post office in Fargo. It was a gamble, because her mental illness made her paranoid, but I went to the bus station in Minneapolis, and there she was. I told her about the will, that she was going to inherit hundreds of thousands of dollars. I gave her the bottle of bourbon as congratulations and then she said she was going to Excelsior to share her good news with — what's her name? Her niece. Emily Hame, that's right. Anyway, I told her not to share the bourbon with anyone, it was all hers. And she said she wouldn't. I believed her, and I still believe her, she didn't share that bottle with anyone.

About Carolyn Carlson, that's not my fault. I didn't mean for anything to happen to anyone but Janet. I told Janet not to share it, and I don't believe she did, or they'd both have been found together on that lawn. Carolyn stole the bottle I gave to Janet, so it's her own fault. Stole it and ran away and drank it behind that movie house. People who steal don't have any right to complain when it goes wrong. I refuse absolutely to take any blame for Carolyn Carlson.

Now, I'm a really good surgeon. I've saved many animals any other vet would euthanize. But my clinic was going under. My loss would have been a loss to hundreds, maybe thousands of pets and their owners. When you balance that against the loss of a sick, unhappy, incurably ill human, it doesn't seem so awful, does it?

Well, does it?

HARDANGER

Designed by: Roz Watnemo
of Nordic Needle

Hardanger is a form of counted-thread embroidery that is worked on even-weave cotton fabric of twenty-two threads per inch. If you are new to the craft, please visit www.nordicneedle.net and click on "Stitches." There you'll find instructions, complete with illustrations, for all the stitches used to make this bookmark. (They are arranged in alphabetical order, so, for example, to begin building the squares that are the fundamental element of Hardanger, go to K for Kloster Block.) Two sizes of pearl cotton are needed to make the stitches — size 5 and size 8. You will also need tapestry needles sizes 22 and 24, and a good pair of embroidery scissors with fine, sharp points. If this is your first project, select a light-colored fabric and a darker thread.

S

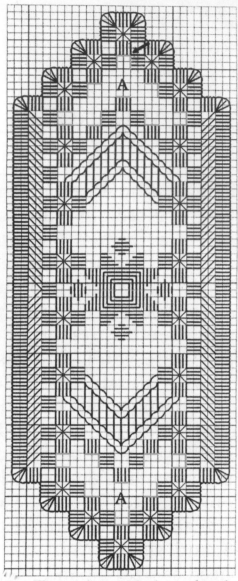

A - Woven bars, picots and webs
Every square of the chart
represents 2 × 2 fabric threads.

352

ABOUT THE AUTHOR

Monica Ferris is the *USA Today* bestselling author of several mystery series under various pseudonyms. She lives in Minnesota. Visit the author online at www .monica-ferris.com.